LOOPER

LOOPER

A COMING OF AGE NOVEL

MICHAEL CONLON

gatekeeper press

Columbus, Ohio

Looper: A Coming of Age Novel

Published by Gatekeeper Press
2167 Stringtown Rd, Suite 109
Columbus, OH 43123-2989
www.GatekeeperPress.com

ISBN (paperback): 9781642373585
eISBN: 9781642373707

Printed in the United States of America

"Don't 'spect too much from anyone,
or you'll be sorely disappointed."

—Uncle Fred

FRONT ~ NINE

1

I stand at the threshold of our TV room with a Craig Raine poetry book tucked inside my armpit, looking at Pop, who's watching Walter Cronkite report breaking news on the Iranian hostage crisis. It's been endless footage of our guys parading around in blindfolds. As I tiptoe past his lounge chair toward the door to the backyard, he puts his hand up to stop me.

"What are you up to, Ford?" Pop asks me.

A drawing sits in his lap with the word "Survey" at the top, along with our last name and address: Quinn, 678 Dorchester Road. I wonder what *he's* up to. Why's Pop got a sketch of our lot? The barnacles on the back of my neck stand at attention.

"Nothing much." I hold my poetry book tightly behind my back so he won't notice. Pop might innocently tell my older brother, Billy, who'll tell my older

9

sister, Kate, and she'll gossip the news to one of her trillion friends because she can't keep her mouth shut, and word would spread like Agent Orange around Kensington Hills that Ford Quinn reads poetry. That's a potential social death sentence heading into freshman year of high school in the fall.

The poem "A Martian Sends a Postcard Home" sticks to my brain like Pink Floyd's "Welcome to the Machine." Great songs and poems will transport your brain into a different universe. Pop doesn't get poetry, but how many dads really do? He'd rather talk about sports, which is fine with me.

Pop stretches for his beer mug and says, "Summer's comin' up. How 'bout playing some golf with your old man?"

He's been bothering me for ages to play golf with him, but I'd sooner play shuffleboard or bingo. Golf's for old, stodgy grown-ups. You'd think it's written in some ancient Quinn scroll that every one of us has to play at least one sport. Brother Billy broke that sacrament last year when he got kicked off the tennis team for smoking between sets. At least Kate plays tennis for the JV high school team. I suppose Pop figures golf is my last bet because I'm a bit too small for football despite decent shoulders, track meets cause my stomach juices to boil, and I might as well be playing with two left hands on the basketball court.

"What's with that survey document?" I smell another Pop scheme coming on.

He turns the document over in his lap to tell me it's none of my business. "How about catching a Royal Knights game tonight?"

The Royal Knights are the local minor-league baseball team and the biggest ticket in town during the summer unless you drive all the way to downtown Detroit to see real pros play at Tiger Stadium. I love the Royal Knights, but kids congregate and smoke cigs under the bleachers at Knights' games. You don't want to be caught sitting alone with your dad.

Outside the window, a head of bright red hair appears in my line of sight. My best friend in the galaxy, Rocket Olivehammer. "No thanks, Pop. Maybe next time." I run upstairs to put away my poetry book, ride back down the banister, and dash out the door with our golden retriever, Chimney, close behind me.

Rocket's at the end of our driveway, bobbing up and down on his unicycle seat. He can't stay still for one zillionth of a second to save his life. "Going to the falls, Ford. Let's go."

His unicycle falls to the ground under his bony ass, and he jumps on my dirt bike. My red Schwinn ten-speed suffered a flat tire, so I drag my sister Kate's girly bike from the garage and speed after Rocket, who's pop-ping a wheelie. Chimney keeps chase down Dorchester Road toward the main drag, Kensington Road. We shoot across a narrow footbridge to an acre of park grass next to the waterfall. The falls has a ten-foot drop, really a mini waterfall but a waterfall just the same. We lean our bikes up against a mammoth oak tree.

The park's empty except for a barefoot girl with tan legs and straight bangs, lounging on a blanket while sipping a Tab from purple lipsticked lips. I haven't seen her before, and she looks like she's fourteen, just like me. My head swivels toward echoing voices coming from a bank of scrub trees by Stone Lake—or Stoner's Lake as the Hills kids call it.

I shove both hands in my pockets—nervy habit of mine—and find the mood ring I'd stashed inside my pants three weeks ago but forgot about till now. I'd wanted to give the mood ring to either Carmen Lazario or Linda Scranton at the spring school dance. Those are the top two girls on my class crush list, but in the end I was too scared to even step on the gym floor, let alone ask one of them to fast dance.

An ugly, familiar face with slanted eyebrows and fanglike front teeth appears from the bushes. Nick Lund and his brown docksiders. Damn. My fine spring day is now in ruin 'cause Nick's sole pursuit in life is to make me freaking miserable. I don't know exactly what I did to earn his Darth Vader-wrath, but ever since the first grade, he can't resist giving me hell every chance he gets. And he's had plenty. I might have poked fun of the huge black mole on his neck, but that was a space age ago. He's wiry, strong, and wears his jet-black hair pompadour style with no part, just like Eddie Munster.

"Having a little picnic, Quinn?" Nick asks. He holds a cigarette between his fingers, takes a quick drag, and flicks the ashes at my feet. Rich Kensington Hills kids only smoke Camels; Hills girls smoke Benson & Hedges 100s. Chewing tobacco has been the fad for a while, but high-end cigarettes are now the new thing in 1980.

Nick's never without his posse, so I look behind him. Sure enough, three boys step out one by one from behind the pine trees that front the waterfall. Jack Lott, Jason Sanders, and Fat Albert, pulling on his zipper after presumably taking a leak. With Lund they make a junior high Fantastic Four. A cloud of smoke trails behind them.

Lund fixes his gnarly gaze on me and points up his chin at me. "Wanna play some dart-out, Quinn?" I can't recall Nick ever calling me by my first name.

"Get lost," Rocket says, who'd defend me against marauding Mongols because he's a loyal friend.

"Are you guys dating?" Fat Albert's uneasy smile accents his fatty jowls, and his eyes dart back and forth among his new best friends, searching for approval.

"You're hilarious," I say. A lame response, but I don't want to invite an all-out assault. In two seconds flat, they might empty my pockets, find the ring in my Wrangler jeans, and give me a super wedgie. It's too late to just ditch the ring in the grass.

It seems like only yesterday Eugene "Fat Albert" Duncan had been the one on the receiving end of the Lund Gang's taunts, diverting attention away from yours truly. Thwacks. Nuggies. Indian burns. But then his parents splurged on a new satellite pay-TV station called ON-TV, where microwaves miraculously beam a signal to your TV from outer space without any commercial interruptions. Overnight, Fat Albert zoomed to the top of the Kensington Hills social Mount Olympus. The Lund Gang's been bragging about watching *Dawn of the Dead*, *Weasels Rip My Flesh*, and *Ten* for the last month. If it wasn't for ON, Fat Albert would still be the target of fat-boy pokes and jokes.

Members of the Lund Gang are the most popular kids in school, and the way the gang treats you is how your own popularity is measured. It isn't fair, but it's true. Life's like that. Some kids just don't care, but I'm not one of those kids. They run the school. Even the sisters from my Catholic grade school, Holy Redeemer, seem scared of the gang, plus they live in the fanciest houses with in-ground pools, Queen Anne billiard tables with fringe pockets, tree forts, you name it.

Oh yeah, and video game machines in the basement. I'd die a thousand deaths for an arcade in my basement instead of a dumb ping-pong table and a Hot Wheels speed track super-loop. Pop won't be buying a Pac-Man machine anytime soon unless one of his get-rich schemes miraculously hits pay dirt. The Quinn's save and scrap for every doll hair, and it "won't be wasted on any video game machines." These are Pop's words.

This summer I'm determined to crack the Lund Gang, and I've got half my foot in the door. First, I live on Dot Ave (short for Dorchester Road), one of the better streets in Kensington Hills—a prerequisite for membership—which has decent-sized colonial houses (though not a mansion like Lund lives in) and large lots, and it's within biking distance to uptown. Second, Jason Sanders likes me, and Jack Lott tolerates me. My problem right now is Nick Lund hates my guts. Lund's the biggest hard-ass kid in school, and the ring leader of the Fantastic Four.

Fat Albert lets a titanic belch escape, followed by a puke of smoke. Normally I'd rib Fat Albert for being such a pig, but I don't dare now that he's penetrated the inner sanctum of the Lund Gang. He's a prime example of why I want to get into the Lund Gang—he's gone from fat loser to funny-cool fat kid in record time. There's an episode in *Lost in Space* where Dr. Smith finds a mysterious silver box in a cave, which gives him green hair and muscles overnight. That's what's happened to Fat Albert, and really any kid who hangs out with the Lund Gang.

"Let's get going, Nick," Jason says. I can't understand why someone as cool as Jason Sanders hangs around a jerk like Nick Lund. Sanders could start his own gang if he wanted to.

Lund shakes his head and shows his fangs. "No. We're not going anywhere until Quinn here plays some dart-out or until he admits he's a total spaz."

In dart-out, when the light turns green, you dart across Kensington Road and back as fast as you can, hoping not to lose your load, or worse, get killed. No stops; that's the number one rule. Just like suicide sprints at the end of basketball practice, only in the middle of honking traffic. It makes bumper skitching in the snow seem as dangerous as ding dong ditch-it. Only a total psycho plays dart-out. Terry Martin got clipped by a bronze LeMans doing dart-out a couple of years back and fell into a coma for three weeks. Now he can't properly pronounce his Rs or his Ds. He's a lifer at the Baskin-Robbins and asked me last summer if I wanted an "asberry taiquiri."

The Lund Gang doesn't know Rocket; dart-out is nothing to him. Rocket would get himself killed by the Lund Gang if he took them on. He's fearless but skinny as a dime. His dad had taught him to face every fear. For example, when he was a little kid he feared rodents, so his dad served him roasted marshmallow shish kebab with mouse meat. When he was older, he'd been afraid to skateboard down Devil's Dive—the steepest, deadliest street in town—so he flew down fourteen times in one day until he no longer felt nervy at the top of the hill. If Rocket had gone to Holy Redeemer, we'd have formed our own gang, and I wouldn't have to worry about asses like Nick Lund. But Rocket goes to public school.

If I dare try dart-out, I'll likely freeze right in the middle of Kensington Road and get mowed down by a Lincoln Continental Town Coupe driven by some banker in a three-piece suit. Billy or Kate probably wouldn't care, but it'd kill Mom and Pop. Worse, they'd find the mood ring I'd hid in my pocket. It'd be embarrassing to let your parents know you were thinking about a girl, even after you're dead.

"You go first." I say this to Lund while queasily eyeing the traffic and hoping he'll spontaneously combust. A weak play on my part, but Lund is crazy enough to try anything, and it buys me some precious time to think my way of out of this mess. Lund tilts his head back and forth, mulling it over.

"What's wrong? Scared?" I want to punch Rocket for saying this, but he never refuses a dare.

"I've done it a million times," Nick says in his cockiest tone. "You've never done it once, have you, Quinn?"

Screw you, Lund.

Rocket gulps from a flask he carries and twists the cap back on. Hawaiian Punch with a shot of vodka from his dad's liquor cabinet. "After we go, you go!" Rocket points at Lund.

"If you're alive," Lund counters with a mocking tone and sneer.

Before Lund can utter another word, Rocket grabs my arm and yanks me toward the cars whizzing down Kensington Road. We reach the curb just as the light turns green. The engines rev, and the cars burp forward. We fly across the street. An old lady's eyes in a VW Beetle turn electrocuted blue. We make it safely to the other side. A cinch.

At the far curb, I hesitate, but Rocket jerks my arm forward into four lanes of traffic. We barely miss a beige station wagon, which swerves onto the curb. The next car stops, rubber tires screeching and horn blaring. A man with no neck opens his window and shouts, "You little bastards, you almost got yourself killed!" He blares his horn, alerting eastbound traffic. Cars slow, and just like that, we cross the finish line.

Rocket wipes his forehead. "That was close!"

The Lund Gang gawks, stupid and speechless. Fat Albert's cig falls out of his gaping breathing hole. The girl on the blanket stares at our spectacle, and I hope she noticed my bravery. Or perhaps she figures I'm just a fool.

Jack Lott does take notice. "Jesus Christ, Ford. That took some guts," he says when we join up again.

I wait for an invitation to the Lund Gang. They require potential members to complete dares for admission to the group. Rumor has it Fat Albert's dare required him to try out as a ball girl (wig, skirt, and bra) for the Virginia Slims tennis tour stop in Detroit. Maybe dartout is just a test for me to enter the gang.

Rocket evil-grins at Lund. "Your turn now."

"Hah. I don't think so. I called your bluff, and you fell for it. Face! Let's get the hell out of here, boys."

So much for passing any dare test. Nick swipes Rocket's flask, takes a swig, and spits it out. "Sick. What's in this crap?"

I turn away when Chimney begins barking at the girl on the blanket. She has jet-black hair with straight bangs down her forehead (not those popular hideous mall bangs Kate and her entourage wear). My dog jumps up and down next to the girl like she's holding a Frisbee.

Why in the hell is Chimney pestering that girl? She never barks, usually too lazy to jump on anyone. Jack Lott gazes at the girl, making my jealousy level skyrocket, and disappears into the pines. Jack, otherwise known as the Human Torch, could snag any girl he wants. In my eyes, he really is a superhero and doesn't need any silver box to make him one like Dr. Smith did.

I stroll toward the girl to grab Chimney's collar, pulling my nutty dog away from her. An acorn drops with a thud next to her naked toes. In the month of May, that's the sign of a dying oak tree. The girl picks up the acorn and tosses it into the rushing falls, where it surfs on a wave before melting into the frothy water.

"It's a wishing waterfall," she says.

Another acorn floats down the stream, heading toward Stoner's Lake. I ask her what she wished for, hoping for a good reply.

A teasing tone escapes from her lips. "For you to give me what just fell out of your pocket." The mood ring glows, winking at me in the grass. It must have crawled up my pants pocket during dart-out. I pick it up and hand it to her, thinking the minute I saw her I wanted to give it to her anyway, but I don't know why.

The girl's cat eyes pull me in like they have some mysterious gravity power.

When you give a mood ring to a girl, you want the color to glow blue—love and joy. I'm not a wanker for thinking this because according to Rocket's brother, Basil Olivehammer, mood rings are based on real science—and Basil knows everything about everything. I don't go for magic or mysticism and wouldn't give you two cents for a Magic 8-Ball, but Basil explained your skin gives off chemicals depending on your mood.

She slips on the ring, and it fits like Cinderella's slipper. I hold my breath and pray hard for blue. Damn. Nothing but ice-cube clear. I'm a bit tongue-tied, so I say the first dumb thing that comes to my mind. "What's your name?"

"Cleo Plimpton. You?"

"Ford … Quinn." Chimney keeps barking and sniffing Cleo like she has a piece of raw steak in her pocket. I grab her collar. "Chimney, all right already!"

Rocket holds out the flask of vodka punch to her. "You want some?"

"Too many calories." She tosses her empty can into her basket, folds her blanket, and slides her feet into her moccasins. "I have to go. Adios, Ford, and thanks for the ring."

I hold my dog's collar tight as she climbs onto her blue Schwinn and pedals toward Kensington Road with my mood ring on her finger. Another acorn falls from the great oak tree, and I pluck it off the grass and fling it into the water along with my wish: for Cleo to—

"She's out of your league, Ford."

Who asked you, Rocket? I think grumpily. But he's right. I watch Cleo ride off into the distance and figure I'll never set eyes on her again.

In that alien poem, the Martian tries to describe Earth things to his fellow Martians, and reading the poem is a bit like trying to solve a puzzle. The Martian compares mechanical things to nature. An open book to a bird. Television to rain. The Martian says books cause humans to melt. Cleo's no book, but she reminds me of some exotic bird who could definitely make my heart melt. Girls are puzzles to me, so they might as well be Martians.

2

A t 3:15 p.m. on the last day of eighth grade at Holy Redeemer School, the doors of the ugly red-brick rectangle building explode open with the screams of a thousand escaping schoolchildren streaming toward the sound of summer's freedom bell.

Amid slaps on the back from schoolmates, I amble across the school's asphalt jungle—where for almost a decade we'd played tackle football and tag, flirted foolishly with girls, et cetera—toward the school bus and thought of all the years I'd spent here starting with Sister Jodi, my first-grade teacher. Hell, I've grown up here.

A pack of graduating girls from my class gather in a huddle in their identical plaid skirts, crying their pretty eyes out because they know this phase of their life is all over. Margaret Spindle, Patty Plaisik, Carmen Lazario, Brenda Simpson ... eight years of memories flash through my brain. Their waterworks stop me in my Hush Puppies. I might not see any of these girls I've grown up with once I get to high school and beyond because Catholic High is an all-boys school.

A kickball-sized tear forms in my eye like the one on the cheek of that American Indian in the spoiled river commercial. At the edge of the parking lot, I dump my books in a trash bin hauled in for the occasion and hope like hell no one spots me teared up, especially Nick Lund. But there's no worry about that because I spot the Fantastic Four leaping into a cream-colored Mercedes station wagon, headed to a graduation party at Peter Lattimore's house to play air hockey and pinball in his basement. My invitation must've been lost in the mail, but Fat Albert bragged he'd gotten one.

On my last bus ride home, Reagan Paulson, a famous local kid actor, plops down into the seat next to me. Kate's friend Vicky Fontaine pinkie swore he gets a check for $79 every time he sings "onion burger, onion burger ... you're sooo good ... give me more onion burger, onion burger ... topped with gooey cheese ... onion burger, onion burger ... you're sooo good" in the local Hamburger Heaven TV commercial. He normally wears his trademark suede suit coat over his blue turtleneck and arrives at school in a brand-new Cadillac Coupe de Ville. Today he's wearing red corduroys, a black leather jacket, and a Tony Baretta-style newsboy cap.

I speak up first. "How did you get your big break?"

Reagan flips open a mirror case, eyeing a tiny pimple on his nose. I figure he hadn't heard me, so I gaze out the window at the cloudless sky. Kids hang their heads out the windows, inhaling the summer scent like that doomed, stranded, tethered cosmonaut seeking oxygen in his capsule after the first spacewalk. A riot breaks out in the rear backseat. Our bus driver, Gus, doesn't seem to care a whit that his riders have transformed into zoo animals. It's the last ride of the year on this godforsaken bus, and the last ride of my life—thank the Lord!

Reagan finally answers. "Television or stage?"

He snaps me out of my last-day-of-school fog. "Hamburger Heaven."

Reagan closes his mirror case. "Caddying." Perhaps he's misunderstood what I said. Before I could think of what the hell he means, he continues. "I started caddying at the country club and carried a bag for a cinema producer." At first I think he said "cinnamon producer," then I figure out he means movies, not spices.

"Anyone I'd know? McQueen, Redford, Clint, Pacino, Stallone? Burt Reynolds?"

He shakes his head. "Producer, not actor. Ever heard of *The Towering Inferno*? *The Poseidon Adventure*? *Lost in Space*?"

Duh. That producer's a genius. Rocket and I have seen just about every movie that came to town for free—even a few R-rated ones. Rocket has a trick for sneaking us into the new Berkshire Mall theater by sticking two matchbooks next to a hinge of the back door as the previous movie is letting out, and we just waltz into the dark theater as soon as we hear the beginning credits coming on.

"Anyhow," says Reagan, "he told me I could be the next Mickey Rooney. At first I thought, what a sick perv, but his creds checked out. He got my foot in the door, hooked me up with a New York agent. The rest is his-store-eee."

"Huh. So it all started with caddying?"

"All the players in town belong to Kensington Hills Country Club. It's got a world-famous golf course." He fishes his makeup case out again, does another quick pimple check as if two minutes could have changed things, and tucks it away again.

I know the private country club because they have a fireworks display every Fourth of July. If not for that, you couldn't get near the place without a royal escort. "Golfers?"

He shakes his head in slow motion. "Nooo, man. Play-ers. Bigwigs. Auto execs."

"Right ... right." I had no i-de-a.

Reagan fishes black Ray-Bans from his coat pocket and perches them above his freckled forehead. "I carried for the actor Robert Wagner. He's Jonathan Hart in *Hart to Hart*, and he's from Detroit. Terrible slicer. You should check caddying out. Worst case, you get a free ride to college if you stick it out for a few summers."

I perk up at this news. A paper airliner zooms over my head and is sucked out the window in the seat in front of me. "Come again?"

He flips his sunglasses over his eyes. "They call it the Chick Evans Caddy Scholarship."

Two fifth graders play tug-of-war with a blue tie in the aisle. The bus screeches to a halt, and I fall forward into the back of the seat in front of me. "Who's Chick Evans?"

He dismisses the question with a flip of his hand. "How should I know?"

I ask him why he's riding the bus today, wondering why he isn't in the backseat of his Coupe de Ville instead of slumming it with the blue shirts. He trails his finger along his lips. "I'm in character. Why else would I be wearing these clothes in this cheese wagon?"

Good question. "What's the show about?"

"What's with the third degree, man?"

A quarter mile of awkward silence follows.

"After-school special," he says eventually. "Cloris Leachman plays my mom, and she's royally pissed I'm getting shipped to a desegregated school." The bus comes to a snorting stop. I get up, and Reagan Paulson gives me a hearty goodbye salute. "Good luck this summer."

Break a leg.

My encounter with the kid actor spreads optimism dust on my brain. If Regan Paulson could rocket his way to local fame from caddying, why couldn't Ford Quinn? On my walk home, after doing the hustle through the Denisons' backyard, I decide to take Reagan's advice and nab a caddying job this summer. Maybe I could get that Chick Evans college scholarship, although Reagan said you have to caddy for four summers to qualify, which means I have to start this coming season.

Pop doesn't have the money to send me to college, unlike most of the Kensington Hills families. My dream is to become an astronaut or astrophysicist, which requires a ton of college courses in math, physics, and astronomy—and cash. Except for Rocket, I've kept it secret that I'm an astronomy nerd, hiding my telescope in the closet on the remote chance a Lund Gang member is bored enough to come over to my house. Telescopes are about as cool as a stuffed Chewbacca in your bedroom, but I've been trying to catch a glimpse of the SolarMax satellite recently launched by NASA to monitor the flares of the sun. There's a whole universe

for me to explore out there beyond the Earth's surface—
let alone beyond the one-mile orbit around Dorchester
Road, Holy Redeemer, and uptown, which I've barely
scratched—and hope I don't get burned.

. . .

That afternoon, I find Virginia, a.k.a. Mom, standing in
front of our living room mirror in her house dress, recit-
ing some self-help drivel from her beloved book, *Mensa-
Netics*, by Osmond P. Peabody. My sixteen-year-old sister, Kate, watches her from the couch. In the midst of
her self-image affirmation, Mom spots me in the mirror
and wheels around.

"Ford, I've been reading in my book about the
importance of goal setting for positive development,
and I have a goal for you this summer."

It's too late to employ the *Jupiter 2*'s force-field
fence against the *Mensa-Netics*'s robot; she's breached
the perimeter. "Virginia, I'm not spending my summer
vacation selling vacuum cleaners." She sells Rainbow
vacuum cleaners door to door.

"No, no, much better." Her eyes light up like she's
discovered the secret recipe that makes Kentucky Fried
Chicken finger lickin' good. "Mr. Doyle from down the

street is sick. He's now in a wheelchair. Can't even make it to the toilet seat."

Mr. Doyle does daily laps around the block while being pushed by his three-hundred-pound wife. "What in God's green acre does that have to do with me?"

A heavy, disappointed sigh from Mom. "Mrs. Doyle's got a new job. She needs help taking care of him, and she'll pay good money. It will make you feel more productive and give you better inner development!"

"No way, Virginia. I can't stand to be around sick people; they make me ill."

"Funny." She shakes her head, and this is followed by a fierce finger wag. "You are not wasting your summer with Rocket on that silly skateboard of yours."

Moms just don't get skateboarding; it's like horizontal parachuting.

I fight the urge to say to her: "Have you ever gone down Devil's Dive at max g-force acceleration? If you had, you wouldn't be asking such a moronic question!" But I only reply with: "Listen, I have a better idea."

"There is no better idea," she says. Mom's been brainwashed by Osmond P. Peabody, and it's made her stubborn and determined to chart my "life path." "Do you know how much Mr. Doyle came through for us when your father was deathly ill?"

The Quinn nostalgia freight train's rolling down the track, gaining steam. I close my eyes, hoping for an early derailment.

"Ford? Did I tell you that story?"

"Only a thousand times."

"Sorry to tell you how you all almost lost your father," she tells me. "The lucky thing is, the week before he got sick, we'd—"

"Just bought a disability insurance policy. Blah, blah, blah."

She folds her arms against her chest, shaking her head in disgust. "Sorry. I guess I'll never mention the worst time of my life ever again."

Do you swear on a stack of your Mensa-Netics books?

"If you'd let me talk already, I could tell you about my plan for this summer," I say. "To get a real job."

Kate jumps up from the couch. "Bagging a few leaves doesn't count."

"Stay out of it, cyclops," I say to Kate. "I'm going to caddy at the country club."

"Caddy?" A loud *hmm* seeps from Virginia's mouth.

"Yeah. It's a real job, and it pays real money. I'd get to meet important people. Plus, you can go to college for free."

Virginia's head freezes in the mirror, and a light flickers in her eyeballs. "I've heard about that! You could be an Evans scholar!"

Yes, that's what I've been trying to tell you, Mom.

Kate scoffs under her sun-bleached hair. "Evans scholar? It sounds like a medical syndrome."

I evil-smile at her, mouth the word "Theo," and Kate knows to shut her trap-hole. I found out from reliable sources she's been secretly dating Theo Nichols for the past few months. Theo's known as a bad boy from the Hills who returned from boarding school this semester after being booted out of Catholic High for high crimes and misdemeanors.

The last straw was a drink bust at the homecoming dance last fall. The brothers pulled wasted and wobbly kids out of the gym and lined them up against the cafeteria wall for questioning and sobriety tests. Theo'd gone undetected by rolling himself up in an oriental rug in Brother Bernard's office. Problem was, he'd slipped into a drunken coma and slept through the night holed up in his cozy rug, which was unfurled in the morning by an unsuspecting Jesuit janitor.

I toss a throw pillow at Kate's head. "It's a scholarship for the best caddy at the country club." She returns fire, and I bat it down with my hand.

Virginia's lips do a pretzel twist, a sign she is thinking hard. "Ford, I know, I know. The Walton kids got those scholarships—Bobby, Patrick, and even Suzy."

"Girls can caddy?" I know squat about caddying, but I'm not worried about Kate caddying. She'd sooner shave her head than lug a golf bag around.

"Yes, girls can caddy! We can do anything you can do. Probably better!" Kate exclaims, rising again from the couch. Kate seems to be absorbing some of mom's self-esteem claptrap.

"Of course girls can caddy," Mom says. "Ford, I'm very proud of you. What a responsible young man you're becoming. College is sooo expensive these days. The Babcocks had to get a second mortgage to send Oliver to Brown."

"Didn't he flunk out his freshman year?" Kate chimes in.

"That's beside the point."

My eavesdropping older brother, Billy, appears with the usual smirk on his face. I brace myself for the insults to come. "Virginia," he says, "why don't you invent something so we can make a million dollars and we don't

33

have to work or go to college?" Billy never disappoints and gets away with murder.

"I'm trying. Believe me."

"Where's Kate working this summer?" I figure I'll call her bluff. "She can join me."

Virginia places her hand on Kate's shoulder. "She's part of my Rainbow vacuum cleaners sales force."

By this, she means two persons. Kate usually spends her summers playing tennis or tanning on the back patio next to Chimney. She normally wraps an album cover in aluminum foil and angles it above her face for maximum sun reflection in her pathetic quest for the perfect tan.

"How can Kate sell vacuums?" Billy interjects. "She's a moron."

"Pipe down, Billy. Kate will do fine. She's been working on her positive self-image." She nods at me. "Now, Ford, I think caddying is a great idea for you."

Billy let out one of his phony Ed McMahon-style laughs. "Caddying? I caddied once, space boy."— You can't hide from your own family you're a space nerd.—"Nightmare. Don't let the 'rents talk you into it. Caddying blows. The bag weighs a ton, and it's boring as hell watching men hit a stupid white ball."

"Don't start, Billy," Mom says. Billy has a knack for starting volcanic fights in Quinnville.

"It's the worst job I've ever had by a mile." He limps around the room like a wounded orangutan, pretending a golf bag is weighing down his shoulder.

"It was the only job you didn't get fired from," Pop pronounces, strolling in from the den, holding a rolled-up newspaper. "They didn't have time to fire you."

Billy was fired the previous winter from his job at Little Caesar's Pizza for mouthing off to the manager. Pop's right. He's basically been fired from every job he's ever had, and he's had scores. Busboy, Amoco gas station attendant, above-ground pool installer, fur store attendant (he delivered Aretha Franklin's fur coat to her mansion and wore it on the way there "because he was cold"), car-drying man at Jax Car Wash, house sitter.

"Look who's talking. What happened to you with your last job?" Billy says to Pop.

Pop stares Billy down. "Don't worry about me, mister, and get your hands off your hips. You kids need to learn to stand up straight."

"Both of you could use better self-images," Virginia adds.

Billy and Pop both burst a laughter pipe. There's one thing those two have in common: poking fun at Mom's self-help pop psychology. I never dare. Every week she tacks up a new self-help goal of the day onto the fridge. This week: "You must believe in your own mental discipline—do not rely on outside forces for motivation. You can do it yourself! Today's goal: Sell one Rainbow vacuum cleaner with an Aquamate accessory."

Unlike Pop, Mom doesn't just dream, she takes action. She sells bagless Rainbow vacuum cleaners. The vacuums use water rather than air to remove dirt. Virginia told me once that the founder of the business got the idea while trying to sweat off a hangover with a cup of coffee in the wee hours of the morning in the French Quarter. A municipal street-cleaning machine hummed by and turned a beer-soaked puke-laden Bourbon Street into a shiny red-brick road. Virginia got sucked into the business when a salesman demonstrated the vacuum on our living room carpet.

"WET DUST CAN'T FLY," the salesman had shouted above the vacuum noise. This new-fangled technology not only removed dirt and hairballs from the carpet but also airborne dust, which supposedly helped Billy's allergies. But what really drew Virginia into the fold was the notion of becoming an "independent business owner."

Finding out my brother had quit after day one, I know for sure I'll caddy this summer. I'll show Pop I'm not anything like Billy, a burden I carry around my neck like a weight, always trying to lift more reps. Luckily, my brother set the bar ankle low.

Virginia sticks two fingers in her mouth and wolf-whistles for a time-out. Chimney's ears flatten, and she gallops out of the room. Mom's whistle could wake you from a coma. "Enough from both of you two!" A light-year of hushed silence. "Ford's caddying this summer."

"Is that right, Fordo?" Pop gives an approving nod. "Maybe they can let you play, too. You need to work on your golf game if you want to make the golf team this fall."

When did I say anything about playing golf, let alone trying out for the high school team?

Billy can't resist. "He'll never make it through one round."

"Patrick Walton is your age and caddies." Pop sits down and pops a Stroh's beer can (he seesaws between Stroh's and Pabst, but a Western beer called Coors is making a run for his money). "He can't weigh more than a sack of flour."

"You'll wish you were dead after about three holes." Billy slashes his throat with his index finger.

"Knock it off, Billy," Pop says.

Virginia sticks two fingers next to her tonsils, threatening to blow just as Chimney sets a paw on the door threshold. "He could get a college scholarship to Michigan or Michigan State, Howard."

"Hell, Virginia, the Walton old man hasn't had to spend a dime on college." He pours beer in a coffee mug full of ice. "He told me once they get room and board, too."

"Don't you have to be like poor as dirt to get that scholarship?" Billy frowns again.

Virginia digs a sarcastic knife into Pop's belly. "It's not like we're rich."

"Oh, yeah, how could I forget, Virginia?"

"Okay, that's enough, Billy," Pop says. He might blow at any moment with Billy's prodding.

My brother laughs, thwacking me hard on the head on the way out the door. "Have fun this summer, golden boy." The back door slams behind him. Billy enjoys rocking the family boat, but I'd rather stay out of the line of sight of Pop's radioactive radar gun.

"When can I start caddying, Pop?"

"I'll call Old Man Walton today and see if Bobby can get you to start tomorrow morning." he says. "Remember, once you start something, you don't quit."

"What about Billy?" He quits everything.

Chimney slinks back into the TV room and drops a wet bone at my feet.

"Let me worry about your brother." Bottoms up. "You'll meet a lot of successful people. Maybe you'll meet some good business contacts."

"Howard, he's only a teenager."

Pop wipes his foamy lips. "It's never too early." He pours more beer down his gullet. "Oh, yeah. The club is closed on Mondays. Old Man Walton told me once the caddies get to play golf for free. You got a good swing, Ford."

Enough with the golf, Pop.

If Billy had still been in the room, he would have told Pop it's never too late. For as long as I can remember, Pop never held down a normal job for too long before moving on to the next, all in the industrial sales category. Mom told me Pop couldn't hold a normal nine-to-five job because "no one can tell your father what to do."

Pop was always trying to think—rather than work— his way out of our financial rut. He once invented a horrible new drink called Swamp Juice. For several weeks we were Pop's guinea pigs, drinking disgusting, syrupy formulas. Pop tried other get-rich-quick schemes: penny stocks, rare-stamp collecting, a percentage share in a Kentucky Derby horse heir that never made it out of the gates of Ohio, let alone Kentucky. Needless to say, there won't be college tuition in the Quinn budget.

I wonder what exactly I am getting into this summer. I know zip about caddying or golf. My lone exposure to golf was our annual Florida vacation when Grandpa Quinn took me to the local golf range. I borrowed his old driver once and smashed a *Titanic*-sized drive toward a bullseye target. The head popped loose and landed in the fifty-yard target circle. Grandpa's eyeballs burned asteroid holes into my frontal lobe like it'd been my fault his old club fell apart. He didn't blow because I was his grandson, but I'd enjoyed a frightful glimpse of Pop's Christmas past. Pop unfairly grounded me inside the condo that day, while Billy and Kate inhaled sea salt air and sipped virgin daiquiris in the cabana on the windy, tar-streaked beach of the Atlantic Ocean.

Maybe I'll meet some cool kids while caddying this summer. Kids who don't know where you stand in the social pecking order, which was basically established in the first grade at Holy Redeemer. Since I'd quit baseball in the sixth grade, I really don't know any public-school kids besides Rocket.

That's one of my problems. My whole life has revolved around the kids at Holy Redeemer. It's where I'd gone to school, attended church, played sports, spent most of my waking moments.

Caddying can't be as bad as Billy suggests, can it?

3

I n the afternoon heat, we pull up to the white plantation clubhouse of Kensington Hills Country Club in
Pop's red Impala. I've dragged Rocket along to avoid
going it alone. He'll normally try anything once.

A boy in an orange Polo shirt greets us with a towel
wrapped around his neck. "Are you a member or a
guest?"

Pop rolls down the window. "Neither. These kids
came here to caddy. Bobby Walton's expecting us."

"He's on the first tee," the boy says. "Pull up to the
curb and follow me."

A minute later, we round a bank of perfectly
groomed hedges without a leaf out of place and stroll
into a postcard from Scotland—perfect rolling hills of
fairway grass and tiny beachheads flanked by the vio-
lent bluish-green North Sea rough. The course reminds

me of the Polaroid photos we receive every summer from Mom's Aunt Shirley, a Foreign Service Officer who'd been exiled to Galloway. She writes us notes in her adopted Scot's tongue none of us can decipher like "Lang may yer lum reek" or "We're a' Jock Tamson's bairns!" or "Haste ye back!"

"Don't move while I go talk to Bobby Walton," Pop says, heading toward a lanky, curly-haired kid near the first tee. I travel in my mind to Aunt Shirley's Scotland.

You're a wee scunner!

Rocket and I sit down at the end of a green bench next to a kid hanging over a half door to a room housing golf bags. Bored boys in green shirts and white pants snap towels at fleeing fire ants on the white concrete.

Golf reminds me of endless sun-drenched Sunday afternoons. Pop's eyes glued to TV golf, drowsing in his La-Z-Boy, and sipping beer from his ice-filled coffee mug. I've heard at least a thousand times how Pop's family lived in Columbus on the fifth fairway of the Scioto Country Club where the Golden Bear, Jack Nicklaus, learned to play. Grandpa Quinn had been promoted from an engineer in Detroit to the plant manager position for a new Ford assembly plant in Columbus—the precursor to the Quinn heyday. Mom's from Columbus, Ohio, and that's where she met Pop. Eventually Grandpa

Quinn got promoted again and again before running a whole division for the car giant.

Bobby Walton waves me over to the first tee and sets a golf bag in front of me that shades my chin. Bobby tells Rocket he'll be caddying for the next group to tee off. I pick up the bag by the handle, suitcase style.

Bobby laughs, saying, "No, like this," and he hangs the strap over my shoulder.

I drag the heavy bag over to the other caddies, standing at the first tee.

A redheaded kid sneers at me with contempt. "You gotta stand in a straight line. This isn't some circle jerk." This gets a snicker from the three other caddies.

"You haven't caddied before?" This kid wears a red badge on his chest that reads "Chip."

"No."

Bobby Walton has thrown me to the golf wolves without any proper training.

"We got a plebe, boys, but we'll teach him the ropes."

I don't have a clue what Chip means by "plebe," but I can kind of guess by just the sound of the word that it isn't positive.

"He's going to bring our tips down." The redheaded kid flicks a tee at me paper-football style. I duck, but it clips my earlobe. "Three points!"

What are we in third grade again, Howdy Doody? This place already reminds me of Holy Redeemer with its ranks and pranks.

"What's your name?" Chip asks with a friendly tone. Finally, someone decent. I tell him. "Listen to me, Ford Quinn, and you'll do okay." I notice his spine has an S-curve. "Remember, if your guy's away, you gotta take the pin ..."

Aunt Shirley would tell him, *Yer bum's oot the windae!*

"Got it?"

I nod. Away from what? I gaze down the fairway and see a mile-long green carpet. Off in the distance, a maintenance crew hangs off a small flatbed truck filled with shovels and large chunks of sod. Perhaps that's a better job for me.

A golfer introduces himself to me as Mr. Sipe and tells me he's a guest, not a member, who hails from Kentucky Bluegrass territory. He grabs a wood from his bag, tosses me a blue head cover, and swings like he's been struck by an epileptic fit—eyes bulging and tongue twisting. I watch the man's poorly glued toupee open and shut but forget to watch the flight of his ball—the main job of a caddy.

After the remaining golfers hit their balls, I traipse behind the rest of the group as we descend down a slight hill from the tee box and into the wonderful world of country-club golf. Chip's player strides down the fairway with his cocky chest out and head high as if he owns the whole damned world. I follow my golfer through tall grass. "Did ya have an aah on mah baaall, son?"

"Yeah, I think it's right 'round here," I lie as we proceed to slog through waist-deep North Sea rough.

"Oh, yeah, here we go." The player crouches down to eye his nestled, hairy lie, and I am treated to his plumber's crack. I drop my heavy bag in the rough next to the golf ball and rub my aching shoulder, already figuring caddying isn't easy-peasy. I hate when Billy's right. The golfer uses his hand as a visor, like a sailor searching for shore. "How far you reckon it is?"

A football field away, I see a yellow flag flapping in the breeze. "I dunno." *Ah dinnae ken,* Aunt Shirley whispers in my ear.

"Really?" He grunts. "Ain't you all s'pose to know that?"

My cheeks turn purple-red. "Are we?"

A ball nearly shaves our heads from the other direction and "Foh-er!" echoes from a distant fairway.

"Well, I'll be a naakeed crawdad." He takes off his hat for emphasis. "You ain't never done this before have ya, son?"

"No, sir."

Mr. Sipe laughs, and his belly shakes from above his bright-orange high-rise polyester golf pants. He yells across the fairway, asking for the yardage. Chip returns fire. "One ninety-five to the front edge, two ten to the stick." Chip's curly black hair hangs just above his hunched shoulders, his thin frame revealing his spine breaking through his tight-fitting green-meshed caddy shirt and white collar.

After he hacks his way up the first hole, Mr. Sipe manages to dribble his ball onto the edge of the green. I stand on the fringe, and he tosses his golf ball at me. I notice Chip cleaning a golf ball with his towel. My towel is bone dry. I spit on the ball and gave it a caddy shine, then take a leisurely stroll across the buzz-cut green to return Mr. Sipe's ball to him.

The head member of the group erupts. "Hey! Don't walk in a player's line, boy."

His words blow me back across the green. *A line?* I scurry back toward my bag with my head down, clueless as to what rule I've broken. A second reprimand strikes me as I mosey back to the spot on the green where I'd just come from.

"Are you deaf? There's a line between the ball and the hole. Do you see?" The member draws an imaginary line with the staff of his club from the hole to his ball to make his point. Turns out golf has its own dress code, language, and purple crayon like *Harold and the Purple Crayon.*

"Sorry," I mumble. *Sorry, my ass.*

In this crazy *Alice in Wonderland* nightmare, there's no way I could know the bizarre rules of a stupid sport with its imaginary drawings. As if the dumb rules aren't bad enough, Chip tells me "reading the greens" is part of my job, along with figuring out which way the wind is blowing. I would have had better luck understanding Bob Dylan songs sung in Danish. Chip gives me a tip on how to read the greens while crouching over his player's putt.

"Just remember one thing. All putts break toward Kensington Road."

All I know is that I want to make a break toward Kensington Road because the bag's weighing me down. By the fourth hole, I stop to rest every ten yards, putting the bag down to switch shoulders.

On the next tee box, Chip bends down, grabs some grass, and throws it in the air. The grass blows across the tee, and the honor caddy barks out the yardage to the pin. He warns the golfers of an enormous golf-ball-eating bunker, stage left. By the sixth hole, my bag's strap is digging welts into my raw skin. Maybe I should have listened to Billy for once in my life.

Noticing I'm lagging behind the group, Chip turns back toward me. "What's the problem, Ford?"

I stop and massage my right shoulder. "Chip, I'm not sure I can make it, both of my shoulders are killing me."

"We've all been there. Try putting the towel under the strap."

I could have used this suggestion a few holes ago.

"Don't worry," Chip says. "We got a break coming up at the end of nine holes. We'll get you fed, so hang in there."

Chip tells me the Scots borrowed the term "caddy" from the French word "le cadet." If I'm killed on this ancient battlefield, at least I wouldn't have to face Pop's firing squad after I quit. This leads me to imagine I'm one of those little green plastic army men, and a boy is moving me around his make-believe warfront in his basement.

On the ninth hole, Mr. Sipe's errant bombing raid falls on an island of white marbled sand, and we embark on an eighty-yard march to secure the desolate beachhead. I surrender my player his sand weapon in this war game for grown-ups. Mr. Sipe swings, detonating a nuclear sandblast. The mushroom sand cloud settles on his toupee, and he curses his ball as it rolls back down toward his feet.

Chip stares down at us from above the green. "Play the ball back in your stance a bit and follow through, sir."

Mr. Sipe salutes Chip and reloads, scoring a parachute landing next to the flag. "Thanks, Chip," he drawls.

I smooth the footprints in the trap with a long-handled rake, thinking I've no desire to be a member of the caddy regiment. I'm the low man on the country-club totem pole—lower than the locker room boy, valet man, or the dishwasher. My brother was dead right. Caddying blows.

We finish the ninth hole as the sun spray paints my cheeks a glossy red and settle on a park bench next to the halfway shack. A sign above the entrance door to the shack warns: "Members Only: No Caddies Allowed." No caddy genes mingling with the country club blue bloods. Modern-day segregation if you ask me. A thin gray-haired lady named Myrtle runs the grill and takes our orders from an open window in the shack. I order a chocolate milk and grilled hot dog smothered in butter, and it melts in my mouth. I figure Myrtle serves members oysters and savory truffles and Grey Poupon on their hot dogs.

Ten minutes later, I'm back on the course, gazing out at the trillion blades of grass I have remaining to conquer on the eleventh tee box. On the back nine, we hack our way through an imaginary jungle with Mr. Sipe's machete posing as a 5-wood. I don't dare make a hasty retreat—I'd sooner face a firing squad than let Pop down. My legs become weak and wobbly. By the end of the fourteenth hole, I am drenched in sweat, my back hunched forward. I try to recall if I've been through anything worse than caddying and can only recall the enema I'd endured during a bout of pneumonia in the seventh grade and the three funerals I've attended.

At the end of the next hole, we stop at the supply line in the form of a small shack.

Thank you, God. A fox in a tight white Polo shirt pours each of us chocolate milk in tall Styrofoam cups—an icy-cold blood transfusion for my weary muscles. There'd be no stopping; everyone keeps moving with cups in hand.

Mr. Sipe and I limp toward home as the sun starts its slow decline, casting a dark shadow on the fairway. On the eighteenth hole—not sure why, but in golf-tongue, Chip calls the shape of the hole a "dog-leg right"—we hunt for his ball in the trees at the sharp turn in the fairway. We find it underneath a pine tree. He drops his ball and searches for an opening. His second swing yields more turf than ball, and it skids toward another pine tree. I drag my dead ass toward the ball.

"Forget it, son. She's buried deep. Just git me another ball if we got any left." Mr. Sipe uses his putter as a cane as we trek down the fairway. "Ya might be wonderin' why I play this game."

"Nope." I'm too tired to talk or care about why he plays the silly game of torture. I swear I see a lizard in the sand trap, but I keep going, too tired to care, even if Bo Derek streaked by.

"It's one of the few sports where ya can play the same game as the pros and on the same field and not just rubberneck on the tube." The golfer's voice rises three octaves. "Damn if Ben Hogan hasn't crossed this path we're takin' now and made par on this hole to win the U.S. Open Championship. I can't go out and play football or basketball without keelin' myself."

I start to take a shining to Mr. Sipe, who tells me he's a traveling salesman. After the round, the group gathers around a small table to fill out the caddy pay cards. The members write in a tip for each caddy, and we part ways.

The redheaded caddy grabs the card from my hands. "Two fifty. Ha! You got screwed. We all got four bucks."

Wow, now you can go buy yourself a new red hankie, Howdy Doody.

"I got a nice bonus on top of my tips," Chip says, pulling a wad of bills from his front pocket. Each player tipped Chip separately for all his help today. "Fifteen bucks. I've done worse."

Showoff. If you tally Chip's total tips and flat fee for the round, he got $29 for the round compared to my paltry $7.50. Howdy is right; I got scammed. I want to suggest we just all throw the tips on the table and split them evenly but figure it'll only get a big laugh.

I wave my caddy stub in the air. "What I do with this?"

Chip folds his cash and places it in a pouch he carries on his waist. "You cash it across the bridge at the caddy shack."

As we hike over the bridge that connects the north and south courses, an older kid with long blond hair screams obscenities over the railing while riding in a golf cart. I peer between the suspension cables over the metal edge and see two boys in green-mesh caddy shirts and white towels, sprinting along the dirt shoulder of Kensington Road.

"Who's that guy?" I ask Chip.

"That's King. He runs the caddy shack."

Howdy Doody butts in with his two cents. "Guy thinks he owns the joint."

"You'll pay for this!" King yells before turning his attention to us as we pass by.

"Chip," he says, holding out his hand like a parking arm gate. "You want to get one more loop in today?"

Chip gives him a "Hell yes!" nod and toothy smile. "I've done thirty-six holes, but they were both singles. Can I carry double?"

"Suit yourself." King jumps into the driver's seat of his golf cart. "Hop in and I'll take you back."

"He's going again?" I ask in disbelief. That's like running back-to-back marathons. By my estimate, if you walk eighteen holes in a straight line that's around four miles. So crisscrossing back and forth from rough to rough like I just did must have added another two, easy. Chip will be logging a good ten miles today.

"He set a club record: three hundred and ten loops last year," Howdy Doody says, watching the cart drive off.

"What's a double?" *More golf lingo to learn.*

"You carry two bags at once." He hunches up both of his shoulders. "It's more money."

I see Chip jump out of the cart, and Bobby Walton places two bags on his shoulder. "Does he ever carry a third bag around on that hunchback of his?"

"Funny, asshole. He's got scoliosis."

I shake my head. Two bags for eighteen holes? With a double loop, you wouldn't have any chance to rest a weary shoulder.

"We better run and get our checks cashed."

I follow Howdy, our towels slapping at the rails of the bridge, and ask him why we're running. "I wanna get out of here before King gets back and wants us to go out again. Duh."

Over the bridge, I step into a mostly empty caddy shack, a one-story aluminum building full of pin-ball machines and ping-pong tables. Damn. No *Space Invaders.* No *Asteroids.* Just the new arcade game called *Pac-Man.* I cash my caddy card, buy a 7 Up and a 3

Musketeers bar, phone Pop to pick me up, and plod back over the bridge to search for Rocket.

After a long wait for two groups to finish on eighteen, there's no sign of him. I wander through the parking lot and around the other side of the clubhouse to the tennis courts, fearful I'll run into Jason Sanders, who's a member at the club. He'd ask me why I'm a caddy. Hills kids from Dot Ave aren't supposed to be caddies. A girl hits a serve on one of the six freshly painted green-and-red tennis courts while a coach looks on, saying, "Throw the ball higher over your head."

Still no sign of Rocket anywhere. I pass a fence surrounding the swimming pool and finally see him sitting on the edge, his freckled back facing me. He's sipping a drink from an umbrella straw, his feet dangling in the blue water. I holler over the fence at him. "Rocket! What the hell do you think you're doing?"

He turns around and waves at me before getting up to grab a towel to dry his wet head like he owns the place.

I meet him at the entrance to the pool. "I could get used to this gig," he says.

"Dream on."

We walk back through the parking lot to wait for Pop's car, and I ask him what happened to caddying.

"I got hot and tired around the first hole." He wraps the country club towel around his waist, and I figure it's Rocket Olivehammer's property now. "I spotted the pool from a bad lie in a fairway bunker on the fourth hole and decided it was time for a swim."

I ask him how he could leave his player high and dry.

"I left him a note that said 'abducted by aliens—help me, please.' The pool's great, but the club sandwiches are lame-o."

Rocket's got some nads. "You ordered food, too?"

He tries an idiot slap to my head but misses. "You just give them your club number."

"But you're not a member, Rocket." I swing back, but he bobs and weaves. "You don't *have* a club number."

"Christ alive, Ford." Rocket smirks and lands a slap to the side of my head. I fake a dive and pull his spastic neck into a Hercules headlock. "You don't think I can swipe a club number from one of these little country-club punks?" he mumbles under my elbow. I loosen my grip on his windpipe. "I told this ten-year-old spoiled brat that my club number was better than his, and he asked me why. I told him if you add up all the numbers, my club number is higher than his." He wiggles free from my arm.

"Then what?"

"Gave him some random numbers, and we compared scores. I asked the kid his last name. Larson. 3699." Rocket smacks me in the jaw and runs for his life, stumbling to catch his towel, which falls around his knobby ankles.

A country club valet shouts, "Hey, no running."

We take off in a mad race to the first-tee side of the parking lot where Pop had dropped us off, which seems ages ago now, before the both of us collapse on the ground in two heaps of belly-aching laughter.

I gather my breath and lean against an ornamental fence. "It was harder than I thought it would be out there."

A comfortable silver roadster with brown leather seats gurgles past with a license plate reading FITZ 683, and I imagine myself in the driver's seat with that girl I met at the falls, pulling up to the valet service. Everything is perfect here, I notice—from the clipped shrubs to the freshly painted white Roman columns to the green shutters.

Rocket interrupts my daydreaming. "You're not wasting your whole summer here, are you?"

I turn toward Rocket, thinking I won't be buying any silver convertible in my future if I don't go to college. "I want that caddy scholarship."

"Forget about it." A quick punch in the gut. "You'll be dead before you get a chance to use it."

I'm too tired to play games with Rocket. I wish I could get as lucky as Reagan, and maybe caddy for the director of *Happy Days*, who'll cast me as the bastard child of the Fonze and Pinky Tuscadero. But we live in the northern suburbs of Detroit, a million miles from Hollywood. No way that could happen twice.

Pop finally shows. I see King and his big blond head riding up in his cart as I step into the car. He stops, his eyes following our car. I duck down in the front seat and shudder.

■ ■ ■

After spending the evening at Rocket's house, where his mom made us Orville Redenbacher's gourmet popcorn, I come home to Pop berating Billy over his report card from last semester, which Pop found under the seat cushion of his den chair. A 2.2 GPA. A big D in gym class.

"Explain to me how you flunked gym class?" Pop waves Billy's report card in his face. "How is that even possible?"

"So my team lost tug-of-war. At least I didn't fail." He grabs the report card from Pop's hand and writes something on the card. "See? D stands for decent."

No, Billy, that'd be D for "doctored." Half the time I want to punch Billy in his sarcastic mouth. Doesn't he give a rip about his future?

"This isn't funny, Billy," Pop says. "No college is going to want you with these grades now."

"He can go to a trade school," I suggest, trying to be helpful.

"Zip it, Fordo." Billy runs his pinched thumb and index finger across his lips. "I graduated from high school, so what's the big deal?"

Pop paces around the room, blowing baby Godzilla flames. "The big deal is that your mother and I have high hopes for you kids. Your grandfather worked at a tool and die shop for years before he became an engineer." His worn black dress shoes stop at my feet. "You have to study hard and get a college degree."

"Pop, you could go to trade school," Billy says, egging him on. That isn't such a bad idea. Except for sales, Pop has no real expertise in anything, except conjuring get-rich schemes.

"Don't worry about me. I have something in the works."

Not again. Please, please, please.

"What, Pop? Tell us." This is just Billy's attempt to distract Pop from his report card.

"Just don't blab it to your mother," he says with a whisper and a wink. Pop can go from mad to manic in an instant if the topic turns to one of his schemes.

"We won't. I promise," I say, moving from my slumped posture to upright, caught in his upbeat tone.

"Okay, then. It's robotics," he says with a bright smile, like we should be jumping up and down in jubilation.

I don't quite understand what he said. "Robots, Pop?"

"Someone already invented that, Fordo," Billy says. "They're called Rock 'Em Sock 'Em Robots."

I can hear Virginia banging pots in the kitchen, getting dinner ready.

"This is no toy, boys." Pop shuts the two doors to the den and sits down. This is getting serious, and I think just maybe he's on to something really good, and I think back to that silver convertible in the country club parking lot, which I imagine is now in my driveway. "Listen up. I got the inside track from my contacts in the auto industry. Robotic technology. Modernization of the work force. Machines will replace factory workers.

They don't go on strike like those union bums or take long lunch breaks."

"Pop, you can barely untangle the water hose, let alone build a robot," Billy says, trying to unnerve him.

"Ro-bo-tics, Billy. I'm investing some seed money into a new company called Technology Now."

Billy the skeptic frowns. "Where's the money coming from?"

My brother's going to ruin the moment, I can feel it.

"I'm selling the shares," he lowers his voice another octave, "that we have left in Ohio Savings Bank."

I shake my head in disbelief, knowing it's the last of Mom's family money. Mom had been conceived from banking stock. Her math-whiz father presided over the Ohio Savings Bank in Columbus despite never having graduating from high school.

"This'll be the big one. Can't miss. At any rate, Billy, you better get these grades up," he says as he picks up the *Kensington Observer* and makes an attempt to shake the print out of the newspaper. "College is just around the corner for you!"

Pop expects all three of us kids to go to college. He never finished himself after getting plucked from chasing coeds at Michigan State and sent to cold-test tanks in Alaska during the Korean War. And he isn't about to let his kids go down the same narrow path. I don't see any options in Billy's future, and now Dad's going to spend the last of Virginia's inheritance. That money could come in handy for college, or at least a new stereo and speakers. I pray Pop hits it big for once.

Just for freaking once.

4

'm minding my own business in the TV room, eating a
Swanson TV dinner and watching a rerun of *James at 15*—
only now it's called *James at 16* because now James is six-
teen—when I hear Chimney yelp outside. This is unusual.
She rarely barks, but she frequently sniffs people like she's a
K9 drug dog at an airport.

Chimney normally won't let me out of her sight,
and I never feel alone with my dog around, even though
I'm pretty lonely half the time, always waiting for Jason
Sanders or Jack Lott or someone from school to call me
up on the phone. I can't spend my whole life with only
one human friend (Rocket). The phone rings a ton in
the Quinn house, but it's usually followed by Mom saying "Kate, it's for you" if she doesn't answer it first. Kate's
got a slew of friends.

"Ford, get the dog," Mom screams from the living room, where she's polishing her silverware set just in case Queen Elizabeth stops by for a visit.

I exhale a thousand sighs. "Ask Kate!" Technically, Chimney is Kate's dog because she rescued her from somewhere, but she never takes care of her for one second on account of how lazy she is, so she's become my dog.

"She's playing tennis at the park." Chimney barks again. "Fooord."

"*What?*" I hope she doesn't blow her whistle. It can blow lids off coffins.

"She's scaring some girl at the Clarks'."

I slam the door behind me, pissed as hell for having to move my legs, which are still sore from caddying, and that was two days ago. My pupils grow wide as charcoal as I see Chimney circling, sniffing, and barking gently at the girl I'd met at the falls last week with Rocket.

God bless you, Chimney. She must have a sixth sense that I wanted to talk to her again. A dog's intuition is so keen they can practically read their master's mind, according to *National Geographic*.

I must be in a dream. I blink hard, raise my head, and she hasn't disappeared. At the end of Chimney's wet, groveling nose is *that* girl.

I hold my dog's collar. "Chimney! Knock it off, will ya?"

"Hey, it's you, Ford."

I notice she's holding a record in her hand and is wearing a red tube top and black painted toenails underneath her flip-flops.

"Cleo?" I ask, pretending to be unsure and too cool, although I can feel my pulse exploding in my wrist.

"You remembered my name."

I've only said her name in my mind a million times since I last saw her and rhymed it in my spiral poetry notebook. *Cleo, you're so real that I feel you could be the real deal.*

"I live over on Foxbury," she says, "the house with the turret."

I know their Gothic home because it sits kitty-corner from a red-brick mansion with a trampoline in the backyard. Rocket and I used to trespass on all the trampolines in the neighborhood until his parents broke down and installed an in-ground one in his backyard. The rubber on his trampoline is worn white from all our jumping—if you totaled the height of our jumps, it would equal the distance to Pluto.

I hear an upstairs window open at my neighbors, and the hairs on my neck quiver like someone's watching us. A ruby-throated hummingbird hovers and sips from a trumpet vine snaking up a telephone pole at the front corner of our lot and zips away.

I wonder why on earth she's next door at the Clarks' house. Mrs. Clark runs some kind of a psychology racket out of her home. I rarely see Old Man Clark, maybe once in a blue moon as he rides off on his motorcycle with his long white beard flapping in the wind like he's a member of Hell's Angels. They have two older kids, Pauley and Jenny.

Cleo bends down and rubs underneath Chimney's chin. "Goood girl."

My dog licks her toes, and I smell the faint flowery scent of her shampooed hair and think of that "Gee, Your Hair Smells Terrific" ad where the high school sweethearts are whispering to each other in the library.

"I was at Dr. Clark's for a therapy session."

"Oh, so your mom's meeting with her?"

That made sense, because Pop constantly complains about therapy-patient cars parked in front of our two houses all day long.

"Nope." Cleo twists her lips like she's itching to tell me something. "Can I trust you with a secret?" She rubs her hands together nervously, and I see my mood ring, still crystal clear.

I nod once, but I mean a thousand times yes. Cleo steps forward two steps and whispers in my ear. "*I* just had a therapy session with Dr. Clark."

I've never known any kids who'd seen a shrink, but what the hell did I know, anyway? Chimney keeps circling and sniffing at her.

"Sorry, I don't know what's gotten into her. She never even barks at other dogs or even squirrels." I hold her collar, but she fights me tooth and hair. "If we ever got robbed, she'd open the safe for them."

She has one hand on her hip and the other in the air like a waitress with a heavy tray. Her eyes narrow with incredulity. "Aren't you going to ask me why I'm seeing Dr. Clark?"

I give her a blank stare, not knowing how I should answer.

"I know it's killing you to know," she says.

Actually, I don't care if she sees a shrink or a fortune teller or Bigfoot's palm-reading sister. "It's none of my beeswax." Okay, maybe I'm a bit curious why she's seeing the psychotherapist next door. All right, curious as hell.

She sits down on a huge boulder on the corner of our front lawn. "Dr. Clark tells me I shouldn't be embarrassed. Seeing a therapist is practically the in thing these days."

Don't tell that to Virginia, I say to myself. She thinks her self-help philosophy can cure all psychological ills.

Cleo crosses her leg, placing her elbow on her knee and a fist under her chin like the sculpture I saw on a school field trip to the Detroit Institute of Arts last year. Chimney lies down next to her. My dog doesn't normally cozy up to strangers unless they're carrying treats.

"Do you have dog biscuits in your pocket?"

She ignores my question, looking lost in her own thoughts. I recall the name of that sculpture just now: *The Thinker.*

"No one at my school would understand," she says. "My mom thinks I have bulimia. I don't feel well, and I've been throwing up a ton." She pinches a millimeter of skin. Bulimia is the preferred dieting method among teenage girls in the Hills. Rib-revealing girls get called away from class and counseled on the dangers of the new diet fad by our school nurse, Sister Godden.

Chimney sniffs Cleo's left hip. I grab her collar. "Maybe she smells a dog or a cat on you."

A loud sneeze. She wipes her lovely, petite nose with the back of her hand. "I'm allergic to dogs and cats. We have a cockatoo my mom lets fly wild in our garden room."

Chimney propeller-scratches her ear, then noses Cleo in the leg. "She's gone nuts." *Why in the world did you say that word, you dimwit?* "Maybe I should take her inside."

Cleo stands up suddenly from the rock and shakes her finger at me. "Dr. Clark told me I'm not *nuts*, and I *don't* have bulimia if that's what you're thinking." She turns her back to me. "You sound like my stupid mom."

A long pause, and the hummingbird returns, hovers, then nosedives into the tubular orange flower hanging over our asphalt driveway. Don't know what I really said to piss her off, but tell myself, *You might want to say something now if you don't want to lose this girl.*

"I wasn't thinking anything"— except that girls might as well be another species—"but why does Dr. Clark think you're puking?"

"She has no real clue." She reels back around to face me. "I have no telltale symptoms of bulimia," she sticks her finger in and out of her mouth, revealing her perfect china-white teeth. "And anyway, Dr. Clark's cool as hell for an adult. You'd never think she was someone's mom."

Chimney paws at Cleo's feet, so I drag her fur coat up the driveway. My dilemma is trying to get Chimney away from her and at the same time not letting this girl out of my sight. She heads down the sidewalk and picks up a record leaning up against her bike, returning to show it to me. The cover shows a guy wearing a scarf with his shut eyelids painted blue.

"Hey," she says, "my mom gave me money to buy this old Gary Wright album today for agreeing to see Dr. Clark. You want to hear it?"

I smile up at God through a gap in the billowy clouds. "Sure." Music might as well be oxygen; I'd die without it. "Follow me," I say, motioning for her to come down the driveway, trying to remain cool. I hear a snickering on the Clark side of the shrubs, like someone has been eavesdropping on our conversation. Had Pauley Clark come down from his secret attic hovel?

In my basement three minutes later, I drop the needle on the song "Dream Weaver," and I'm suddenly transported by the music to outer space, tethered to a spacecraft. The song will put you in a trance like the melody is scientifically designed by a musical hypnotist. After I come down to earth, we sit on the couch, and my legs won't stop a nervous fidget. Meanwhile, Chimney whines from the top of the stairs, clawing to open the door.

What is up with that dog?

It dawns on me that I've never been with a girl in the basement alone, let alone anywhere else, and wonder if I shouldn't make some lame move on her, but then I remember we aren't on a date. Then again, she's wearing my mood ring. Guys are always thinking of moves on girls, but I'd heard Paula Constance from Holy Redeemer actually made a first move on Larry Turner, a normal kid just like me, in the balcony of Kensington Theater during a midnight showing of *Young Frankenstein*. Thoughts swirl dizzily in my head but are interrupted by Mom's Rainbow vacuuming upstairs, which is louder than a KISS concert.

I go over and turn up the stereo and sit back down next to her. My left fidgety leg and her right leg are a shoe box apart. An eerie silence goes by before I think of something to say.

"Did you happen to see Pauley Clark next door?" A Pauley Clark sighting is as rare as a Fabergé egg. And I want to know who's snooping around behind the shrubs separating our house from the Clarks'.

Cleo pops off the couch and roams around my basement, eyeing my kid stuff. "No, why?"

"Pauley's my sister Kate's age, I think, but he doesn't even go to a regular school." Pauley's a big mystery to me, just like the rest of the Clarks. He just moans from the upstairs window like he's the hunchback of Notre Dame. "He hardly ever goes outside."

"That's odd." Cleo grabs a Stan Smith tennis racquet from underneath the ping-pong table and does a forehand swing. "You play tennis?"

"Not much, you?" I hate tennis because the wannabes are so damn pretentious with all their Bjorn Borg headbands, perfect white Tretorn shoes, and private lessons at the indoor courts at the Kensington Tennis & Racquet Club. Kate plays tennis (Billy was excellent before he quit) but refuses to play with me unless she's desperate because I fire moonballs into the air, and she just gets fed up chasing the ball, normally throwing down her racquet in protest.

"I used to play, but I don't have the energy anymore. Mom's worried about that, too. Won't get off my ass." Her shoulders slump, and she plucks the tennis strings while leaning against the ping-pong table. "What are you doin' this summer?"

I want to say "spending the summer with you," but I'd just sound like some smart-ass jerk. "Caddying at the country club."

Her eyes perk up. "Oh yeah?" She does a slow-motion backhand. "You'll probably see my stepdad at the club someday. He plays there almost every morning."

Her parents must've divorced or her real dad's dead, but I don't want to bring up a potentially prickly subject. I hear Chimney growling at the door and pray Virginia doesn't bring down a load of dirty laundry with my underwear on top. "What's your stepdad do?"

"Golf."

Perhaps I'll caddy for him this summer. "No, I meant for a job."

"Archaeology professor at the University of Detroit. He's an expert in Ancient Egyptian stuff like pyramids, pharaohs, and mummies." A fake serve scrapes the tiled ceiling, causing flakes to float to the floor. "That's why he nicknamed me Cleopatra, but my real name is just Cleo." With her straight black bangs, she could have played Elizabeth Taylor's daughter in that old movie *Cleopatra* they run every single Easter.

"Ford is short for Gifford." *Now what in the world did you say that for, you idiot.* No one's heard that name since kindergarten when "Gifford Quinn" rolled off Ms. Lewis's tongue during roll call on the first day of class, which spawned mirthful giggles. Pop came up with my name on account of Grandpa's bigwig gig at Ford Motor.

Cleo traces the lines on the palm of her hand. *Am I in your future?* "You go to Holy Redeemer, Gifford?"

"It's Ford. Since first grade. Are you Catholic?" Maybe she'd gone to Our Lady of Sorrows, which is on the other side of the Hills, but I'm pretty sure she's a public schooler.

"Funny, Giff ..." She laughs out loud and places the Stan Smith on my ping-pong table, which is covered with my plastic yellow racetrack.

Please don't let her think I still play with Hot Wheels. I eye an old comic book, an issue of *Daredevil and the Black Widow*, on the floor in the corner and pray to Thor she doesn't think I'm still reading comics, too.

"We're atheists unless you count Egyptian goddess worship."

Sign me up. "Did the ancient Egyptians have a church?"

"Of course, Giff. They worshipped at the Ramesseum temple." She sits back down next to me. "I usually tell people I'm agnostic instead of an atheist."

Hmm. She told me. I guess I'm not just anyone. I ask her what the difference is. She flicks her bangs out of her eyes. "Agnostics believe there is no way of knowing if God exists or not. Atheists think there is no God. Period."

She isn't like the other girls in my class; she's strange and mysterious. Her matching gold wristbands and headband glitter under the fluorescent ceiling lights. I'm thinking summer vacation might be really, really good this year.

"Does Jack Lott go to Holy Redeemer?" Cleo asks out the blue, bursting my bubble dream.

Skipping static fills the basement as the A-side ends. The stereo arm makes its way back in place. "Yeah, Jack and I did eight years together at Holy Redeemer Prison. What about him?" I get up and flip the record to the B-side, "Love is Alive," hoping she says she and Jack are first cousins, and any chance of the two of them dating are DOA.

"Just wondering, that's all." Cleo bounces off the couch and swings her hips back and forth to the music. "I saw him at the club the other day playing in a tennis tournament and heard he was Catholic."

Who the hell cares? Jack's a member out at Devon Hunt Club, but there is no way I'm going to tell her this and make her think he's any cooler. All the well-to-do kids from the Hills are members of some private sailing, tennis and golf, or hunt club. "They were playing at Kensington, but I was too sick to play, so I sat and watched. He's pretty good." The song ends, and she stops swaying. "A real hard serve."

Unlike mere mortals, Jack Lott doesn't need to pretend he's a superhero because he is a real hero to us

Holy Redeemers. Scoring touchdowns, making last-second winning basketball shots against our rival, Shrine Academy, city champion in the 100-yard dash, top-ranked junior foil fencer in the state. Oh yeah, and a great tennis player, too. A Norse-looking musclebound kid, and good natured to boot.

Jack's twin older brothers, Tony and Graham, are sports legends in the Hills, too. Graham had been the starting quarterback on Catholic High's state football championship team. Tony Lott had been slotted to throw the javelin at the Olympic trials before President Carter boycotted the summer games in Moscow because of the Soviet Union's invasion of Afghanistan. What an epic bummer that was. Years of training pissed away in an instant.

I realize if Jack Lott is my competition, then I need to up my lame game and say something negative about him, but I can't think of one stinking thing. Plus, if he finds out, I'll have to go into the Witness Protection Program.

"I'm pretty sure he's got a girlfriend." This isn't necessarily a lie because I've never known him to be without one going back to the second grade, when he dated Stephanie Crow, a third grader.

"I would think so," she says, with a dreamy, faraway tone to her voice.

What the hell does that mean? "I would think so."
She digs through my record collection and pulls out and puts back a Bay City Rollers cover. Who still listens to those S-A-T-U-R-D-A-Y guys? Kate, that's who.

A few years back she'd gone bonkers about the scarf-wearing bandmates from Scotland and ordered a Rollers Kissing Kit from *16* magazine at the height of Rollermania. The Rollers got their idiotic name when the drummer threw a dart at a map of the United States, landing on Bay City, Michigan, which is only ninety minutes from Kate's bedroom. One weekend my sister convinced Virginia to drive her and Betsy Carmichael to Bay City so Kate could write a pathetic letter to the Rollers mailbag at *16* magazine, saying she'd visited their namesake. They not only published it but mailed her a signed poster of all four Rollers in their knee-high socks along with a T-shirt that read "Rollers 4-Ever." The highlight of her life so far.

Cleo skips over Kate's lame buys and picks out *Frampton Comes Alive!*. She's got decent musical taste. Nice.

She holds the album cover to her chest. "I looove this album."

"You can borrow it." I almost take those words back; my albums might as well be my closest friends, right along with Chimney and Rocket. On second thought, if she borrows something, she'll have to bring it back, and then I'll give her another album … and so on and so on…

"I have it," Cleo says in a who-the-hell-doesn't-have-this-album? tone. "I just made a new mixtape and included 'Baby, I Love Your Way.'"

I don't own the technology to make a quality mixtape yet because my cassette player won't plug into my old stereo, but I'm saving up for one with my caddy earnings. Cleo clunks the Frampton album back in the rack.

"Oh yeah, I did see his sister."

She's lost me. "Jack Lott's sister, Bailey?" Bailey Lott is infamous for getting gonged on *The Gong Show* while balancing on a ten-foot-high tightrope, singing the "The Star-Spangled Banner."

"No. Pauley Clark's sister. You mentioned something about never seeing Pauley."

"Oh, Jenny Clark." Jenny puked her drunk guts up in our driveway once, and Pop wrongly blamed Billy for the mess. Virginia somehow knew the truth and wondered out loud at me over breakfast why Billy didn't try to blame it on Jenny. He even cleaned it up with the garden hose. "She's my brother's age."

"Well, she's gorgeous as hell. Reminds me of Susan Dey from *The Partridge Family*."

"People say my dad's a dead ringer for Reuben Kincaid." Chimney must have nosed open the door because I hear the muffled pound of pawbeats down the stairs. She prances by me and hovers guard next to Cleo. *What in the world, dog?*

Cleo glances at her Cleopatra watch, which reminds me of the Martian in the poem who tells his fellow Martians that humans wear time on their wrists. I just want time to stand still. "Oh, I gotta go, Giff." She takes two steps toward the stairs before stopping and whirling back around. "Maybe I'll see you next Friday?"

The electrical fuse box in my heart blows. *Pretend cool, Ford.* "Sounds like a plan." Vinyl from my shaky hands slides back into the jacket sleeve. I watch her disappear up the stairs while I choke Chimney with her collar.

Wait, what? I run upstairs and outside and catch up to her in the patch of grass between our driveway and the Clarks'. "What's next Friday?"

She slips out of her flip-flops, puts them in her basket, and mounts her bike. "My next therapy session. What else?" She places her hand in a gun formation and fires at the Clark house before weaving her way down Dot Ave.

Next Friday I'll invite her back to my house for 7 Ups, peanut butter Space Food Sticks, and basement music after her date with Dr. Clark. Waiting for 168 hours to see Cleo will feel like an eternity. I haven't looked forward to something like this since fellow Holy Redeemer Veronica Brophy invited me to a KISS concert at the Pontiac Silverdome last year. After bragging around the world about my good luck, I'd waited for hours on my front porch, but Veronica never showed. Cleo wouldn't do that to me, would she?

5

Whenever Rocket has something exciting to tell me, he can't wait one second, even if it's after midnight. I've just fallen asleep when I'm woken up by rocks pelting my window. I open it and see Rocket standing in our yard with a flashlight in his hand. "Get down here."

I wipe a century of sleep from crusty eyes. "Unless you tell me Jimmy Hoffa's eating Ding Dongs in your kitchen, consider yourself dead."

"No. This is better than that." He holds up something in his hand, but it's too dark to see. "Don't be a stupid putz. Get your ass down here or I'll give it to someone else."

I crane my neck out the window as far as I can but still can't see what he's got. Chirping crickets are about the only thing you hear at night in the Hills. If you count the chirps for fourteen seconds and multiply it by forty, you'll get the temperature. Seventy-two degrees, I calculate. Rocket won't let up until he shows me whatever moronic thing he's found, so I slither down the stairs, careful not to wake Virginia, and find Rocket waiting in the same spot.

"What's so important at this—"

"This will blow your mind." He slowly brings his arm around, flashes two concert tickets in front of my face, and focuses the flashlight beam on the tickets.

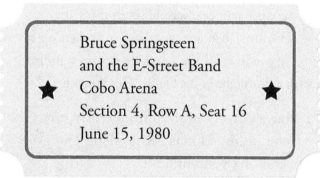

Bruce Springsteen
and the E-Street Band
Cobo Arena
Section 4, Row A, Seat 16
June 15, 1980

Must be some mistake. "You're going to see The Boss?" I eye the ticket, double-check the date, and can't believe my eyes. No mistake. *Front row!*

"No, idiot." He shoves me in the chest. "*We're* going. *You* and *me*. Tomorrow night."

I jump up and down so high I practically skim a low-hanging cloud. So far this is the most epic moment of my life. I feel the ticket to make sure it's real, and it is, because it's got the date and everything. It might as well be a million-dollar bill. "How'd ya score these?"

"It doesn't matter." Sometimes it's better not to ask Rocket too many questions because you might not want to know the answer. He sprints around our yard like a spaz, and I chase the flashlight's beam under the bright moon. I can't believe my good fortune. In just twenty-four hours, I'll be ten feet from The Boss and the E-Street Band. I've played the album *Darkness on the Edge of Town* so many times I've had to replace the needle on my turntable.

Billy has every Springsteen album, but they were in his bedroom, where I'm forbidden to go. Then he fell into a weird jazz phase—mellow Pat Metheny-type crap—and didn't notice when I nicked some of his old rock albums last year. Most kids wouldn't pick *Greetings from Asbury Park, N.J.* as the most brilliant Springsteen LP, but I do. "Blinded by the Light" and "Spirit in the Night" not only rhyme if you say them right after another but are probably the most badass, triumphant, poetic songs ever written.

Greetings from Asbury Park, N.J. also has an ace album jacket. The front and back of the album have all the words to the songs, and a flap covers the front, and when you turn over the flap you realize it's a fake postcard in Bruce's own handwriting with a list of his bandmates and a picture of him for the postage stamp, smiling with his mustache and scrawny beard.

Normally I listen to Rocket's albums because he has scores along with his brother Basil, and we debate the greatest Boss songs ever. I don't have enough money to buy many albums of my own, but one caddy loop can buy me one album. Nick Lund once claimed he saw The Boss eating clam chowder at Baker's Keyboard Lounge in Detroit before a gig at Cobo Arena. Nick has a story for everything and would probably one-up you even if you had a date with Joey Heatherton, so you're generally better off just shutting the hell up. I don't know why everyone can't see through Nick's bullcrap like I can.

On the morning of the concert, I rise early, pull out each Springsteen album in chronological order, and figure I'll stay inside and study the lyrics of each song. With my luck, the Soviets will decide to drop a nuclear bomb on today of all days. I replace the stylus on my turntable with a new one I bought uptown at Vinny's Hi-Fi and close my eyes to the aching sounds of "The River."

Just a few lines in, my solitude is rudely interrupted by a throbbing knock at the door. "Get lost, cyclops." *What does Kate want now?* Always accusing me of stealing her hairbrush, zit cream, or *People* magazine.

"Open up."

Great, it's not Kate. It's Pop trying to ruin my glory day.

"It's unlocked." I pull my headphones down around my neck.

"You need a ride to the country club, bud?" He's wearing a bright smile along with his breakfast apron, after chugging liters of Maxwell House. Mornings are the peak time of the day for Pop. "I made your favorite. Pancakes and bacon. Give you some energy for caddying today."

No way I'll kill Pop's good mood; they're far and few between, so I nod. "Sure, Pop." I wasn't planning on caddying today, but I figure one loop would get me enough cash to buy one Boss T-shirt at the concert.

A full stomach later, Pop drops me off at the Kensington Hills Country Club just before nine o'clock. Like on my first day, I sit on the green bench near the first tee. I calculate that if I bag a loop by 9:30, I'll be home by three o'clock tops, just in time to get ready for the concert. I've only been to two real concerts in my life. The Beach Boys at Pine Knob and a fake Beatles band when I was twelve at the Masonic Temple.

While I'm daydreaming about the concert, Bobby Walton barks at me from his podium in front of the first tee. "Did you check in at the caddy shack?"

I shake my head, and he tells me to report to King across the bridge. Apparently I got a get-out-of-the-caddy-shack-free card for my inaugural round.

I descend the bridge to a sea of green shirts snapping towels. I wade through the crowd and enter the caddy shack. King sits in a chair with his boots on the counter behind a booth with a glass window, the kind you see at party stores in bad neighborhoods. A hearty knock on the glass and King looks up from *Time* magazine, and then glances down again to resume reading. I knock again and again.

"I'm not blind!" King shouts.

"Bobby Walton told me to report here."

He closes the magazine cover, showing a drawing of President Carter under the title "Debacle in the Desert," then takes his feet off the counter. "You're new here, aren't you?" He says this with a bothered, critical tone.

"Yeah, I just started Tuesday."

"Sign your name here, pleon." (I learn later that a "pleon"—a kid with ten loops or less—is the lowest form of caddy matter; even plebes rule over pleons.) King hands me a notepad with three columns for the three caddy ranks—honor, captain, apprentice. I scribble my name under the apprentice column. Just like at Holy Redeemer, I rank on the lowest rung on the ladder.

"When do I get to go out?" I ask King.

King coughs out a hoot. "When ... I ... call ... your ... name."

"How long will that be?" I check my watch; it's 10:15.

"We'll get you out by high noon." He opens his magazine. "Now go piss off, pleon."

A soft knock. "Do I get paid for sitting around here? Is there a clock where I punch in or something?"

King whirls around, sticks his blond whale head out the open door, and rings a bell.

Silence.

Movement in the shack stalls. All eyes on me. Even the pinball players hold the silver balls in suspense on the edge of the machines' flippers. "This pleon thinks he should get paid for sitting on his ass. Do you think we can find him some work?"

I've poked a hornet's nest.

The caddies erupt in a chant. "Shithouse, shithouse, shithouse."

"Gandy, get him the mop."

A tall fellow with a cowboy hat, long sideburns, and brown dingo boots pulls out a mop and bucket from a small closet. I take Gandy for one of King's henchmen.

"Congratulations, you get shithouse detail, pleon," Gandy says. "It's part of the initiation rite of all our boys and girls here at Kensington Hills Country Club."

Gandy hands me a foul mop and bucket and leads me to the shithouse—a brick outhouse with two urinals and one toilet. I'm assaulted by the stink of urine and have a sneaking suspicion that I won't be paid for this work.

"Fill the bucket at the faucet outside the building." He reaches into his pocket. "Here's some soap. Scrub the floor and toilets. Get the boogers above the urinal. King always checks that." He lifts his Stetson a tad off his forehead. "Oh, see that writing over there?"

I nod. In scrawled cursive above the urinal, someone has scribbled "Bogart's an A-Hole."

He points to the graffiti. "You best clean that up."

"Who's Bogart?" I mumble.

"Jesus, you really are a pleon," Gandy remarks. "Mr. Bogart's the caddy master. The head honcho. The big dick. You got a lot to learn."

As water pours into the bucket, I stare at the bridge, tempted to run for it but come to my senses, not wanting to risk antagonizing King. It'd be curtains for caddying here. Instead, I decide to take my lumps and obey King's orders. I mop the floor clean, using my fingernail to dislodge several pieces of dried boogers. I pour the dirty water down the drain and wash the floor one more time.

After my mop duty, I warm myself on a bench in the sun, wondering when my name will be called and checking my wristwatch every ten seconds. 11:30. I do a double take after noticing a priest carrying a golf club in one hand, sauntering down the bridge trailed by a caddy. Maybe God is trying to tell me something.

Four caddies play basketball on a concrete court, shooting the ball at two hoops with chained nets. Other caddies are playing horseshoes and smoking cigarettes. Taking pity on me, a kid who looks like he's strolled off the movie set of *Quadrophenia* (I saw the flick last year at the midnight showing with Jason Sanders but fell asleep thirty minutes in) sits down next to me with his black hair cut mod-style, wearing punker Doc Martens boots and an Army parka, a mile too baggy for him, with a UK patch on the shoulder. His neck shows a small knife wound. A green caddy apprentice badge shines on his coat next to a bunch of other buttons with odd phrases:

"Blackburn Mods!" "Scooters 4 Life," "The Specials," "Mods Are Back."

He taps me on the shoulder. "Oi, mate. Can I scrounge a melvyn off ya."

I don't know what he's talking about. He pinches his thumb and index finger together, presses them against his lips, and puckers up. "Ya know, a cough and drag?"

I shake my head. "I don't smoke, bloke." He tells me his name is Owen Rooney and asks me how many loops I've carried.

"Just one, you?"

He flashes me a pair of fives. "Country cousin." Just evolved past pleon stage. "You dig The Jam or The Chords?"

I've never heard of these British bands, so I change the subject. "Didn't realize caddying would be this hard."

"Not 'alf bad if you stick with it ... How 'bout The Clash?" He pulls a short switchblade out of his pocket and starts whittling a small stick. "'ang in there. Gets easier on your bones after a few rounds."

I give Owen a half smile, thinking maybe this kid isn't half bad, and then I quiz him about what he knows of this country-club version of *Lord of the Flies*. "Aren't there any golfers? What's the deal with sitting around here all morning?"

"Cos loopers outnumber them twenty to one." A rabbit's foot hangs from his belt loop. "You've got to get 'ere early in the morning to get out straight away."

Nothing worse than getting up before the sun rises. "That sucks."

He whittles away on his stick. "Well, if you wanna avoid the queue, get 'ere around six in the morning."

A roar comes from inside the shack. Through the window, I can see a group of caddies crowding around a pinball machine. I turn back to Owen. "I get up that early once a year."

A kid across the way tosses a horseshoe and misses. A chain net swallows a basketball. Wood shavings fall on Owen's black high-top boots. "Sounds like you just like milkin' the day."

"We drive to Florida every year for spring break to visit my cousins in Cocoa Beach," I say. "My dad always stops at the same Holiday Inn just past Atlanta. He gets us up at the crack of dawn. I fall asleep in the car and wake up in the Sunshine State."

"Never been, just Brighton Beach where the sky's usually pissin' rain." He pauses. "It's a bloody contest."

"What is?"

"Seein' who gets 'ere first." A red, white, and blue basketball rolls over, and Owen kicks it back to a caddy in Deadhead threads. "Rat and Chip always get here first."

"I've met Chip, but who's Rat?"

"Don't worry." Owen trims his stick down to a sharp point at one end. "You stick 'round long enough, you'll meet 'im."

I nod over at the shack. "What's up with numbnuts?"

"King's a real prick, so stay away from him."

My newfound friend slips his knife back into his pocket, stands up, and then bends down, shoving the pointy end of the stick into the ground. He pulls out a golf ball from the pocket of his parka, and places it on his newly crafted tee on the grass between the shack and the basketball court.

"Grab me that ol' twig behind you," he says.

I hand him a rusted five-iron, leaning against the shack. He steps up to the ball, aims, and whacks the ball down the middle of the makeshift basketball court, over the fence, and out of sight across Kensington Road.

"Hey!" the Deadhead says.

Owen gives him the Italian salute, and says, "Piss off, maggot!" He gives me back the club like I'm his caddy and yanks his new tee from the ground, shoving it in his pocket.

Owen sits down with his back against the shack. "By the way, make sure you don't let King see you leave any earlier than six o'clock, or you'll be in his doghouse. A hard flick of the wrist, and a golf ball rises a mile above his head. "Bogart gets on his ass if he runs out of caddies." The ball lands in his hand, and he pulls another golf ball from his parka and hurls it to the heavens.

"I need to get home by five because my friend's got tickets to Springsteen at Cobo."

"Sounds like it's robin. Me brother Jake saw the bloke at Hammersmith Odeon." Head still, pupils tracking the flight of the golf ball.

A blonde girl appears and leans against the shack, using the window of the building as a mirror to smear on lip gloss. She smacks her lips and gives herself a satisfied smile. She turns around in her white overalls, her eyes landing on us before she strolls into the shack.

"Hey," I say, "get a load of her."

Saturn's dimpled moon crashes to Earth and bounces onto the court. "That be Gigi Arnold."

Huh. Cute as a dumpling covered in vanilla pudding.

He exchanges his golf balls for a magnifying glass, roasts an ant on a sun grill, and turns it on the girl. "Lovely set of bacons."

Don't know if he means her legs or something else. "By the way, why do you do this?" Maybe he wants an Evans scholarship, too.

"Me three older brothers carried. Besides, we could use the bread. All goes into the family pot. Pocketed seven quid yesterday." He tells me his family moved from England last fall, and I ask him where he lives now. "We're artful dodgers at the Palms Motel, but Mum and Dad are searching for a new flat in the Valley. Hills might as well be posh Chelsea, and the links here're beautaful."

The Valley's the poorest area in the county and to Hills kids might as well be Mars. Of course, Owen is from East London, practically another galaxy away.

King's voice booms from the shack, shouting out names. Owen Rooney jumps up and dashes inside. He comes back out a few seconds later and says, "Check out some Bowie. I'll start ya in the beginner class. See you baked, mate."

Then he runs across the bridge in his clunky boots for his morning loop, stops, and yells back at me, "Do ya wanna play some golf with me Monday?"

I give him a thumbs-up. (Pop would love to see a golfer in the family besides himself; perhaps it's something the two of us can do together as I get older.) I barely understand two words Owen says, but he seems nice enough for a Britwit, as Billy calls them, and it's nice to meet a stranger in a strange land. I'm finding out Kensington Country Club is a place where you just learned on the go.

In the shack, a bunch of green shirts surround a pinball machine, coaxing a player, who I can tell is racking up bonus points by the sounds of the bell. The pinball machine theme is Charlie's Angels, the trio of girls in their standard pose, toting guns, tight jeans, and cleavage. Farrah's belt buckle earns a bonus point. The crowd sounds a collective groan and a high-pitched "Shit!" echoes throughout the shack. The game ends, and the crowd melts away. Gigi Arnold gives the machine a smack on the side with the palm of her hand, then saunters away. The machine chirps back at her. King calls her name to caddy, and she says, "'bout time, for fuck's sake."

After what seems like a lifetime, King calls my name for a loop. Across the bridge, Bobby Walton gives me a large brown bag even heavier than my first one. Another guest bag. This day I know where to line up, the holes to expect, and the basic rules. I look out at the sea of green turf and wonder on which hole I'll drown.

A boy with a blue captain's badge that reads "Timmy" inspects my bag. "Ha. You've got a hacker."

I don't know what he's talking about. Timmy hasn't even seen him hit yet. "How do you know?"

"His sticks are in tubes." He turns up his snotty nose. "Only duffers use those."

I peer down at my bag. Each club has its own plastic black tube like a sheath for a sword.

A wiry man with slick brown hair comes over and slaps me on the back. "We'll have fun today, son."

I hate back slappers, and I'm not your son. The member throws a tee in the air to get the party started. The tee lands, pointing toward my player. His tee shot rockets straight before comet trailing out of bounds. He hooks his mulligan (golf lingo for a do-over) too, and the ball disappears toward the fence. Timmy was right. The man would hook and hack all day long.

At the halfway shack at Number 9, Owen Rooney passes by me after filling out his caddy card on eighteen, and I ask him how his loop fared.

"'E's a right Arnold." (Arnold Palmer=farmer=spends all day in the rough.) Owen can go home, and it's only 2:30. My group slow-pokes from tee to tee, but I'll still easily make the Springsteen concert and have time for a quick nap before we go.

By 4:30, I finally make it to the eighteenth hole. I grab my caddy pay stub and jog toward the bridge, feeling the excitement build for the most epic night of my life, and wonder what song Springsteen will open with tonight. Probably something off *Born to Run*, like "Thunder Road" or "Tenth Avenue Freeze-Out" to get the crowd on its feet. Like that's even necessary at a Springsteen concert. King appears from over the arch of the bridge and stops his cart next to me.

"Get in," he says in a gentle, breezy tone, just like the bluebirds singing in the trees in the fine warm air this summer afternoon.

I wave King off, my mind a million miles away on E-Street in Bossland. "I'm going the other way." *Maybe he'll open with "Spirit in the Night?"* Golf carts with rattling clubs zoom by me and disappear across the bridge to the north course. Owen had told me if the famed south course was full, members have to settle on the eighteen-hole course on the other side of Kensington Road.

"Hop in, I'll drive you," King says, smiling. I hesitate but hop in the cart anyway. Perhaps he isn't such an asshole after all. King pulls hard on the steering wheel, and the tires spin into a screaming U-turn. Straight back toward the first tee, not the caddy shack.

"Hey, where are you going?" I protest.

"I'm not going anywhere, but *you* are."

A sonic boom rips through my heart. "But I have plans tonight."

His foot floors the pedal. "Members come first. Your ass is mine while you're still on country club grounds." Brakes squeal to a halt on the cart path in front of the first tee. Bobby Walton hoists a gigantic red-and-yellow golf bag and plants it in front of my Converse high-tops. Three caddies loiter in the hot, boiling sun with bags at their feet. I figure Bobby Walton will excuse me from caddying because I have Springsteen tickets, but before I can ask him, an old man with black hair slicked back in vampire style steps out of a cave door next to the caddy bench. "Good, you found one, Walton." The caddy master turns toward me. "What are you waitin' for? Get out there!"

I stutter and mumble "But I have tick—" before stumbling out to the tee box, dragging the golf bag with me, too scared to plead my case to Bogart. His tone makes it clear he's in no mood to grant me a day pass.

An electric rainstorm is my last hope because steel clubs are lightning rods. But God's floor is a swirl of blue and white colors with no black clouds in sight to save me. The only rain is dripping down my sunburned cheeks, which I rub away quickly with my green-striped caddy towel.

I can forget The Boss.

My heart sinks as deep as the sandy bunker I pass on the first green. A hate for everything in the world crashes down on me like a miniature Hindenburg exploding in my brain. Rocket will be wondering why I didn't show and will probably call the morgue. He knows I wouldn't miss The Boss unless I'm dead, which sounds good to me. But I can't give up my future for one concert by quitting now. I try not to imagine the empty seat next to him in the front row at the concert.

A million trampled blades of grass later, I pretend I'm at the concert, where at least I get to make the song choices. Virginia's Mensa-Netics technique of envisioning where you want to be in life is surprisingly helpful, but I'd never tell her that, so I decide to open with "Badlands" (my third all-time favorite Springsteen song) and close with "Blinded by the Light," saving "Born to Run" for the encore.

Four dreadful hours later, while on the eighteenth green, I add "Rosalita" as the second encore and "Spirit in the Night" as the third. After I finish my round in darkness, I trudge across the bridge, turning my pay stub in to King.

In the empty shack, a lone light bulb hangs from a ceiling above King's lopsided head. "You need a caddy shirt." He disappears below the counter, emerges with a folded green-mesh shirt, and hands it to me. I unfold the shirt, admiring the country club crest—a horse's head and golf bag. King eyes my pay stub. "You owe me a buck."

I have to actually pay *to miss Bruce & the E-Street Band?*

"The shirt costs twelve fifty, you only made eleven-fifty for two rounds," Bogart's henchman continues. "You owe me a buck. You do know simple math, don't you, pleon? Or don't they teach you that at the flunky school you must go to?"

Nobody attacks my school, not unless you've paid your dues there. "I just graduated from Holy Redeemer." I'm not used to talking about grade school in the past tense, and it feels strange, like a part of me has washed away like jellyfish drifting off in the ocean waves.

"A Hills kid?"

"Yeah." His question triggers the thought of my brother—Billy the Hills Kid—and I know he wouldn't put up with King's bullshit for two nanoseconds.

"Why in the hell are you caddying?"

I ignore the question and fish a dollar out of my pocket, handing it over to him. Not every kid in the Hills is Richie Rich.

"You can only wear white pants. White overalls are okay, but no shorts. Now get lost, pleon."

No problem. A-hole. King must think I'm officially a cadet in his green shirt brigade. Ten sorry minutes later, the headlamps of our Impala flood the dark, empty parking lot next to a row of empty guest golf-bag holders. The tires crash against the curb, and I know its Virginia. On second thought, maybe I will quit. Caddying is demeaning and demoralizing, like life in general. A glorified prison camp. I jump into the passenger seat and slam the door shut.

"Virginia. That was awful."

As we turn onto Kensington Road, I know what's coming. You'd think she's programmed by NASA. Always the same launch protocol. I start the countdown as soon as we roll out of the dark country club parking lot after she flattens the edge of a tulip bed. T-minus three, two, one...

Engage car cigarette coil. Ignite Pall Mall. Roll down window.

Inhale. Exhale perfect Saturn booster O-ring.

Extol Mensa-Netics.

"Osmond P. Peabody would say, 'You need an ambitious—'"

"For the love of God, Virginia," I say, my eyeballs retreating into my forehead. "Not now, please."

She has two hands pressed firmly on the steering wheel, and her nose straight ahead. "Tommy Bradley set a goal seven years ago. Now he's an Eagle Scout, and he's—"

"Applying to Yale. You've told me this a million times."

Another O-ring orbits the sun visor before accelerating out the window. Two taps in the ashtray. Black, ashen moondust. A programmer turns a control knob in Houston.

"Winners establish good habits and a goal."

I toss my sun visor in the back seat. "Mom, you're preaching again. Save it for Sunday mass."

Virginia believes she can do anything if she sets her mind to it. Any failure can be traced to poor self-image and bad habits. I'm sick of Virginia proselytizing Osmond P. Peabody and his self-help philosophy of Mensa-Netics.

On Dot Ave, the crew prepares for reentry to the Quinn atmosphere. Smoke fills the cabin. Warning alarms sound at Mission Control. The Impala touches down on our driveway. I cough and fall out of the car along with a pallet full of leaking Pall Mall dust debris. Mom gropes in the dark for two cartons of milk from the milk chute and pushes one into my chest.

"Ford, you're *getting* that Evans scholarship." I hear footsteps on the Clark side of the hedge, followed by a muffled snicker. *Pauley?* The Clarks remind me of my planned rendezvous with Cleo after her next therapy session. Virginia, I'm *getting* Cleopatra.

6

few days later, I wake from a deep-space nap after another caddy round, zombie-ramble down the stairs, and find Pop hunched over a land survey spread out on the dining room table.

Oh yeah, that stinking land map again. He punches numbers on a calculator and scribbles notes on Virginia's stationery. A bathrobed Virginia leans against the wall, eyeing Pop with a mug of Sanka in her hand. I sit down at the table and order Cream of Wheat from Virginia, but she ignores my request.

"I can't believe you blew the last of the family stock on robots, Howard." She leans over and plucks a stock statement from the table and waves it in her hand. "That was my mother's money. Have you lost your mind?"

"Robotics, not robots."

She clenches her teeth. "That's doesn't make it any better."

"I was swindled," Pop says. "Stockbrokers should all be rounded up and thrown in jail. They're street hustlers in three-piece suits. Don't worry, though. I got a new idea."

"That's what I'm afraid of." She puts her mug down on the dining room table next to Pop's map. "Now listen to me for once. Jim Walters may have an opening down at the funeral home selling caskets. A new walnut line is coming in from New York. Penny Walters tells me they're gorgeous. You could make a nice commission selling those."

"I wouldn't be caught dead working for Walters in that clip joint. Bury me in a pine box." He expels a frustrated sigh. "Can't you see I'm busy, Virginia?"

His head rises from the survey map, and he nods to himself. The light had finally dawned on Pop. Dirt's gold in these Kensington Hills. Real estate developers are modern-day prospectors, and the classifieds are the modern-day gold mines. With a down payment from Grandpa Quinn, Pop had bought our beige-painted two-story colonial for fifty grand in 1960 from the local Lutheran church. Pop hadn't realized he'd purchased the mother lode at the time. House prices rose and rose throughout the decades.

"No house in the neighborhood sits on two lots. Our house does."

Our family room—a converted, screened-in porch—overlaps the second lot. Remove my TV room and there's room to build another house on the vacant lot.

The die has been cast. Pop's determined to sell off the lot, and a wrecking ball will level the room where I've spent the better part of my lifetime toasting my buns on the box heater behind the old brown couch during the winter months, watching endless episodes on Saturday morning of *H.R. Pufnstuf* and the *Land of the Lost*.

A dreadful thought occurs to me. "Where am I supposed to watch TV?"

He shoos me away with the back of his hand. Virginia peeks over Pop's shoulder. "Howard, are you sure there's room to build next door?"

"Don't you worry, Virginia. It's foolproof."

"That's what you said about factory robots."

He slams two fists on the antique maple. "Robotics!"

Nosy Kate, who is standing in the foyer next to the dining room, pretending not to listen while waiting for a ride from one of her dopey Hills girlfriends (or maybe badass Theo Nichols), butts in on Pop's master plan. "You are not murdering my elm trees!"

And just like that, Kate and I have become allies.

"Do you know how much it costs to cut one down each time one of them dies?" Pop replies. The Dutch elm disease had mercilessly invaded the Hills five years ago, slaughtering innocent elm after elm on Dorchester Road. Map in hand, he strides out, slamming the front door.

"He's going to tear down our family room right now," I shout.

"Don't be silly, Ford," Mom says.

We all rush to the window, pull back the curtain, and press our noses to the glass. Pop paces off the side lot with a devilish grin. The problem with Pop is that once he gets a money-making scheme in his head, he won't give up short of a lobotomy. A few minutes later, he returns, winded. "Virginia, what's the name of that real estate fellow who always advertises in the church paper?"

"Fitzgerald. Joe, I think."

"Are we selling the house, Pop?" That's a fear of mine, because if we move to the wrong side of town, I can forget admission into the Lund Gang.

"No, Ford, just the side lot."

Just the side lot? "But what about the TV room?"

"It'll have to go to make room for whoever builds a house next door. You can use the den," Pop declares.

"You can't even fit a couch in there ... it's the size of a shoebox."

"We'll buy you a bean bag."

A horn blasts from outside, and Kate bursts out the front door. A view from the window screen reveals a red Firebird Trans Am humming in the street. Yep, the dopey boyfriend. "You Need Love" from Styx escapes from the windows. Kate hugs the driver, and they roar off down Dot Ave.

Figures you'd like that suck-wad band, Theo Nichols.

■ ■ ■

One thing I notice after my first week on the job is that the caddies at the club are, for the most part, radioactive nerds. You know in their real world they are the losers who are picked last for dodgeball at school. None of them would have had a chance at getting into Lund's Gang at Holy Redeemer.

But at the country club, we're all in the same gang, helping each other out. There's always the exception, like Wally Mitchell, who's always trying to start a towel-snap war, but even Wally isn't too bad, and you know he gets royally picked on at his school because he has zits that are turning into pits on every centimeter of his face. The honor caddies are on top of the pile for sure, but they're razed enough in their own life not to needle us plebes too much.

At the club, I don't have to worry about a hair out of place or saying something stupid, ruining any chance of getting into the Lund Gang. I don't have to laugh at dumb jokes to be cool. If a caddy says something stupid, I tell him it's stupid. You could never say that to certain kids at school unless you want shaving cream in your locker.

There's an invisible boundary line at the country club that loopers are forbidden to cross, in the form of a path of stone pavers that runs past the pro shop, bag room, and lead to the pool and tennis courts. The stone path turns into yellow brick just past the practice putting green. No caddies are allowed on Yellow Brick Road—that's what we loopers call it. There's no reason for a caddy to venture past the practice green unless he's running an errand for a member to fetch cigars or miniature Jim Beam bottles from the locker room attendant. It's strictly off limits to mingle with the country club elites. You don't want Bogart all over your ass unless you wanted a guest hacker with a heavy bag.

That afternoon, I carry an insurance salesman's bag with my hat pulled tight over my forehead and trespass onto the forbidden Yellow Brick Road, past a man in checkered polyester pants lining up three balls on the practice putting green. I round the fenced-in pool and put the bag down next to a brush pad for golfers to clean their spiked shoes at the men's locker room entrance. I bide my time for a bagless plebe.

Ten minutes later, a kid with a green badge and bad posture comes down to fetch fresh towels from the locker room attendant. I gesture to my bag. "Can you carry this bag down to the bag room?"

"Piss off."

I open my palm and flash him a Lincoln. "There's five bucks in it for you."

He quicksilver snatches the bill from my hand. "Why didn't you say so?"

I continue down Yellow Brick Road searching for Rocket. He told me he was coming to the country club to try the chicken salad sandwich and to settle the score with King after giving me the late loop on Boss night. The pool area is vacant except for a lady in a golf skirt with her legs crossed, sipping a lemonade through an umbrella straw. I stroll back down Yellow Brick Road and freeze when I see him.

Bobby Walton puts a bag on the cart next to a girl's. Rocket jumps into the front seat with her, and they ride over the bridge to the north course. He's playing a round of golf with some member's daughter. A red-faced King comes marching up from the other side of the club, where employees park their cars.

"Hey, Quinn," King says. "What the hell do you think you're doing in the member's area?"

"Just runnin' an errand for Bobby Walton," I lie, trying to sneak past him, but he switches lanes to block my way.

"You happen to know who would have filled my car with whipped cream?" He leans up close to me like he's sniffing my shirt. I take two steps backward. "Is that the errand you're talking about?"

I back away from him another step, but he keeps pace. "No, why would someone want to do that?"

"The valet spotted a skinny kid with bright red hair runnin' this way." The rim of his hat covering his whale-like head touches my nose. "You seen anyone fittin' that description, Quinn?"

"Can't say that I know anyone like that 'cept Will Robinson."

"He was nosing around the shack asking me if I liked Bruce Springsteen, and if I've ever seen him live in concert." This has Rocket thumbprints all over it.

"Have you?" This time I step forward—an inch or two, but forward just the same.

"Springsteen blows," he replies, stepping back. "Now go get some towels. You got some work to do."

I give him a true character test. "Have you even heard of the song 'Badlands'?"

"What?"

"That's what I thought."

My hatred for King has reached the boiling point, but Rocket got him good with the whipped-cream routine. Caddying is supposed to be a job. I feel like I'm a private in the army. Of course, I can leave anytime and just flip him the bird, but I have a bad habit of sticking things through to the bitter end. I don't know if I'm trying to be the anti-Billy or suffer from a genetic disorder that skips a generation, but I'll tell you this: King isn't going to make me quit, and Virginia is right.

I sure as hell am getting that Chick Evans scholarship come hell or high water on the sixteenth hole.

7

Pebbles fall in sheets on my head in a drowsy dream before I wake to a rainy June morning. My clock reads 9:08. I slept through my caddy alarm, but then I remember today's not just any Friday; it's Cleoday.

With hours to kill, I read my thick book on the *Apollo* missions, rereading for the umpteenth time how *Apollo 13* ran low on rocket fuel and had to boomerang around the moon using its gravitational power to coast back to Earth (some so-called astrophysicists call it the "slingshot" effect, but that makes no Quinn-sense because slingshots go straight and never return.)

By noon, the sky clears, and I head out back to play with a boomerang I'd bought at Kresge's to study the physics of the toy. The aerodynamics of a boomerang can be shown in a trajectory graph:  After a thousand chucks toward the Clarks', none of my throws come close to landing back in my hand. I would have quit after a few crummy tosses if it weren't for Chimney's fetch and returns.

After lunch, Cleo finds me in the backyard trying to spin a basketball on my finger like Meadowlark Lemon, but three lousy revolutions is all I can muster. A minute earlier I'd put Chimney in the house so she wouldn't bother Cleo and had grabbed his-and-her pops—7 Up and Tab. Cleo wears flared jeans and a yellow Bob Seger & the Silver Bullet Band tour T-shirt cut into a midriff. God invented that trimmed T-shirt for me.

She picks up the boomerang and hurls it to no one. It curves around a majestic old elm before landing back in her hand. Wow! I grab the drinks off the patio table and give her the pop. I'm not sure what to do with her next. I try to avoid awkward silences lest she think I'm boring as all get-out. Virginia's down at the Olivehammers' for Friday bridge, Pop's gone job hunting, and Kate's wasting time down at the public swimming pool with Theo. Not even God wants to know where Billy might be.

We sit on the grass sipping our soda pops, not making much conversation because I have no clue how to talk to a girl. The silence slowly chokes me until Cleo breaks the silence. She mentions to me a few girls she knows from school are heading to cheerleading camp at Ferris State this week.

"How lame is that?" she asks, but I notice some sadness in her voice, like she kind of wished she'd gone, too. But that's exactly what I like about Cleo; she isn't the cheerleader type with her Egyptian bangs, pyramid-shaped earrings, and thick gold-colored wristband.

"I went to space camp once," I admit like a blithering moron. A stuttering effort to recover. "In the fifth grade ... I mean ... ages ago."

She gets up on her knees, curling her legs underneath her. "Did you know that Nut was the Egyptian Goddess of the sky, Giff?"

I raise an eyebrow at the word "nut" and can't take it back.

She laughs. "I'm not a nutcase!" She pours half her Tab in the grass. "Too many calories."

Doesn't Tab have just one calorie?

She asks me about space camp, and I tell her that camp's where I got completely hooked on space travel and astrophysics. The camp was at the Kennedy Space Center in Cape Canaveral and my dad's brother, Uncle Mitt, and his family lived down the way in Cocoa Beach. Our family drove to the scorching hot Florida spacecoast for a two-week summer vacation. I'd been within spitting distance of the first *Apollo* flight launches to the moon and rode in the same lunar modulator simulator used for training by Jim Lovell, Alan Shepard, Pete Conrad, Alan Bean, and Neil and Buzz.

I share with Cleo a few space facts. Did she know in four billion years the Andromeda Galaxy will collide with the Milky Way Galaxy and form a giant elliptical galaxy? And she shares with me facts about Egyptian astronomy. The ancient Egyptians observed the movement of the stars to predict the annual flooding of the Nile, the southern airshaft of the Great Pyramid points to Orion's Belt, the Sphinx's eyes gaze directly at the constellation Leo. We both know Ptolemy was one of the most influential astronomers of all time, but who doesn't know that?

"Hey," she says, putting her hand on my shoulder. "You got a decent telescope?"

Time on my wrist stands still.

"Yeah. It's in my room." Rocket is my only friend in the world who knows I own a geeky telescope for stargazing, and now I've broken my vow to keep it that way.

Cleo springs to her feet. "Let's check it out." She grasps my hand, pulling me into my house and upstairs to my bedroom. On the bottom step, deadly panic sets in as I scan in my mind the juvie things in my room: an Estes Electric Launch Rocket Kit, a walkie-talkie (Rocket has the other), chemistry lab kit, electric football game, *Star Wars* Death Star Space Station (includes a trash compactor, laser cannon, elevator, escape hatch, trash monster), a mountain of baseball cards, toy soldier footlocker, loads and loads of books, and of course, my Gabriel 40 Power Observer Refractor telescope (a birthday gift from my late Uncle Fred). On the top of the last step, it dawns on me it's daytime; we can't see diddly-squat in the sky right now. I won't get my chance to show off my expertise in astronomy.

How dumb am I to think she just wants to see my telescope?

In my room, Cleo grabs *The Outsiders* off my shelf. "I love this book!" A spiral notebook with an STP sticker on the front falls on the floor and spreads open. I tremble and freeze for an ice age because I'd scribbled several poems in the notebook. A clumsy reach to close the book, pick it off the floor, and shove it safely back on the shelf next to *A Martian Sends a Postcard Home*. Fortunately, she puts S.E. Hinton's book back on the shelf without noticing my semi-autobiographical book of poetry verses. Instead, she plucks an orange Nerf ball off the floor while I pull out my telescope and assemble it on a tripod next to the window table with a clean sight line between backyard tree limbs. The bedroom door thumps shut, causing me to turn toward Cleo in delight.

Is she thinking what I'm thinking? She leaps up off the ground, revealing bony ribs underneath her midriff shirt, and dunks the sponge ball down through the plastic rim hanging from the top edge of the door in Doctor J-style. *You dope, that's why she closed the door.*

The ball bounces my way. She dives for the ball, and I snatch it off the carpet before she can claim it. A bank shot good from fifteen feet, then a mad scramble for the ball as it rolls past my Venus flytrap at the foot of my bed, but she snares the ball first. I block her way to the hoop, but she elbows past me for an epic layup, and I grab her by the waist, and we somehow tumble to the ground in tangled limbs.

A mixture-scent of Butter Up tanning lotion and peppermint Chiclets leaks into my nostrils. She loops her bare leg around mine, and we roll over so our faces are pressed together, and I think I'm in heaven while trumpets sound in my ears. We press our lips together. The high-pitched tune grows louder and more familiar in my brain, and Cleo removes her lips from mine. Her neck arches up as she lies on top of me and next to the orange Nerf ball.

"Did you hear that?" she remarks. The sound of a shrill whistle pierces through the screen window. Virginia's stupid wolf whistle. *What's she doing back so early?*

"Fooord!" A three-step dash to the window. Eye on the target through bionic telescope. Virginia in her Sunday best for Friday bridge club. *Damn.* I can kiss this chance with Cleo goodbye. She'll tell Pop if I have a girl in the bedroom and give me some moronic lecture about girls like she knows anything.

"We gotta go, Cleo. My dog's escaped." *Thanks a ton, Virginia. GOD!*

I rush her down the stairs and out the front door before Virginia sees us and gives me the third degree. Cleo skids to a stop and glowers across the street at a yellow AMC Pacer that's parked in front of the Carters' house. Laney Carter struts out her front door with a gold purse and gets into the jellybean-shaped car.

Although she's my age, I don't think much about Laney Carter because I've rarely set eyes on her even though she lives across the street. Ralph Lord has, though. (Ralph's uncle once wrestled both The Sheik and Bobo Brazil at Cobo in a tag-team match under the professional name Atlas Lord.) He lives in the house behind her on Glouchester and owns a decent pair of Army binoculars. He'd told me once that Laney Carter spends all day writing poetry (I dig that*)* in her back-yard hammock and spinning her hula hoop between her bikini top and Bermuda shorts. Anyway, Laney goes to a K-12 all-girls private prep school called Glendower in South Kensington—the Palm Beach of the Hills. (I've spent hundreds of rainy days and nights exploring the universe at Glendower's epic planetarium, not to mention one midnight laser show to Pink Floyd's haunting, seizure-inducing *Dark Side of the Moon*.)

Cosmic lightning beams ripple through Dot Ave asphalt from Cleo's retinas. "I hate that bitch."

Huh? "Laney Carter?"

"No … Pippa." She bites down hard. "Farnsworth," she says, dragging out her name in contempt. "Don't ask me why."

A girl in the passenger seat flips Cleo the middle finger, and the car jolts down Dot Ave. I've never heard of any Pippa Farnsworth, and I don't ask her why she hates her guts so much. Perhaps Pippa is her nemesis, like Nick Lund is for me. It's shaping up like we have lots in common.

After Cleo leaves, I stand dreamy eyed, pondering how this Egyptian princess is different than all the girls I've ever known in the entire universe. Chimney suddenly appears and drops the boomerang from her slobbering mouth, and I pluck it off the ground and launch it toward deep space, and it nearly nicks the Clarks' gutters before plunging back to Earth. Chimney spots the space debris, and the chase is on. I dive for the falling object but not before the hound snatches it out of the air. I fall on the grass with a heap of fur, resting my back on the grass with bits of Cleo thoughts hovering in my mind I'd never dare share with anyone.

I yank the boomerang out of my dog's jaw. The momentum spins me around, and I face our giant, aquarium-sized living room window. And there's Pop, peering at me with a sourpuss frown and that stupid survey map in hand.

No way Pop'll ruin my mood today. Chimney chases me upstairs to my bedroom, where I spin ELO's "Do Ya" and make a new entry in my poetry notebook:

Thisisgoin'tobethemostepicsummereveeeerrrr!!!

8

"There's a big party down at Harkness Park tonight."

Rocket tells me this while he strums his acoustic guitar in my basement in the dying hour of a summer day. He knows two songs: "Stairway to Heaven" and "Hot Blooded," which is two more than I can produce.

"Who's going to be there? Public kids? Catholics? Stoners? Preppy penny-loafer Hills kids?" Maybe Cleo will be there.

"How should I know?" Rocket turns his guitar upside down and places his guitar pick on top of it. "You show up and find out. It's a public park ... it's not like anyone can kick you out." Rocket never spends a split second thinking about how he might fit in like me. I agonize over every little thing. He picks up the guitar pick, puts it between his crooked teeth, and bites down. "Arrr yee innn?" I flash him the thumbs-up sign.

We have a couple of hours to kill before heading to the party, which might as well be a lifetime. Rocket gathers three ping-pong balls off the floor and juggles chin-high circles in front of me.

Does he ever stop moving for one second? He's a fine juggler, though.

Rocket balances a ping-pong ball on his snub nose while I blow tiny Bubble Yum bubbles. The ball slips off Rocket's nose, and he yells, "Gumfight." He isn't asking me, he's telling me.

"You're on." I throw him a cherry-flavored pack, rummage through an old trunk next to me, and pull out two straw cowboy hats. I toss one to Rocket. Gumfight on. We don our hats, face off, and assume gumslinger pose: shoulders up, elbows bent, gum stick in hand, knees bent slightly forward, feet planted firmly on ground, toes pointed in. Loser pops first.

Blow hard.

Gum balloons grow from our mouths, stretch across the room, forming pink zeppelins before mushrooming into hot air balloons. POP! Score one for Quinn.

Wipe. Reload. Assume gumslinger pose.

After four messy gumfights, we hit the fresh evening air. Rocket jumps on Billy's ten-speed and flies out of my driveway, red hair trailing behind him like a flame from a drag car.

"Where the hell are you going?" I shout after him. Parties don't start till after dark.

"To get some stuff for the party," he yells back at me as I catch up with him at the end of the block.

"What stuff?"

He smirks. "You'll see."

I assume Rocket means sparklers or firecrackers. His favorite holiday is the Fourth of July, when he always manages to finagle from some friend of a friend an odd assortment of Kentucky fireworks—M-80s, Cherry Bombs, Magic Mustard.

Rocket skids to a stop at an uptown parking lot for Dawson's Insurance Agency. The sun lags below the taller buildings of downtown Kensington Hills, casting a shadow across half the city. A man in a wrinkled blue suit eyes us suspiciously before hopping in his yellow VW Beetle and driving away.

"I give," I say, using my snarkiest tone. "Are you buying life insurance?"

A hazard sign appears: Rocket's thin devious grin. "I'm gonna get us some booze."

Terror strikes. "Is Basil here?" Perhaps his brother has left a six-pack behind the dumpster.

"No, but Farmer Jack is." Farmer Jack's is the local grocery chain.

"That's called stealing."

"No, it's called livin'." Rocket throws me a foul snicker. "You should try it sometime. C'mon, ding-dong." He waves me along.

"Thanks, but no thanks." There's no way I'd ever lift anything, let alone beer. I'm no Boy Scout, but stealing is stealing.

"Fine," he replies. "Then just watch and learn, brother."

Rocket drops the bicycle on the ground and struts out of the alley toward Farmer Jack's. I squat down on a parking curb, hoping Rocket's simply pulling my leg, but I know better. To pass the nervy time, I fish out a set of Topps baseball cards from my back pocket, shuffling through them, and notice some Wacky Packs cards mixed in. Ron Guidry, Larry Bowa, Milk Muds, Cap'n Crud, Gaylord Perry, Cracked Jerk, Minute Lice, Roy Smalley, Kentucky Fried Fingers, Tommy John … Oscar

Gamble. Only one Detroit Tiger—our former weak-hitting, sure-gloved shortstop, Tom Veryzer.

A police siren blares in the distance; my bones quake with fear, and I crane my neck around the corner and go back to reading through the stats on the back of each baseball card fifteen times—Fred Lynn averaged .333 for the Red Sox last season. That's ace squared. But still no sign of Rocket. *Should I go in after him?* No. Rocket works best alone.

Three more nervous shuffles through the cards. I stand up and gaze down the alley, and a flash of red hair accelerates toward me at Mach speed, pushing an overloaded grocery cart. My cards spill out of my hands, and I scramble to pick them up.

"Quick, follow me, Ford." We duck behind the dumpster, and a rodent darts through a crack in the brick. "I got it." Rocket pulls a sweating case of Stroh's beer from the cart. "The blue gold, man." He rips into the box, and out come two blue cans. I poke my head around the dumpster for spies but only notice a suspicious pigeon perched on a telephone line above our heads. Rocket pops the tabs on the beer cans and forks one over. Before I manage to take a few poisonous sips, Rocket tosses an empty one into the dumpster and reaches for another can.

Another pop from an opening tab. "Damn. I forgot to get some chew." I ask him how he'd managed to steal the beer. "I've done it like five times." A satisfied smile on his lips. "No problemo."

He must be putting me on. "With who?" I'm pretty much Rocket's only friend.

"Me, myself, and I. While losers like you are caddying their asses off in the blazing sun, I'm drinking beer." He downs the last sip of his beer. "Hurry up and drink that thing, Ford. We got a party to go to, bro."

Empty cans rattle in the dumpster. We hide the grocery cart in the alley after Rocket shoves a carton of Pop-Tarts in my hands and rides off into the retreating twilight toward the park. Rocket balances the case of beer on top of his handlebars, half covered by his Ted Nugent "Double Live Gonzo!" T-shirt. He drinks a beer along the side streets of Kensington Hills, his front wheel wobbling past the immaculate houses while I munch on a cinnamon Pop-Tart.

Just past Hillsdale Lane, the case slips off Rocket's handlebars and crashes onto the ground, sending beers rolling out one by one down a hill and into the road. A car honks. A mom with two kids in the back—each pressing their puzzled, smiling faces to the car window—runs over a beer. Tires crush exploding beer cans. We jump off our bikes and make a mad dash to collect the beers before jumping back on our rides toward the party as darkness settles in.

We reach the long path sheltered by rows of pine trees leading into the park. Voices echo from the open field. Kids mill around, Bic fireflies spark in the air, some guy's lip-locked with a girl next to a bonfire.

Is that my sister Kate and her jackass boyfriend, Theo? Jason Sanders comes up to me with his arm around Polly Ledbeder. I hand him a foamy beer. Jason gives me a "right on" nod and a toothy smile.

"Where did you score these beers?"

"We're not giving away our source," Rocket says. He's never had any use for my Holy Redeemer friends.

"Suit yourself." He turns to me. "Quinn, you want to go swimming at the country club tomorrow?"

"Sure." *Hell yes!*

Jason looks toward Rocket. "You, too, if you want."

"Is she coming?" Rocket nods toward Polly, trying to get Jason's goat. Sometimes I think Rocket wants me to be his only friend, thinking if I make it in tight with Jason Sanders or Jack Lott, I'll leave him behind. I'll *never* do that to him.

"Nooo."

"Then I'll pass. I'm allergic to country-club air, anyway. I get all stuck up." Rocket lifts his freckled face to show his nostrils. "By the way, I don't need *your* invitation to use the club."

Rocket couldn't care less about who people hang with, what country club a kid belongs to, or where on the social pecking order his parents stand. When Sanders is really bored, he calls me. Nick Lund and Jack Lott must be at the annual summer camp with a bunch of other Hills kids at Otsego Lake. Every summer I've wanted to go to camp with the other kids from school, but Pop has never had the extra cash to send me.

A Jimmy Connors junior clone comes huffing and puffing toward us. "Fat Albert got busted with a beer ball." He wipes his forehead with a red, white, and blue wrist sweatband. "The cops are coming."

As news of the police raid spreads through the park, kids scramble through a narrow dirt path that leads to the park exit. Jason Sanders grabs Polly's hand. "I'll pick you up at noon tomorrow, Quinn."

■ ■ ■

On a hot summer's day, the kind where the walls are sweating before ten o'clock, I dress quickly, throwing on the nearest shirt on the floor next to my bed, and wait on our concrete front steps. The Sanders' black Cadillac drives up in front of my house, and I dive into a waiting, open door. With two drumsticks, Jason, a fantastic drummer (he fancies himself a "percussionist" because he also plays the xylophone and bongos), strikes the back of the front leather passenger seat occupied by a barking terrier, tapping along to the song on the radio, "I Want You to Want Me" by Cheap Trick. A brass ashtray cover on the side door serves as a cymbal. *Tat-tat-tat-tat-tat, clang.* His mom roars off down our street under elm trees that hang like awnings along Dot Ave.

At the club, we saunter straight through the front door of the clubhouse and into the men's locker room to change into our bathing suits. Sweat forms on my forehead from the humid, suffocating locker room air. We pass an elderly man with one foot on top of a bench at the end of a row of lockers, applying brown polish to the tip of a leather golf shoe. Another man with a pot belly traipses by, wearing nothing more than a towel around his waist.

We change into our suits, and Jason leads me outside and into the pool area, encircled by a large ornamental fence. A boy of about ten sweeps a dead horsefly from the water with a new Prince tennis racquet the size of a snowshoe. He looks me up and down with his upturned nose. "Hey? What do you think you're doing here, caddy boy?"

How's the little twerp know I'm a caddy?

"Your shirt." Jason nods at my chest. "You better take it off. Caddies aren't allowed to swim in the pool."

Those epic TV mini-serials flash through my brain—*Roots* and *Rich Man, Poor Man*—and give me a partial seizure. *You can't just waltz in here with a caddy shirt, you dope. You've embarrassed Jason, and now you'll never be invited back.* I might as well be carrying a sign above me head that reads "I'M A LOWLIFE CADDY."

"Yeah, you might contaminate the pool." The kid has a gap between his two front teeth wide enough to fit a harmonica between. "I hope you took a shower."

Jason threatens him with a fist. "Get lost, Frankel."

The kid snarls. "Don't worry, Sanders." He flicks his racquet, and the wet horsefly soars across the fence onto Yellow Brick Road. "I wouldn't swim in this caddy-infected pool now."

Before this moment, my green-mesh caddying shirt has been just a green-mesh shirt. I've forgotten caddies are second-class citizens at the club, servants for the spoiled members. I shed the *Scarlet Letter* shirt, roll it up, and hide it under a lounge chair.

For a hot day, the pool is empty, unlike my public swim club, which would be wall-to-wall bathing suits. The members' kids don't know how good they have it.

Sanders dives into the deep blue water and disappears into the depths of the pool. I dive in after him.

Waterlogged and spent, Jason and I spend the next hour in lounge chairs, sipping cherry-flavored shakes. Across the pool, a gaggle of girls with bouncing pony-tails stroll past with tennis racquets in tow and proceed out the latched gate. Only the backs of their heads and white tennis outfits can be seen. A girl swings her head as if swatting a fly with her taut brownish-blonde pony-tail. I eye her tan legs as they disappear from my view toward the girls' locker room, but she's not Cleo.

A rebel yell from the other side of the pool. Two guys with goggles and Speedos appear out of nowhere and launch themselves into the deep end. One lands a majestic belly-flop. The second one flashes a toothy grin I've seen a zillion times in the past eight years and grabs his knee, jackknifing into the pool. A tsunami roars across the pool and propels a jetsam across my feet. They sink deep into the pool and resurface, spitting chlorine water into the air.

Half of the Lund Gang. My day's ruined before it barely began.

Lund perches his wet chin on the side of the concrete pool. "Well, if it ain't Quinn."

A whale surfaces, his blowhole sending a stream of water onto my chest—Fat Albert. Nick Lund enjoys a hysterical laughing fit, coughing up pool water from his porpoise mouth hole. Jason dives in over their heads, disappearing to the bottom before surfacing like Sub-Mariner. I'm left alone with Lund and Albert.

"Is Sanders your only friend?" Lund wears a permanent smile like a sharp-toothed hyena.

"Didn't I see you caddying the other day?"

Shut your fat face, Fat Albert.

"Why the hell are you caddying for?" Lund asks.

"Only once in a while, just to learn about golf." Why tell anyone from the Hills my only way to pay for college is through a caddy scholarship?

Lund isn't buying it. "You learn about golf by playing golf."

"I'm savin' up some cash." This is a slippery slope toward disaster.

"For what? A queer disco album?" Lund again.

"Yeah, a disco album. Hilarious." That's as far as I want to go with Lund.

Sanders dog-paddles by, clueless about Lund's taunts as he heads to the diving board at the other end of the pool. Lund pulls himself out of the pool, and we stand toe-to-toe. "You want in to the Fantastic Four?"

The Lund Gang's assumed the identities of the Fantastic Four as follows: Lund—Mr. Fantastic (*please*), Fat Albert—The Thing, Jack Lott—Human Torch, Jason Sanders—Luke Cage a.k.a. Power Man.

"For real?" A happy dizziness wobbles me off my axis.

Lund assumes jack-knife formation. "I never ask twice."

"Sure, then." It'd be boss—no, a life changer—getting into the Fantastic Four. As a freshman in high school this fall, I won't have to worry about looking over my shoulder to make sure Lund hasn't stuck a stupid note on my back like he did last December: "I love Sister Martini." I'd sat through the whole first period in Mr. Crable's history class wondering why the back of the class thought the Normandy Invasion was such a laugh riot.

Sanders backstrokes to the edge of the pool. "Your buddy here is testing for our gang," Lund says to him.

"Diving test?" Sanders points to a cloud-high diving board.

"Game on," Lund replies.

I think ahead to the cool things I'll be doing with Nick and the boys. Last winter, the Lund Gang scored front-row tickets at Olympia to see the Dead Things

(Red Wings) play hockey. Maybe the Wings will be play-off ready when I arrive next season with the Fantastic Four + One.

"Okay, then, Quinn. The test to get in is a front flip from up there." Lund points to the high dive. "You get sixty seconds."

"I'll time it," Fat Albert says.

At the Kensington Hills public swim club, Rocket and his fiery red hair would launch off the high-dive pad after a running start near the ladder. He would tuck in his limbs and fall straight down like a cliff diver. That's why we call him Rocket. My problem is that you can't be afraid of heights if you want to be a space traveler, can you? Heights make my windpipe close and pores water. I normally climb stairs because elevators make me woozy. The kid down the block in a wheelchair, Zach Bartholomew, had dove off a high dive and cracked his cranium on the side of the pool. Joey Mason witnessed the fall and told me the deep end had turned red as a girl's period. Though Zach is paralyzed from the waist down, he dates a nice-looking girl, Patsy Lindsey, who rides in his lap all day long. I've been practicing partial flips on the Olivehammers' in-ground trampoline. Not the soaring, crazy front and back flips Rocket does, but baby flips just the same. Astronaut-in-training.

In T-minus sixty seconds, I can enter freshman year in the Cool Zoo Crew rather than the Putz Patrol. Rumor has it if you break into the Fantastic Four, you have your pick of super heroes, since the three have been taken and the fourth's the Invisible Girl. As I circle the pool toward the diving board, my mind rifles through the superheroes in my comic book collection at home. I narrow it down to three: Iron Man, Captain America, The Question.

I scale the high-dive ladder, hanging on for dear life with each nauseated rung, and enter Apollo's Command Module headed for the moon's gravity. I step up on the board with my knees shaking, amble onto the launching pad, eyes half closed from fear, telling myself not to gaze down. A stiff wind sweeps across my waistline, and I reach back, grabbing the top of the ladder to steady myself.

Two steps.

The board dips from my weight with each lurch toward oblivion, like it's made of papier-mâché. The boys whoop with laughter down below, their heads bobbing in and out of the deep end. At the end of the diving platform, I stop and open my eyes wide, still afraid to peer down into the abyss.

"Twenty, nineteen, eighteen, seventeen..."

I freeze from fear and survey the view of this world from up here. Lunar land rovers posing as golf carts. An oasis of purple-green grass dotted with craters filled with ivory sand. The golfers and caddies on Number 7—the farthest hole from the clubhouse—are specks on a green page. A group strolls up close on Number 18. A caddy stoops over from the weight of the bag, arches his chin my way before handing his golfer a putter.

You only have ten seconds left. T-Minus nine, eight, seven, six. *Just climb back down the ladder.*

"Five, four, three ..."

Two. One. Ignition. Think three feet above the trampoline. Boosters firing. Blast off. Suspended in space. Head over heels. Tuck. Spin. Flip.

Plummet.

Legs tad beyond vertical.

Plunge.

Stomach meets my esophagus.

Splash!

Skull fractures wide open.

Sink.

Dead weight hurtles to the bottom.

Quinn has landed. One big splash for Ford, a giant typhoon for Quinnkind.

I tunnel up for air through the bubbling water, fighting toward oxygen and the new life that awaits me on the surface. Before surfacing, I make my decision. Definitely The Question. I pop up the side pool ladder and onto the concrete surface with the strength of He-Man. Yeah. Forget The Question and his tattered trench coat. Call me the naked-chested He-Man. Three of the Fantastic Four stand by the edge of the pool, dripping wet next to their new superhero.

"Awesome dive," Sanders remarks.

"I guess he's in," Fat Albert says, turning his head toward a tight-lipped Lund.

Sanders holds up his hand, and I gave him an epic high five. "Pick your superhero. Aquaman? Green Lantern?"

"Nope." Lund crosses his arms and shakes his head. "Not even close, Quinn. You didn't complete a whole flip. You landed on your ass. You're supposed to hit the water hands first. Plus, you were one second late by my count."

"Nick, he came close enough," Jason Sanders says.

"We're the Fantastic Four," Lund spits back. "There's no such thing as the Fantastic Five, anyway. Plus, the

Human Torch isn't here to vote in a new member." Jack Lott would have voted for me, but he's probably playing tennis at his club.

"By my count he made it, Nick."

I knew I could count on Jason!

"Fine, Batgirl." He nods to Sanders. "You two can be the Dynamic Douchebags. C'mon, Fat Albert, let's catch a sauna and"—he snaps a towel at Fat Albert's meaty thigh—"burn some of your fat ass off."

Lund whispers something into Fat Albert's ear that elicits a gargantuan-sized grin from The Thing. "Sanders, are you coming or staying with Captain Caddy with his amazing ball-washing ability?"

Sanders tilts in the wind. Lund grabs a green-striped towel, wraps it around his tan neck, and saunters toward the clubhouse. Fat Albert takes one step to follow Lund before thrusting his bulkhead around and shoving his two large hands into my chest.

Capsize.

Drowning.

Touching bottom.

Rising back to sea level from the abyss, I break the surface of the water and find myself alone. Sanders has abandoned ship. I try to be mad at Jason but can't blame him. Lund has some kind of control over him. Why does Jason Sanders need Lund? Power of a group leader. Think Jim Jones serving cyanide-laced Kool-Aid in Guyana to his followers at the Peoples Temple. I realize that I could have performed a double flip within five seconds and Lund still wouldn't have baptized me into his cult. Did I really think he was going to let a caddy into his exclusive club?

Rich kids don't caddy. They use caddies. I can forget the Dumb Lund Gang.

9

A fter being denied entrance into the Fantastic Four, I sulk in my room and decide to write a hateful poem to vent my anger.

Nick's a gnarly prick, and I'd like to stick a picket up his wicket.

A stake penetrates my heart. I notice that a thin empty space the size of the spine of a spiral notebook exists between *The Outsiders* and *Salem's Lot,* but it might as well be a mile wide. The next hour is spent turning my room upside down.

Nothing.

Kate! I rush into her room and rummage through it, finding nothing except her diary, which is locked. Another half hour rifling through her things, but I can't find the key or my notebook, so I kidnap her diary for ransom. Who else could have stolen my notebook? Billy could care less about my life, Mom never cleans my room, Chimney can't read, so the only suspect left is Kate.

Then it strikes me out of the blue. Cleo? We'd rushed out of my room so fast, maybe she grabbed it on the way out the door. Not sure why she would do that. One thing does dawn on me: Kate threw a huge sleepover the other night with tons of girlfriends. Practically the whole neighborhood showed up, so I slept over at Rocket's house.

After an hour of simmering panic, I walk Chimney uptown in a dark, vile mood and tie her leash to a lamppost in front of Olga's Kitchen. I order the usual three things from Olga's helpers: three-cheese Olga, plain original Olga with ketchup only, baklava for dessert.

Nothing cheers me up more than Olga food. I leave with a crumbling baklava after I see the Lund Gang in the back of the restaurant. Nick Lund's giving Peter Lattimore's younger brother a nuclear nuggie while Fat Albert holds the helpless kid's arms behind his back.

On the sidewalk, a man in a Levi vest is petting Chimney. He owns a mustache and sideburns down to his jawline. I untie Chimney's leash from the lamppost, but my dog doesn't twitch a muscle, just sits at attention for the man. Chimney normally wouldn't sit for the King of Prussia.

Is this guy trying to pinch my pooch?

The man removes his thumbs from his vest pockets. "This your dog?"

"What's it to you?"

He smooths my dog's wrinkled coat. "I know this dog."

"She gets 'round." *Get lost, buddy.*

He crouches down and rubs under Chimney's chin. "No. I mean I trained her."

"Not possible." Chimney knows one trick—fetch. "It's like she hears a foreign language when people speak to her."

"Roll over!" Chimney rolls over.

Maybe he's hypnotized her. The original Olga, Virginia's substitute bridge partner, strolls by, heading for her kitchen.

"Play dead!" Chimney plays dead on the hot concrete, tongue hanging out and panting. The man pulls a dog biscuit out of his pants pocket and gives it to Chimney. He has my attention. Chimney doesn't follow commands from some stranger. I figure this is one of those scenarios you hear on the news every so often. Mother gives up baby for adoption and now wants her back a year and five hundred diaper changes later. There's no goddamn way this creep is stealing my Chimney away from me.

I tug on her leash, itching to get away as fast as I can before Nick and Fat Albert ruin my lunch. "We have to go."

"Too bad we had to let your dog go from the training center." The man puts his thumbs back into his vest pocket. Chimney sits frozen in front of him, waiting for another command. "You don't know?"

God pulls the trigger on his sunray gun, and shafts of light strike my forehead. Olga rushes out the door with a mountain of Styrofoam, leaking vapors from lamb and beef piled high in her arms. Chimney's nostrils quiver, but her eyes remain fixed on her master.

The man won't let up. "Tank is a cancer dog."

"Her name is Chimney." I follow Olga's Olgas down the maple-lined street.

"Wait!" he shouts. "I'm a medical dog trainer. I train dogs to detect cancer in humans. Tank—or rather Chimney here—was good, but we couldn't keep her because she kept chewing up the furniture."

That sounds like Chimney.

"Well, tell Kate I said hello." The man starts to stroll away.

Kate? "Wait. Did you say Kate?"

The man stops. "Yes. Your sister came and got her. I guess she never told you?"

A dreadful thought occurs to me, and I think I might piss my pants. "How does Chimney know someone has cancer?" Chimney pants in the heat, her rubbery tongue unfurling onto the sidewalk. I spot a Styrofoam hat turning left at the Kresge corner.

"She can smell it." His finger touches his nose. "Blood, kidney, bladder. All sorts."

An electric eel crawls up my spine. No wonder Chimney's obsessed with Cleo. I break out in a cold James Brown sweat. Cleo. "I gotta go."

An evil hoot of laughter jerks my ear to the door. Nick Lund marches out of Olga's with Fat Albert trailing behind, an Olga burger falling out of his blubbery mouth. "Quinn. Where the hell are you going? I got something for you." Nick holds up his thumb and two fingers in nuggie pose. Fat Albert grins and nods his head in approval. I wish Chimney was trained to kill, but I have more important things to deal with than those two bozos.

It's an exhausting sprint home. *Cleo has cancer?* I debate telling Mom, but she'll think I'm crazy. What if the guy is putting me on, and it's all some gag? I'll be the laughingstock of the neighborhood.

Why would a guy make a thing like that up? Out of breath, I stop running and wonder what to do. *Kate will know for sure, because she found Chimney.*

I find my sister in the mudroom sorting Rainbow vacuum cleaner accessory boxes containing extension wands, power nozzles, and dusting brushes. She's become Virginia's little sales disciple. I snatch a box from her hand. "Did you know Chimney's a cancer dog?"

"Yes, that's why I picked her." She grabs the box out of my hand, and hoses uncoil onto the floor. "I'm a Cancer, too."

"That's true. You are a cancer."

She stacks boxes over her head; Virginia's inventory has filled the mudroom from floor to ceiling. "Yes. We are very loyal and able to empathize with other people's pain and suffering." She'd lifted this line from the placemats at Ping's China Express, where Billy had been fired for sticking chopsticks up both of his nostrils and then handing them out to customers. "You can leave now."

"OH MY GOD, Kate. Really? Chimney is a cancer dog, as in the *illness.* NOT THE ZODIAC SIGN!"

A box of Aquamates crash to the floor. "Chimney has cancer?"

"Forget it, Kate." Damn if Chimney isn't a cancer dog, after all. I run out the door with no time to waste.

On the front step of Cleo's Gothic-style house with its blue slate roof and turret, I freeze with fear. How do you tell someone they might have cancer? Or that they might die? A voice trickles down from the upstairs window. "Giff? Is that really you?" *Rapunzel?* "I'll come down in a sec."

I reach the front door just as Cleo's mother yanks it open. She stands sternly with her hands on her hips, wearing a cropped and fluffed Princess of Wales haircut. "Can I help you, young man?"

"I'm here for Cleo. So is my dog." I know it sounds dumb, but that's how it spills out of my mouth.

"Cleo can't see anyone because she's not feeling well." She points her needle nose at Chimney. "And she's allergic to dogs."

"That's why I'm here." I take a step toward the door. "You need to take Cleo to the doctor."

"Excuse me?" She starts to close the door.

Cleo comes down the stairs and wedges her thin frame between the door and her mother. "We've been to a million doctors, Giff … She thinks it's up here," Cleo says, pointing to her head.

I lose my grip on Chimney's leash, and she charges forward, bumping past Cleo's mother, barking at her daughter.

"You need to control your dog, young man." She nudges Chimney back out the door with her foot. Cleo tries to step onto the front porch, but her mother blocks her with the back of her hand. "What's going on?"

"Chimney doesn't usually bark at anyone."

Cleo's mother bares her teeth, and Chimney growls in response. "Well, she's barking at my daughter!"

I shake my head. "You don't understand. Chimney was trained as a medical dog." I'm not about to tell her she might have cancer. "I think she's trying to tell you something, Cleo."

Her mother's eyes throw darts at me. "I know my daughter better than you and your silly dog." The door slams in my face.

I sigh. What kind of fool am I thinking she'd believe a kid and cancer-bloodhound dog? I sit down on their stoop, thinking of what my next move is to save Cleo, and hear Cleo's window shut above my head along with her mother's muffled, angry voice before finally pulling Chimney down the front walk as she scrapes her paw nails on the concrete. After I arrive home, I decide to ask the only doctor I know on Dot Ave for help.

The neighborhood therapist from next door. Dr. Lorraine Clark.

■ ■ ■

Hail pelts my window, and my groggy, sleepy head clears. It's not raining. Must be Rocket again.

Get lost, I've got a million logs to saw. He better have Stones tickets this time because nothing's more precious to me than sleep. Then I think he must have scored some Who tickets, and the hair on the back of my neck flares. Owen Rooney told me they're coming to the Pontiac Silverdome this fall. I've left the window down, and it sticks in the summer humidity. Shove, shove, shove. I should just go back to sleep. No one's out there. Must be just my imagi—

BAM! A shaft of moonlight shines on a person on the grass like a spotlight on a singer on a stage. A Cleo-shaped girl. *Is that her?* I manage to open the window and crane my neck out. "What are you doing out there, Cleo?"

"Mom and I had a huge screaming match … I had to get *out* of that house." *Why are you here?* I say in my head. *Maybe she really likes me?* "Let's go somewhere," she says.

My head pokes out the window. "Where to?"

"Anywhere."

There's only one place I can think of at this late hour. I grab my walkie-talkie, thinking Rocket might still be awake, and ghost-drift down the stairs and out to the side yard. Cleo's leaning up against a tree, holding a knapsack in her hand.

"Hold on a sec," I say and turn on the walkie-talkie. Radio static fills the air. "Roger. It's me." A loud belch returns. He's awake.

"Identify location," he says.

"Home. Where the hell are you?"

Two large burps. "Mission control, I have made contact with an alien life-form. It uses crude language and has ... if I think I know who it is ... a striking resemblance to a Sleestak. Requesting permission to remove all vital organs for examination. Warning: Idiot alien may be hostile to human life."

A giggle erupts from Cleo's mouth. "Giff ... who *is* that?"

"Houston, I've detected a strange female alien species. A thousand alien-spawn eggs may be released on our planet, and we'll be washing dishes for these lizardy half humanoids for the next millennium. Do you read, Mission Control?"

"Shut up." I want to draw and quarter Rocket. "Identify location."

"Desolate crater. Aliens have transported me to their cosmic lair." Translation: backyard tent.

Nowhere else to go in my house because Virginia sleeps with one eye open and can hear a spider bark. I look at Cleo. "C'mon, then."

Three houses down, we enter Rocket's cave and sit Indian style. Two sleeping bags, a lantern, a half-eaten bowl of fossilized Grape Nuts, a radio, and *The Book of Lists*. He's left us alone, thank the Lord. I turn off the walkie-talkie and switch on the lantern, illuminating Cleo's long angular cheekbones and magnificent, dark eyes. Rocket's left a dorky *Star Wars* lightsaber next to his bag (*God, she'll think I'm ten years old*), and I slide it underneath and outside the tent but accidently bump the light switch.

"What's that?" The lightsaber floats brightly in midair and slashes across the backyard in the hand of a headless horseman. That was close.

The old tattered *The Book of Lists* begs me to pick her up (it's banned in school libraries for obvious reasons). Rocket and I have spent thousands of hours going through the book, so I know my fave lists. "3 People Who Died During Sex," "10 Women Offered $1 Million Each – If They Pose Nude for A Girlie Magazine," "24 Feats of Physical Strength" (Frank "Cannonball" Richards took a cannonball into his stomach at close range.), "The 8 Most Valuable Baseball Cards." (#6 Gil Hodges, $50). And Rocket's fave: "10 Beans and Their Flatulence Levels" (self-tested for veracity, to my dismay).

I flip open the book like I don't know every list by heart and page through to a topic I think she'll be interested in and tell her the list: "21 Best-Known Stuffed or Embalmed Humans and Animals."

"Well? What are they?"

"You have to guess ... that's the game."

"Oh, okay." She ponders an answer and rolls her eyes to the ceiling. "I got one. King Tut."

"Brilliant. That's number one. First guess."

"I knew it!" She laughs out loud and smacks me on the shoulder, which makes me smile. "Give me another one."

"Irving Wallace's 12 Favorite Dinner Guests from All History." This one's calculated on my part.

Cleo goes from Indian style to up on her knees. "Jesus Christ, I dunno."

"That's number four on Amy Wallace's list." She tells me she wasn't even guessing with that answer, then volunteers Robert Redford, but I tell her they have to be dead.

She rocks her spine back and forward. "Let me think." A long pause. "Abe Lincoln."

"Number five." She guesses a trillion famous names—Elvis, Marie Antoinette, JFK, Leonardo, Anne Frank, Lennon, Lenin, Houdini, Gandhi ... but can't name one more on the list. Uncle Fred or Galileo are numero uno on my personal list.

Cleo grabs the book out of my hand. "Who's number one?" She throws the book at me. "I should have guessed ... Cleopatra."

Blush from my cheeks makes the tent glow red. A whippoorwill whistles singsongily from a tree.

"Hey," I say, "do you want to jump on Rocket's trampoline?"

"Jumping makes me sick." Her eyelashes are painted long and black to match her hair. "And really, any physical activity."

I forgot she's sick, and I hope Chimney's just dead wrong. "It's an in-ground one."

She's out of the tent in an instant. I bring the lantern outside, and after we take off our shoes I take her hand to lead her onto the rubber surface. She takes my other hand so we're jumping up and down holding hands together so we don't fall, like a couple of third-graders. She stumbles, and we lose each other's grips. I jump solo, higher and higher and higher before I do a few routine moves. A sit to a stand. A knee to a stomach. Stomach to back to knee to stand. I'm showing off now while Cleo wobbles on the springs, watching my spastic moves. You get a little tingle in your belly every time you jump too high.

You can square—no, cube—that feeling and multiply by infinity, and then you'll know how I'm feeling with Cleo right in front of me. This is a bit what floating in space must feel like. Suddenly she plops down on the trampoline, and she goes all quiet and teary eyed. Have I done something to upset her?

A cold northern wind sweeps across the lawn, and she shivers. "Freezing my ass off." She has no meat on her bones to keep warm with.

We duck back inside the tent. A loop of black hair dangles loose down her face. She blows it out of her way, and I'm hypnotized as it billows around her eyes. A dog howls on a nearby lot, and a windy gust shakes the tent, crushing one side for an instant before straightening out again.

A humanlike hand enters the opening in the tent and tosses a grenade inside. What's Rocket doing now?

Get freaking lost! Just a box of Spaceman candy cigarettes. I owe him one for not playing the third wheel. It's his own tent and backyard, after all. I pull out two candy cigs and give one to Cleo.

There's a bit of a lull while we suck our fake sweet cigs, pretending to be cool, and I finally get around to asking her why she's sitting in a tent with me this late at night. "You haven't run away from home, have you?"

"Yeah. And maybe now my mom'll understand." Cleo gets all squirmy, casting her eyes at the tent floor. "I've been mad as hell at my mom, but I never thought once of hitting the road until tonight."

I wonder where I'd run off to besides Rocket's tent.

"Your mom might start to worry where you've gone."

"Mom's usually down for the count after three rounds of 7 and 7s."

She begins to unload her feelings on me and tells me her parents divorced when she was only four. Her mom's a control freak, and Cleo's old friends want nothing to do with her because they think she's become weird. Her mom hates the Egyptian clothes she wears, threw *Go Ask Alice* in the fire last winter when Cleo was only halfway finished, and wants her to take some of her pills because she thinks Cleo's depressed.

Cleo tells me she and Pippa Farnsworth used to be soul mates, but they've had a falling out over some boy. I don't want to hear this last part because I'd be tempted to dismember any other guy she might be interested in with a pickax. Anyway, she got fed up with calling Pippa and never getting a return call, and then Pippa spread BS rumors about her dropping acid, and now her other friends won't return her calls.

We stop to listen to a whippoorwill chorus. "I won't change for anyone. My mother, Pippa. They can all go to hell."

I ask about her stepdad, and she says he doesn't judge a soul, gives her tons of space, and she can't understand why he *ever* married his mother. She tells me she ran away from home tonight after a verbal brawl with her mom (she refused to eat her dinner and take a pill), and she just can't breathe in her house anymore.

Cleo's No. 2 pencil thin but tells me she was pudgy as a toddler, and her mom never let her eat a thing, especially ice cream, and every time she heard the ice cream truck bell ring and the kids screaming with laughter outside of her house, she'd gaze out the window with envy and wish she was dead. I think of Chimney's sense of cancer smell and wish she hadn't said that.

"Why don't you move in with your real dad?" I ask.

"My dad's got a new wife. *Darlene*," she says with sneering contempt. "Anyway, he moved all the way over to Dearborn so he can be close to Metro Airport 'cause he's a pilot. But he's promised me forever we'll fly to Paris or London someday." She picks at her black, chipped toenails. "Right now he's stuck with the Delta route to Columbus. Like I would ever go there."

It's Virginia's hometown, but I don't say a thing. Rocket's left a transistor radio in the tent, and I turn it on to search for music, and Ernie Harwell, the Tigers' announcer, says hello to a kid in right field from Wyandotte. I twist the knob and tune it past commercials, pause on that mesmerizing funk-music station with the DJ called the Electrifying Mojo ("may the funk be with you"), and then past that pukey, midnight music show called Pillow Talk with the deep, slow-throttle voice of Alan Almond.

"STOP." I turn the dial back. Chuck Mangione's flugelhorn fills the tent with mellow dentist music, and it dumbs my wisdom teeth and numbs my brain cells. "I love this station … perfect before going to sleep. And that dreamy voice."

I don't say anything to Cleo about Chimney and our weird encounter at her house for fear I'll chase her away or make her even more freaked out than she already is, but she can't run away from home without getting some kind of medical checkup. Maybe she can live in

157

Rocket's tent all summer, because his mom never checks it, his dad's always traveling for work, and Basil's too cool to step foot in a camping tent unless it's with some far-out hippie girl at the Sleeping Bear Dunes up north. I'll think of something to coax Dr. Clark down here to give Cleo a medical exam, if a shrink is even qualified to detect cancer. One thing I know from every doctor visit I've ever had is a swollen neck is a sign of something wrong. It's the first thing they grope at before they bring out the wooden tongue depressor.

We each curl into the two sleeping bags, and at some point I realize she's really not going home tonight. She rolls her bag over so our two blue sleeping bags are touching like two mummies in an Ancient Egyptian tomb built for two. I start to tell her one more list: "8 Cases of Spontaneous Combustion," but she's fallen asleep. In a low bass Allan Almond-voice, I say to her, "Sweet dreams, Cleo."

Phyllis Newcombe comes to mind from the list. She died at age twenty-two, combusting into nothing but a pile of ashes while waltzing at a smoky dance hall. Before I turn off the lantern, I hover it above her neck to check if it's swollen but only see a faint freckle and the most perfect, lovely neck in the world, fitting for an Egyptian princess. I wouldn't trade this night for a lifetime backstage pass to Springsteen's concerts.

After I wake up the next morning, I think it must have been a dream because she's gone, but I can smell her raspberry perfume on her sleeping bag, so I know it was real, and feel like I've never felt before. After unzipping the tent to a ribbon of purple-pinkish sky, I stretch my arms wide and gaze around, but she's nowhere to be found. I return to the tent and roll up her sleeping bag, wishing I could bottle her scent, and find a scrap of paper.

> *Giff—I have to get home before mom wakes up and knows I've been gone all night and throws a crazy fit· I guess I lost my nerve· If there's one favorite person I'd like to have dinner with, it's you (alive, not dead!) & I know you'll be famous one day· Cleopatra·*

I stare at it in awe and realize something.

I think I love Cleo.

BACK~NINE

10

A tall hedge separates our driveway from the Clarks', and I peer through the bushes, working up the nerve to approach Dr. Clark. Kate's catching rays on a towel in her bathing suit in the lone footprint of sunshine in the backyard portion of the driveway.

Rocket whirls up on his unicycle and spins round and round Kate. "Are you spying on Jenny Clark, Ford?"

Since the beginning of time, he's floated from house to house on that pole on a wheel of his, up and down Dot Ave without a care in the world. He clips Kate's towel, and his cycle tilts perpendicular, but he somehow rights the ship and pedals past me.

Get lost, Rocket. I have something important to do, and I don't need him messing it up.

I eye a thorny gap in the branches for signs of a Clark, but all I see are car parts and the ruins of old motorcycles. Pop's carped from the beginning of time, *What are they runnin' next door, a chop shop?* The Clarks are a source of fascination and fear for me. All the houses in my neighborhood are King George colonials surrounded by well-kept lawns, but the Clarks live in a spooky brown-striped Queen Victorian ringed with oily crabgrass and discarded oil filters.

Rocket keeps pestering me about why I'm looking next door. "I need to borrow some brown sugar for Virginia from the Clarks."

"I forgot!" Kate tears off her sunglasses, and springs to her feet. I haven't seen her move that fast since David Cassidy's tour bus was rumored to be parked uptown. "The Clarks have a new litter of kittens, and Mom said I can have one!"

Did she run this by Pop? He despises the Clarks and wouldn't be caught dead living with a Clark-bred cat.

We arrive at the Clarks' front door. Two tepid knocks on the door by Kate are followed by shuffling footsteps from inside the house. Rocket idles on the front walk on his unicycle. The door opens wide and Pauley Clark appears, wearing only a towel around his waist. His brown, shaggy hair falls just above his naked shoulders below his doughy, pimply cheeks.

"We're here for the kittens, Pauley," Kate says, folding her arms. "Your mom said we could have one."

"So you guys want some pussycats?"

A sinister chuckle escapes from Rocket's lips, and he collapses his unicycle. I figure we're dead meat if we dare step into the house.

"*I* do, not them," Kate says, pointing her thumb at us.

"C'mon in, then," he says, opening the creaking door. "They're in the basement."

I sense a trap, but I say nothing, too nervous to talk. We follow him inside, stepping past an ancient rug below an antique bronze chandelier and onto a creaky worn wooden floor. I look around the house and am surprised at how normal everything appears, except for a few animal paintings on the wall and sculptures of naked ancient Greeks. The house smells like a mixture of cigarette smoke and sweet licorice. Books are piled everywhere—the floor, the shelves, a window seat. A library with no librarian to put the books away.

Kate's eyes dart wildly. "Where's your mom?"

"Heh, heh, heh," Pauley gurgles. "She's in with a psycho, doing a therapy gig."

Rocket perks up. "A real lunatic?" I elbow Rocket to shut him the hell up.

"Probably, but we're going to find out for sure."

"What do you mean?" Rocket skips a step to catch up with Pauley.

"You can hear everything through the heating vent down in the basement."

"Maybe we should come back when your mom's done," I suggest, thinking nothing about this feels right. I'm freaking out, but I try to stay cool.

"Don't worry about my mom. She's busy. You'll hear."

We make our way down the basement stairs. Pauley flips the light switch. Five kittens peer up at us from a large blanket next to the furnace. The kittens are pressed up against their mother's stomach, whining, their little lungs not large enough to sound a meow.

Kate gently picks up the smallest kitten in the litter. "Oh, how cute." The black cat barely fits in the palm of her hand. She pets the kitten's head as it tries to squirm away.

"C'mon, you two," Pauley whispers. "Let's enter the psycho session."

Rocket treads on Pauley's naked heels. I stay put with my sister, who holds the kitten close to her chest. The scrawny kitten's claws have already latched on to my sister's heart. She has her kitten. Rocket's voice whisper-booms from the other room. "Quinn, get your butt over here ... you gotta hear this stuff."

I step through a curtain wall and see Rocket and Pauley standing on top of an avocado-green-colored Maytag washer and dryer, their ears glued to a heating vent.

At least Pauley has put some clothes on—a painter's smock. Rocket reaches his hand down and pulls me up next to him. Dr. Clark's voice is crystal clear, the patient's muffled.

"Tell me again, how did that make you feel?" Dr. Clark's voice.

"Like total crap."

Faint, but I can just hear the words.

"Say it again."

"Total crap."

Becoming clearer now.

"Louder."

"Total crap."

"Louder."

"Total crap."

Stereophonic sound now.

"Good."

Rocket tugs my collar toward the wall for a better hear, and I tumble into Pauley, who teeters on the edge of the washing machine before crashing to the ground on a heap of dirty clothes along with a loud "Hey!" He scrambles back on top of the Maytag. Rocket triples over with hyena sounds, and I mouth the words "Shut up!"

"Did you hear something?" the patient says.

Kittens croon beyond the curtain wall.

"Please continue."

Pauley nods in recognition. "Mom's tryin' her Confrontational Therapy Method," Pauley whispers, "bringing out the repressed feelings of the patient. We'll know if it works if she cracks ... I've heard her do it a million times ... and got a crap load of tapes upstairs."

"You record this stuff?" I ask. Pauley just smiles and turns his ear toward the ceiling.

"Now, he sheltered your true feelings?"

"Yes."

"And he buried your child spirit, right?"

"Yes."

"And if he were here right now, what would you say to him?"

"You bastard."

"Now, what would you really say to him? C'mon, you can do this, you've come this far."

A garbled sound rattles down the aluminum vent.

"What? I can barely hear you."

"You bastard."

"Louder."

"You damn bastard."

DOLBY Stereo.

"Louder, Martha, louder."

"You goddamn bastard."

"LOUDER."

"YOU GODDAMN BASTARD."

"Okay, okay. Excellent."

The house shakes with those words. Rocket's no longer grinning. Asteroids are bursting through his retinas. I shoot him a knowing look because I've heard that loud voice yell "ROCKET!" a thousand times before.

Rocket's mom's having a session with Dr. Clark. Rocket flies up the stairs, shrieking like a boiled raccoon. The front door opens and slams shut.

Kate comes over with her black kitten, stroking its head as it sleeps in the palm of her hand. "What's up with Rocket?"

The shouting upstairs turns to whispery nothings. Footprints stomp above my head.

"Pauley?"

Dr. Clark's coming!

Footsteps patter down the stairs, and my head puppet twirls to find somewhere to hide while sweating puddles form at my feet on the concrete floor. Pauley leaps down from the washer, runs to the furnace, and grabs a kitten. I follow his lead, get tangled in the curtain, free myself, and pick up a white kitten, clutching its itty-bitty skeleton fur against my chest.

Dr. Clark descends the stairs, her long gray hair flowing behind her. "Pauley, I didn't know we had visitors. You should have told me."

"They're here for the kittens."

She scans my guilty face. "I know *that*, Pauley. I heard someone slam the door. Who else was here?"

"Rock—" Kate starts to say.

"Terry came by," Pauley interrupts her. "He's thinking of getting a cat."

She frowns, skeptical. "I thought he hates cats?"

Kate, oblivious to the wiretap operation, rubs her chin against her kitten's tiny head. She has no clue why Pauley's covering for Rocket, but she knows my friend and probably figures he's done something totally stupid and Pauley's in on it.

"It's for his girlfriend," Pauley lies, brushing his rumpled hair out of his face and dropping the kitten back next to her mother.

"Well, it looks like you've found a kitten," Dr. Clark says, shifting her attention to Kate.

"Isn't she adorable?" Kate strokes her cat's thimble-sized head with her thumb.

"Is that the one you want, or has your brother found one, too?"

"No, we'll take this one," Kate says. I put the kitten down, and she limps over to her sleep-deprived, nursing mother.

"She's the tiniest one, Kate," Dr. Clark says. "Are you sure you want that one? She may not survive."

Kate swallows her kitten in her arms. "Oh, I'm sure. I'll never let her go."

"What name will you call her?"

"Fluffy."

"You have to keep Fluffy away from Sheeba from now on," Pauley says, nodding toward Fluffy's mom. Kate gives Pauley a distrustful leer and smothers her Fluffy, who's buried beneath her arms. "Once a kitten is touched by human hands"—Pauley opens his mouth wide and brings his crooked teeth together—"the mother cat will *bite* the kitten in the neck until it's dead."

"Oh, Pauleeey." Dr. Clark flicks her hand at her son likes she's batting away a fly. "Don't listen to him, Kate."

Once at home, Mrs. Olivehammer's therapy session has left me in a state of electric shock. I wonder if Virginia ever ventures next door, and if she does, how much Pauley knows about my parents' life that I don't. Then I remember she has her Mensa-Netics philosophy to lean on. I sit frozen, petting Chimney's velvety coat on the living room shag. The doorbell rings, and panic seizes my lungs. No one is home except me. I open the living room curtain a fraction, peek outside, and see Dr. Clark at our door.

We're in a heap of trouble now. I close the curtain, hoping she didn't see me, and a minute later trim it back again. She's left. I release a gallon of oxygen. *Why'd she leave so quickly?* A half hour later, I trip over Rocket's unicycle on the doorstep on my way to his house to cheer him up. *Phew! She was just returning it.* Probably figured it was mine since she hadn't cornered Rocket in her basement.

As I skip from sidewalk crack to sidewalk crack, I worry about Rocket's parents and hope for his sake they aren't headed to Splitsville City. He's never told me a thing, and I've never heard them fight like my parents do, but maybe that's better for parents than having nothing left to say to each other. Fights can be good because they get things out into the open rather than simmering and festering inside until things erupt like Mount St. Helens did last May. If that's true, Mom and Pop will never get divorced.

And maybe that's how Dr. Clark's confrontational therapy is supposed to help Mrs. Olivehammer.

The Clark house no longer has the same mysterious Halloween feel to it, and the next day I return without any fear, bringing Chimney with me. Dr. Clark and her welcoming smile answer the door. We stand under the chandelier in the foyer while I explain to her Chimney is a cancer-sniffing dog, how she sticks to Cleo like glue, and Cleo might be dying. She asks for the skinny on the dog cancer training center, and I tell her all about Mr. Levi-Vest Man. Dr. Clark kneels down, closes her eyes, placing both of her hands on Chimney's floppy ears like she has X-ray vision. An eternity passes.

"Good girl, Chimney, good girl." Chimney yawns and slobbers gobs of spittle on her hand.

Somehow Dr. Clark knows by touching Chimney that I'm not fibbing. She agrees to "investigate the situation" with her medical contacts and to speak with Cleo's mother.

"I've met *that* lady," she says in a harsh tone but doesn't disclose how.

And something about the tone of her voice gets me to thinking Cleo's mom might also be getting therapy once a week from Dr. Clark. A gnarly notion sprouts in the pit of my stomach. If I somehow found out good old Pauley records Cleo's therapy sessions, I'll drop him from a scrapped Apollo command module for a nuclear splashdown on the shore of Three-Mile Island. He'll be space-wrecked forever.

11

On a steamy Wednesday afternoon in July when the blades of grass are fainting from thirst, I finish up a loop with Owen Rooney, the Brit I'd befriended my second day on the job. I can carry two rounds now without passing out. Bobby Walton stuck me with Mr. Toadrey, the worst tipper in the club, who smells like a foul mixture of Musk English Leather and Noxzema.

Mr. Toadrey's playing partner is a Detroit Zoo zoologist, Glenn Lerch, nicknamed Lurch because he's ten feet tall and rarely speaks unless it's about his stupid pet iguana named Dragon. Dragon normally sits contentedly in the large front pocket with his little green head poking out as long as you drop Razzles on his red lizard tongue every other hole. But you have to keep an eye on him because Lurch allows him to roam free in the sand traps, and before you know it you'll be chasing his spiked spine down a cart path or up a tree. Bobby had given Lurch's bag to Owen, which was okay with him because he has a soft spot for reptiles.

After our loop, Owen and I escape onto Kensington Road through a hole in the fence on Number 9 on the north side of the club. You have to wait until there's a gap in the foursomes between the eighth and ninth hole before you make a run for it. A large volcano of a trap at the 150-yard marker on the ninth hole provides cover if you spot a golfer. If King or Gandy catch you, it'll be shithouse detail for three weeks and shouldering for hackers with bags as big as Volvos.

Once outside the fence, Owen asks, "You wanna come stay over at my place tonight? We'll get in an early loop."

Heck yeah.

Owen gives me a grand tour of the Palms Motel: an indoor pool, a video arcade, a ceiling-high fake palm tree in the lobby.

Man, I can get used to swimming and playing video games all day long. We have the total run of the motel the whole afternoon: swimming in the palm-tree-shaped pool, playing Nerf basketball in vacant Room 4, swimming again, and stuffing our mouths with Orville Redenbacher popcorn in the arcade. The motel owners are smart enough to have both *Space Invaders* and

Asteroids in the arcade, and naturally Owen gets free tokens, so he can play until his fingers fall off.

In Room 9, Owen has hung a "Do Not Disturb" sign on the knob, and band posters serve as wallpaper: *Quadrophenia* (of course), The Ramones, Sex Pistols, and The Jam. A nice Fender bass leans against the wall in the corner, and Owen picks it up, switches on the amplifier, and does a mod bass line that sounds like a wounded elephant. "I'm taking bass lessons down at Strings 'N Things." Maybe he can start a punk band with Rocket.

At dinner, Owen's older brother, Jake, announces the Kensington Hills Country Club will be hosting the 1980 PGA Championship this summer. I don't think much of it; there's no way I'll ever caddy for a professional golfer in a major tournament and one of the biggest prizes in the world of professional golf.

"Don't worry, boss," Jake says to me. "There are other jobs you can do. Hold a group's scoreboard or rake sand traps ... either way you'll be 'tween the ropes." After playing a bit of golf myself lately and caddying for a load of hackers, I'd shine golf shoes to get near a real tour pro.

We wake the next morning at 4:30 and rumble down the quiet streets of Kensington Hills in Jake's battered orange wood-paneled Ford station wagon. In the darkness, the clubhouse sits lonely as a pyramid in the desert; a single car hums in the lot with its yellow parking lights on.

"Who's that?" I ask.

Owen eyes the make of the car. "Chip."

"Jackson Pollock!" Jake slaps the steering wheel, and black-and-white fuzzy dice waffle from the rearview mirror. "Chip beat us here again. He's got no life."

The caddy shack won't be open for a couple of hours, but first come, first served rules at the club. Chip gets first pick of the player he wants to caddy for this morning.

"Where's Rat?" Owen asks, picking his head up from reading song lyrics of the album jacket from Secret Affair's *Glory Boys* with a magic penlight.

"He's been at the club so long he doesn't have to sign in at the shack ... might as well be doing life behind bars." Jake turns off the overhead light in the station wagon and reclines the seat. "For Rat, this is his life."

We'll get a little shut-eye till the sun rises. With our heads resting on our balled-up towels in the back seat, we listen to Larry King on the radio interviewing Burt Reynolds and Dolly Parton, and afterwards the man who invented the Slinky.

"Good night, John-Boy." I fall asleep to the sound of Larry's throaty voice and Jake's wild snoring.

Two restless dreams later, Jake slaps us awake with his towel. "Rise 'n' shine, Teddy Boys."

"Bloody hell, Jake." Owen throws a Bazooka Joe gum pack at his brother's head.

Because we're on top of the loop list, we don't have to spend two minutes at the caddy shack, and we're on the first tee before dawn breaks above the majestic oaks. I'm handed a bag with a King Tut wash towel, but the significance of the ancient boy ruler doesn't register a thing in my sleep-deprived brain.

Jake reads the nametag on my player's bag: Valentine. "Wot a lucky bloke ... he's a real corker."

A second later, a golfer approaches me dressed in plaid yellow-and-orange golf pants and eyes my green badge. "I've heard you caddied, but I haven't seen you out here before."

Rust crumbles out of from sleepy eyes; I'm barely human at this hour of the morning. "I don't normally get here this early."

"Then you're missing the finest part of the day." He gives me a wink and a mile-wide smile. I hate when anyone smiles at me before noon unless it's a girl, but he seems nice as all get-out. Although still a green plebe,

I'm not exactly a rookie, having notched almost twenty loops on my caddy belt. Once you reach forty, you're automatically promoted to the rank of captain with a blue badge, no questions asked, plus $2 more a round. If I carry two rounds a day, I'll be Captain Quinn in no time.

Jake warns me "morning golfers" take their golf as serious as tour pros. I want to show this Mr. Valentine I'm not some caddy hack and "know me onions" as Owen's fond of saying. By now, I've memorized the distances from various spots on the course stone-cold. For example, the creek that runs through the fairway on Number 5 is ninety-eight yards from the green. A terrific tee shot will end up in the creek, so you better alert your player to the hazard if the member doesn't remind them. A driver on Number 15 will end up in a monster trap or the woods behind it. A 3-wood is a better play.

A few feet from me, Mr. Valentine takes short, smooth practice swings with his driver. Fresh grass clippings kick up and float down around his white-tipped golf shoes. He loads the tee and knocks the ball out of sight on a string down the middle of the fairway, leaving behind shoeprints in the dewy turf.

Mr. Valentine shoves his club into the bag while another player tees off. I slip a purple velvet cover over the driver so the irons won't scratch the blonde wood's precious surface.

"I toted bags once, too," he tells me while putting his tee behind his ear. "Good way to pick up poor swing habits. Do you play the links?"

"Links" is Scottish for golf course but technically means the rough grassy terrain between the sea and the land. Mom thinks I should study French in high school because it's the rage in the Hills, but I'm learning a language all on my own this summer.

"Yes, sir. I've been playing quite a bit this summer." Golf's as addictive as nicotine or alcohol. One great shot brings you back to the course for more.

The course is just waking up as we make our way down the fairway. Dew has swamped the grass. All four tee sheets have found the short grass and have made wet comet trails ending at the balls. Glimmering yellow morning light floods a warm coat on our chilly start to the day. The group goes at a breakneck speed like one big oiled machine churning down the fairway without the usual chitchat you endure from the afternoon beer league. Just solid whacks on the ball with the occasional "well done" or "you smoked that drive" and on to the next hole.

Until that round, I had not seen a golfer hammer the ball straighter or farther than Mr. Valentine. He swung the club with a smooth arc, as if the club weighed no more than a dove. On my round, he cards a 71. All pars and a birdie on Number 17—only pros shoot a round of par or better at Kensington Hills. Turns out he's a "scratch" golfer, which translates to professional grade. Now I understand why Chip arrives before sunrise every day. To be in *this* foursome. The name on the bag tag means more than just avoiding a dreary wait in the shack. A normal round with four slackers and hackers will take five hours. Mr. Valentine's group finished in just over two, rarely venturing into the rough, never stopping for anything except to watch the flight of the shots soaring toward the flag like eagles diving for a fish strike.

After our round, the three other players pay Mr. Valentine a wad of money because he won all three bets in their gambling game called "Nassau." He hands me a hefty $20 tip for barely doing anything at all but walk in a straight line, except helping him read a putt on 17 after one of the other players pressed him (basically a double-or-nothing dare).

"Let me see your hands," he says before I leave. I hold out my hands, wondering if he thought I stole something out of his bag. A caddy named Brad Elston got canned for pilfering a pack of Camels and a Jacques Restaurant matchbook from a member's bag.

"No, your palms." I turn them over and assume he'll tell me my fate like some fortune teller. "Do you have tendency to slice the ball?"

Maybe he is a fortune teller. "How'd ya guess?"

"I didn't guess. I'm looking at your calluses." He retrieves a 5-iron from his bag. "Here, grip this club." I weld my hands together on the shaft. "Your grip's a bit off." He shifts my left hand a tad clockwise, adjusting the shaft just below the middle set of my finger creases. "The V of your right hand should point to your chin."

It's nice he's taking an interest in me; most members don't know you exist unless you give them the wrong distance to the hole, and then they want to take your head off.

"Keep your elbows together."

I fold in my elbows and take a short practice swing. He drops a tee at my feet and nods. A free and easy swing sends the tee flying across Yellow Brick Road. "Nice. This grip will give you a nice draw on the ball."

With a "draw," the ball will hook slightly at the end of its apex and give you a nice long roll.

"You know, the thing about golf is it's character revealing," Mr. Valentine says. "People cheat using a foot wedge to get their ball out of the woods, can't seem to count their strokes on a poor hole, or get mad as hell when it's just simply a game." A sly grin appears, probably conjuring up some past golfing escapade. "Yep, golf's an ego leveler, especially on this course." He gazes out at the course he's just conquered like it's his mistress, and I guess at some point in his life he must have had a professional golf career in mind—perhaps real life got in the way.

With this grip change, I would manage to thrash Owen for the first time the following Monday. The game of golf is growing on me, and I decide to play every chance I get this summer, along with getting some early loops on the bag with the likes of Mr. Valentine.

■ ■ ■

On a blistering summer evening, an owl's muffled foghorn blows outside my TV room. I inhale sizzling Pop Rocks and devour Kate's *People* magazine. Hollywood's bionic couple are Splitsville, a white family fights to keep a black child—but a Connecticut judge says no—and Carol King's daughter turns punk rocker.

Earlier that day, I'd bought a Rubik's Cube at Kresge's, and now it taunts my soul from the couch. I've pissed away two hours thinking about losing out on the Lund Gang diving-dare test, furiously turning the cube. Nick Lund once told me that no matter where your colors stood, you're only twenty moves from solving Rubik's Cube. The best I could muster was three colors in a row on one measly side.

Freaking impossible! Billy strolls in and ignores my presence as usual. *Whatever.* He picks up Rubik's Cube, and I don't give his frantic spins a second thought.

Ninety seconds of solitude.

"Did you hear about Lee Majors?" Once in a pale-green moon, I'd try to bond with Billy, but five years separating siblings might as well be a quarter century. "Turns out he's a six-million-dollar idiot. Who breaks up with Farrah Fawcett?"

Billy tosses the cube on the window seat. "I'd like to give her a bionic whirl. He'd break her in half. If you're the Bionic Man you can only date the Bionic Woman."

I put the magazine down. "I guess you're right."

"Like you would have any clue." Two long strides and he snatches the magazine from my hands.

"Hey, come back here. I wasn't finished reading that!"

I turn my head and witness a miracle. The cube glows red from the couch—on one side! I pick it up and rotate the cube from side to side. Yellow, green, red, orange, blue, white. Solid color squares on all six sides. Billy solved the cube puzzle? *Inconceivable!* Billy's a bloody genius. I rush upstairs and knock on the door of his forbidden roomdom.

"Go away, Ford." A shoe brick thumps the door. "Now!"

I press my teeth to the door. "How'd you do that?"

"What did I say?" Billy never ignores me if I threaten to enter his room, so I pound on the No Entrance sign he'd taped to the door. He opens the door a sliver. "What don't you understand?"

"Have you ever tried Rubik's Cube before five minutes ago?" I've hidden the magical cube behind my back.

He opens the door a bit more. "No. Why?" Caught red-handed. Stoners would sooner play *Dungeons & Dragons* than waste time on Rubik's Cube. He doesn't know the degree of difficulty of the mind-bending puzzle. I show the solid colors to Billy. He has no idea mere mortals are lucky to get one solid row of colors. He snatches the cube from my hand, twists it to cover up his secret brilliance, and tosses it down the stairs. "It's not hard if you're not a spacetard." He slams his door shut, opens it again, and flings the *People* magazine past my face. Cover girl Farrah Fawcett tumbles down the steps.

How fast you can solve Rubik's Cube on your first attempt is directly proportional to your spatial IQ. Rocket's brother, Basil, told me this to prove he had an IQ of 140. I hadn't timed Billy, but I know it was around ninety seconds because I'd only made it halfway through the article on Carol King's daughter's obsession with the

Sex Pistols before he'd stolen my magazine. That gives Billy an IQ close to Einstein's. The son of a bitch has fooled Mom and Pop for years. A Quinn myth was perpetuated by Uncle Fred after he claimed Billy beat him in chess when he was only five years old. We had all figured it was a joke because Billy has never showed any intellectual curiosity. There'd been faint clues throughout his life that only dawned on me after the Rubik's Cube incident. He can solve math problems in his head by adding from left to right, there's no maze he can't crack in microseconds, and he can take apart a transistor radio and put it back together again. And then there's the clincher: He never gets lost. He's got a sixth sense of direction.

Pop and Mom are just not smart enough to know how brilliant Billy is because for some reason he's hidden it from them. I know better now. I have to work hard to get good grades or I'll never become an astronaut. Billy isn't stupid; he just doesn't give a crap. Why's he throwing his life away? Maybe we aren't related after all.

. . .

On my way home from Rocket's house a few weeks after Pop's lot-sale scheme, I slip past a silver MGB convertible roadster blocking the driveway, and my heart leaps, thinking my car-dealership-owning uncle is visiting from Cocoa Beach, and we'd spend a few days buzzing 'round town with the top down. Turns out it isn't Uncle Mitt's car at all. The license plate reads: F-I-T-Z 6-8-3. I've seen that car at the country club.

Frozen panic fills my veins.

My TV room. I flash through the mudroom, grab a treat from the kitchen, and see Mr. Fitz puzzling over Pop's treasure map in the living room. I lurk in the den, gobbling Twinkies, listening in on the two.

"It's not a buildable lot, Mr. Quinn. You need an extra fifteen feet for setback."

"Who's going to notice?"

"Mr. Quinn, the new owner will need a building permit from the city before he pounds one nail."

"So we're dead? Is that what you're saying?" Pop's voice rises in steady volume. "Just plain dead?"

I swear I can see Mr. Fitz shaking his head through the bookcase. "No, no. Not at all. We have to obtain a zoning variance from the city. Just a bit of red tape we'll have to cut through, that's all."

"Why didn't you say so? Do I need a damn lawyer now?"

That could be a deal killer. Sweet! Lawyers cost a ton of money we don't have.

"They're worse than stockbrokers. Criminals in ties."

You tell'm, Pops!

"Save your money. It's just a formality. I'll do all the talking."

Don't believe'm, Pop.

"Okay. Let's talk about price."

I rearrange the den in my mind to fit my TV on the shelf. The old 8-track player stereo will have to go, and the gazillion *Encyclopedia Britannica* volumes, along with Virginia's *Reader's Digest* collection.

"A similar lot over on Grover's Lane just sold for seventy-six thousand dollars. No variance required."

My ears suddenly tune to Radio FITZ. *Seventy-six grand for one measly vacant lot?*

"Where do I sign?"

Where indeed. That'd pay for some college. I guess I can trade my TV room for college tuition, but it'll still be a close call.

12

Today's the day Dr. Clark arranged for me to finally see Cleo at the hospital, along with Chimney—strictly in a medical capacity because dogs aren't normally allowed in the hospital.

While I slept last night, Khomeini freed a single hostage "for health reasons," and everyone knows it's a publicity stunt by the Iranians because there're still thirty-two of them left blindfolded in some hellhole prison in that desert country. It's all everyone's talking about today on the TV. Pop's raving mad about it. Pimples, a caddy regular at the club, told me during a loop that the shahs of Iran are like the Kennedys of America. Political royalty. This struck me as interesting because Ted Kennedy is running for president against Carter, who backs the shah. Not really sure where exactly Iran is on the map or why they hate our guts.

What I do know is my forensic search for my lost notebook has turned up nothing over the past weeks. I wonder who's laughing out loud at my wanky poems. Probably Kate and her clueless friends who wouldn't know the difference between Robert Frost and Sylvia Plath. I'll gladly trade Kate's diary for my notebook but don't want to make the first desperate move because I haven't found her diary key and don't want to read cyclops's deepest thoughts anyway, which is an oxymoron, of course.

Chimney and I meet Dr. Clark in the hospital lobby and follow her to Cleo's patient room. Hospitals have a foul clean odor all their own, and this one's no different. A sign reads "Oncology," which I'm pretty sure is a fancy word for cancer. A lump grows in my throat, and I pinch myself not to tear up.

It hits home now how Virginia felt when Pop almost died. I've heard the story a zillion times from Virginia. When I was in the second grade, he'd awoken in the middle of the night with a horrible pain in his gut and drove himself to the hospital while Virginia slept soundly at home.

Two days later, the doctor had cut him open from his hip to his belly to get to his gallbladder. He got sick after the surgery with a fever and internal bleeding, and he couldn't shake it off. On a snowy night, while I was sledding with my cousins down my uncle Mitt's steep front yard before they moved to Cocoa Beach, the surgeon came out into the hallway with his mask pulled down under his chin and told Virginia, "Sorry, Mrs. Quinn, but it doesn't look so good."

Twenty minutes later, a flat line crossed the screen. As Pop reminded us, "I was a goner." Virginia had sat in vigil, made the sign of the cross over her chest, and hailed Father O'Brien from his rectory chair. Before the good father had had time to gather his collar and cross, Pop had rebounded, the flat line turned wavy, and the next Monday he was sitting up in bed drinking coffee.

Pop recovered from his illness that spring, though he was half the man he was before the operation. He'd been a heavyset chain smoker. Once fat and happy, he became thin and grumpy. After the doctors made him quit smoking, he turned to drinking Pabst Blue Ribbon instead.

Dr. Clark doesn't turn left toward the cancer ward but rather makes a hard right toward the psychiatric unit. Chimney pulls hard on the leash toward the cancer ward, sniffing killer cancer molecules like hot dog biscuits fresh from the oven. I tug on her reins and lead her toward the psych ward. We pass a few rooms full of patients. A man karate chops an imaginary villain. Two nurses hold the man's arms down before stabbing him with a needle. A nurse spots me and closes the curtain shut. Another man, bald as Kojack, sits straight up in bed mumbling some pig-Latin curse.

"Dr. Clark." She stops and turns around. "You went down the wrong hall." I yank my thumb. "The cancer rooms are back there."

"Well ..." Something seems to be caught in her throat. "Chimney was sort of right."

I scratch my head behind my ear, a nervy twitch, and ask her what she means by that.

"Chimney found a tiny melanoma, a form of skin cancer." She rubs my dog's floppy, silky ear. "It was just on the surface of Cleo's skin near her hip bone, and it wasn't making her sick yet."

A woman runs out of a patient room screaming, "Aliens are in the bathroom and they've made a mess!"

"If she's not sick with cancer anymore, why is she still in the hospital?" Uncle Fred told me once the longer you stay in the hospital the more likely they'll find something else wrong with you just to jack up the room charges.

She twists her mouth end into a knot. "Some people *think* they are sick, when they're not."

"You mean she's faking it?" No wonder kids are screwed up when you consider how adults can never answer simple questions straight up.

"No, not at all. She thinks she's sick, which is just as debilitating. It's called somatization disorder."

Big words don't help, either. "Sounds made up."

She nods. "Precisely."

"I just want to see her."

"That's why you're here. She won't eat and refuses to believe anything the doctors tell her."

I can't blame her one bit.

"She'll only believe what Chimney says."

Chimney doesn't talk, Dr. Clark. "You mean if she doesn't bark, she'll think she's cured."

"Right." Dr. Clark bends down and says, "You can do this, Chimney. Good girl."

I knock lightly on the door and hear Cleo's weak voice tell us to come in. Chimney lounges down next to her bed. Cleo wears a light-blue hospital gown over her frail frame and has an IV line attached to her arm but looks as beautiful as ever. I wonder why she has an IV line if it's all in her head but just figure it's only sugar water and won't harm her. (This is the closest I've ever been to a girl's bedroom that isn't Kate's.)

She's still wearing the mood ring I gave her when we first met. The liquid crystal glows amber—nervous and unsettled. The week before, I'd finally bought a new Technics stereo with my caddy earnings. It plugs into my cassette tape player, and I made my first mixtape for Cleo so she can listen to it in the hospital. I choose a bunch of songs I think she might like, including, "One (is the Loneliest Number)," "Love is Like Oxygen," "Rock with You," "Upside Down," "God Only Knows," ELO's "Livin' Thing," and The Vapors' "Turning Japanese." I put the mixtape and a brand-new *That Was Then, This Is Now* (which I haven't gotten around to reading yet) on her bedside table next to an orange pill bottle.

There isn't any talk between us about her condition. Chimney's not barking or sniffing Cleo, so I know in my heart her skin cancer is gone, but I guess Dr. Clark already told me that. She reaches out her skinny arms, pulling an IV line with her. "Put Chimney in the bed with me, Giff."

Why is she in the hospital still if her cancer's gone?

I lift Chimney into the bed and pray she won't bark. She pants silently at her feet on the end of the bed, licking her rear paws. Dr. Clark's feet shuffle uneasily underneath the curtain. She's told me what to ask her.

"Looks like you're cured. Chimney isn't barking or sniffing."

A smile comes across her lips. "That was a close call, Giff. If it wasn't for Chimney, I'd be in serious trouble." She grabs a Polaroid picture off a side table and shows it to me. A picture of her hip, covered by a large bandage where they sliced off her skin cancer. "Dr. Clark wants me to look at this every time I feel sick as a reminder I'm cured, but how does she know they got it all or it didn't travel down my leg? My leg itches *right now.*"

She scratches her leg, and I realize she's in the mental ward because she can't shake the feeling she's sick when she's really not, like Dr. Clark told me. "Will you hold my hand?" she says. "I'm scared."

"You're fine now. Chimney's sleeping." Her tail swings back and forth, probably dreaming of a nice run in a sunny meadow. "My dog would be making a huge fuss if she thought you were still sick." I'm trying to avoid the "C" word.

"You think so?" She reaches over, palms facing up in the air for me. I hold her hand. Her skin is soft and thin like cellophane, and my heart's melting like a stick of butter in a microwave. The last time I held a girl's hand was back in the 7th grade when Polly Ledbeder grabbed my hand and we stormed the Holy Redeemer gym floor to "Crocodile Rock" during the Fall Dance.

Cleo has a faraway look in her eyes and turns her head toward the window. The sky's a swirl of pink and gray. Inmates scream down the hall. "Do you ever wonder what's beyond the planets? What's in the next universe?"

Just about every waking hour. "I'm trying to deal with my own universe."

She gives me a weak punch in the shoulder. I know it's stupid and selfish for me to have said that. Cleo wants to know there's a universe beyond the living, but all I can talk about is my own small, pathetic world.

"I'm serious." She shifts in her bed so she's now lying on her side. Her eyes are like two black marbles. "If we die, maybe we get transported to a different place in the universe. We don't become dust. I don't mean physically, but like our souls."

Her parents are atheists; they won't have anything to say on the subject without sounding like frauds. Perhaps I'll convert her to Catholicism after she gets released from the hospital and we start dating like a real couple.

"I'm sure that's true," I finally say.

"How do you know *that*?" She lifts her chest and her eyes lock onto mine like a fighter pilot on an enemy pilot. For our future's sake, I better come up with something plausible.

"Souls exist." Every book of poetry I've ever read talks about loneliness and death, and eventually the poet just can't resist writing nonsense about unearthly souls.

An innocent foal must have a soul, and if you take a lamb to slaughter ... Or something like that. If my Catholic teachers talked about souls, it hadn't registered.

She scoffs at me. "Is that just something they tell you at church?"

"No, science."

Her tone tightens. "You better not be fooling with me, Ford."

"It's true. It was proven by Hunter McDougal in 1907. Did you know that?" This isn't a lie. I read it somewhere, maybe in one of Rocket's *Mad* magazines—the one with the title, *PSSST! KEEP THIS ISSUE OUT OF THE HANDS OF YOUR PARENTS!* or in one of my *Omni* science magazines.

"Get out!" She shoves me in the chest with what little strength she can muster. "How'd he prove it?"

"The scientific method. He weighed people before and after they died. The soul weighs exactly twenty-one grams ... the weight of a hummingbird."

"A hummingbird? Huh. I like that." Her pupils drift up toward the ceiling. "You're not like other boys, are you, Giff?"

That's what I think about her—that she's not like other girls. She smiles, seems satisfied, and squeezes my hand tight. Her eyelids droop before closing.

I hold her hand for another good twenty minutes. Just Cleo, me, and our forty-two grams of soul. And eighty-five pounds of a sleeping Chimney.

■ ■ ■

Twenty minutes later, a nurse dressed in blizzard white pulls a cart full of liquid vials, pill bottles, and a glass of water backward into the room. She flips open a patient chart, spills four pills out, and crushes the pills into dust, all while her back is turned to me. A glass of water is filled with powder. I mouth to a sleeping Cleo, *We need to get you out of this place.*

Florence Nightingale turns, startled, and drops the glass on the floor, shattering an ocean of pill water on the floor, causing Chimney to jump out of bed and lap up the dusty puddle. My life turns into a slow-motion reel as I make eye contact with the nurse while grabbing my dog's leash, which slips from my hand, and I rush after Chimney, who's galloped out the door and slid sideways past Cleo's mother, who's entering the room wearing a mask of pure hatred.

"You!"

A mad dash through the hall chasing a blur of fur, past a man who looks familiar, but I don't have time to exchange pleasantries. I lunge for the end of the dog leash, then I'm yanked on my stomach toward the cancer hall led by hound nostrils. I reach an open exit door, pound down three flights of stairs, scramble through the lobby and a sea of wheelchairs, white uniforms, and gawking onlookers, and burst out into the parking lot as Dr. Clark drives away in her battered VW Beetle. I don't bother trying to flag her down.

Chimney's looking sluggish and thirsty, so I take a small detour toward the cider mill located on this side of town, where I know they have a dog-drinking fountain next to a plaque that says "Gristmill Est., 1837." I have to practically drag her to the mill, wondering what's wrong with her, then I recall the drug-laced water she lapped up in Cleo's room. She takes a few sips and collapses on the ground, falling into a deep coma sleep.

After gorging on a gallon of cider fumes and imaginary donuts waiting for Chimney to revive, I worry about what's going to happen to Cleo if left to her mother in that psych ward. They should just let Cleo work through whatever it is that's making her sick and not fill her with poison like her mom wants to. But what do I know? I'm no doctor. She seems perfect enough to me, and no one's perfect anyway despite some parents trying to raise them that way. Sometimes I wonder if country and hunt club kids like Cleo, Jason, Jack, and even Nick have it harder in some ways than the rest of us because their parents expect too much out of them, with their moms and dads devoting too much time fiddling with their kids' heads and lives. Pop would have fallen under this umbrella as a kid, and it might explain a lot about him.

Owen Rooney told me he hardly sees his dad because he's too busy working the late shift at the GM assembly plant and sleeping all day at the Palms. And if you ask me, Owen's turned out all right. Loves music, caddying, video games, cycles, all things mod. And as far as I can tell—life. I ponder all of this and lean up against an oak tree to watch the flowing, muddy creek water and wonder if I should stop uptown on my way home to buy a new notebook to write some of these thoughts into a new poem.

But then I think again. Owen and Rocket are a bit alike: They just "do" and don't think. Maybe people like Cleo and I think way too much about life.

13

The weeks go by, and I fall into a routine. If I don't go to the Palms Motel after caddying, I usually go straight home to take a nap. Waking early and carrying a bag for eight hours makes you exhausted. One Tuesday in mid-July, I crash on the couch after carrying a second loop in the blazing afternoon sunshine. Chimney's dead to the world on the floor, and *Lost in Space* is playing on TV. Penny is in a tizzy because her pet space monkey Debbie has escaped from the *Jupiter 2*.

Pop comes home red faced and flushed, sees me sprawled against the cushions, my eyelids half shut. He shuts off the TV and declares, "Boy, you guys are useless around here. I'm getting the hell out of here!"

I don't know where he went or why he left. I'd been up since 6:30. How much has he worked today? I'm the only one with a full-time job in the family.

Pop's exodus hit me hard. He'd left in rages in the past but always came back before dawn. Maybe he's gone for good this time. His job isn't going well; I know that because he comes home every day around three or four o'clock. Most Kensington dads don't do that. There's only one thing I can think of that would make him this upset: the side lot plot.

During Pop's absence, Rocket's mom, Mrs. Olivehammer, sits vigil with Virginia on our brick patio. Every late afternoon they slug down tea, whisper, and laugh out loud into the fading sunlight.

By day four, Virginia straightens up and discards her tissues and is recruited by Mrs. Olivehammer into her burgeoning army of door-to-door sales moms of the National Mix-Fare Federation. No more Rainbow vacuum sales. Before Pop returns from the village of Godknowswhere, our mudroom floor has grown knee-high with boxes of various Mix-Fare products—chocolate powder, plastic shakers, skin lotion, cleaning liquid, fruit bars, and Mix-Fare this and Mix-Fare that. Dr. Clark becomes Mom's first customer, buying liters of something called Super-V, an earth-friendly cleaning product good for dishes, floors, counters, and even mouthwash. Mom's enthusiasm and the thought of drinking milkshakes all day gives me the itch to work for her home-based business instead of lugging a golf bag around for hours in the humid Michigan weather.

One morning, I pick up the Mix-Fare milkshake mixer, pour brown granules into a plastic container, and pull a milk carton out of the fridge. "Virginia, I think I'll sell shakes to my friends instead of caddying." Milk goes into the mixer, and I give it a firm shake.

Virginia is flipping through a manual on the merits of Mix-Fare pyramid sales. "No, Ford, you've got a job. Mix-Fare can't give you a college scholarship, but caddying can."

I gulp down some Mix-Fare chocolate shake. "You don't get caddying—"

"Now, listen to me, Ford—"

"But, Mom—"

"Don't 'Mom' me. Your father never got his college degree, and look where it got him." She picks up the Holy Redeemer directory, a treasure trove of future Mix-Fare recruits, and writes down names in her sales notebook. "How could I have forgotten the Pinkertons? They know everyone in town." She plucks a pencil from behind her ear and scribbles down their name into her book.

"Why'd Pop leave?" I surprise myself by asking this, but I'm not a little kid anymore.

She presses hard with the pencil, and the tip breaks. "What?"

"You heard me."

Virginia closes her notebook. "The neighbors are fighting the lot split."

Mom tells me Laney Carter's dad from across the street is a lawyer and has started a petition opposing Pop's zoning variance. One evening, I see Mr. Carter and his long, crooked neck in his brown suit and bow tie, carrying a clipboard, knocking on doors, his head tilting to one side like he was edging the grass with his earlobe.

All of our neighbors sign the petition except for the Clarks and the Olivehammers. Pop hates lawyers and now despises almost everyone on the block.

■ ■ ■

A week later, I'm woken up by a wonderful smell and know he's back home. I'm relieved and go downstairs, a bit scared of what he might say to me or I might say to him. Bacon is piled high on a plate covered by a piece of paper towel to soak up the grease. He turns away from the oven, and all he says is "Hey, Fordo. One egg or two?" like he'd never left. That's all right with me. I'm glad he's home and the "D" word hasn't been uttered.

For a short while, even Pop gets sucked into the Mix-Fare sales frenzy, and Mom is cashing in her chips from his leave of absence. Soon he is delivering boxes around the neighborhood to Mrs. Dee with the trampoline on Derbyshire Road, and Mrs. Lynch on Rutland Grove. She even drags him to a sales meeting to hear the latest marketing pitch and to learn about the new product line. The Mix-Fare squeeze mop has been scientifically designed to spread Super-V cleanser over every horizontal surface of your house. There were late-night meetings with friends, Mom trying to build her sales force after a bridge game, repeating the mantra of sales multiples while touting the success of her competitor, the giant of all door-to-door sales, Amway. "They're selling product in Japan! Do you have any friends overseas?"

For a moment, I thought we were going to be living on easy street, and paying for college would be like buying a Mars bar. Pop would no longer mope around the house and could join the Kensington Hills Country Club set instead of playing golf at the nine-hole municipal dog tracks. *Mom has actually done the impossible*, I tell myself. The combination of Mom's self-help philosophy and the Mix-Fare Federation proves as unstoppable as Godzilla in downtown Tokyo.

I never saw Mr. Fitz and his silver convertible parked in our driveway again. The Kensington Hills zoning board denied Pop's variance. Kate's elm trees and my TV room are safe from the buzz saw for now. Pop railed on and on about lawyers, how he hated Carter, and how he was going to plot his revenge on our spiteful neighbors. Now he refuses to acknowledge the existence of any of the "petition-signing Dorchester rodents" as he calls them. He keeps a list in the den drawer, and I catch Pop reading it over every so often with knife eyes. He talked about running for the zoning board but didn't carry it through. What else is new? He hates politicians worse than lawyers. There's only one person he despises more than Carter and his backstabbing neighbors: Mr. Fitz.

The way Virginia described it to me, Carter had carved up Mr. Fitz at the zoning hearing, chewed a mouthful, and spit him out at the feet of the board members. Instead of arguing the merits of the variance, Carter exposed Mr. Fitz as an unscrupulous land developer intending to turn the idyllic Hills into high-density urban sprawl. Carter handed the seven male board members a purchase agreement showing Mr. Fitz's intention of developing low-income housing on the western edge of the Hills on forty postage-stamp parcels.

Pop pounded his fist on the table. "What's that got to do with the fifteen square feet of my land?"

Seven—zero. Variance denied. No lot split. No pay day for the Quinns. As the chairman's gavel sealed the verdict, Pop's outstretched hands reached to straighten Carter's crooked neck. Mr. Fitz slowed his attack with a hip check. The gavel fell hard a second time.

"Order!" A young man seeking a variance for a circle driveway subdued Pop.

A week later, Pop received a restraining order, prohibiting him from coming within fifty feet of Mr. Carter. Pop's blood always simmered on the surface of his vessels, but the Carter affair raised his blood temperature to a constant boil on Dot Ave. The Carters become arch enemy number one.

. . .

For months, Virginia had been pestering Billy about taking the college entrance exam. With his land deal dead, Pop turns to Billy while we sit around the dining room table eating pork chops and Rice-A-Roni.

Pop cuts into his pork chop like he's sawing a piece of wood. "You're taking the SAT."

"No, I'm not, Pop." He throws me a "shut your mouth about the Rubik's Cube" glare.

Chimney and I sit on the sidelines. Her tail stiffens—a sign that another Quinn storm is brewing from the living room. Fluffy paws an imaginary villain.

"You can't get into a four-year college without taking it," Virginia pleads with my brother.

Billy pokes at his rubber broccoli. "They only test you on math and verbal."

"What the hell else is there?" Pop asks.

"You wouldn't get it."

"I do."

"Fordo, you better stay out of this." Billy narrows his eyes at me, warning me again not to reveal the Rubik's Cube incident. I understood what Billy means. Standardized tests don't measure your ability to solve Rubik's Cube or navigate north or south if you're dropped in the middle of the Iranian desert like our guys who tried to save the hostages. Billy's a walking compass.

"Goddamn it, Billy," Pop says. "For once you're going to apply yourself and take this test. Your future's at stake."

"You mean your future."

"What do you mean?"

Billy stands, biting his lip. "You just want to tell the neighbors or whoever that I'm going to college and not some dropout."

"He hates all our neighbors," Mom says.

Pop's face turns Mars red, and he comes around the table. Billy brushes his long hair out of his eyelashes, pushes his chair from the table, and stands toe-to-toe with Pop. Two Quinns ready to come to blows.

"What are you going to do, hit me?" Billy dares, knowing Pop has never done such a thing. Mom pushes herself in between them. Pop backs away. Just a bluff on both sides.

"You're just afraid you'll fail like with everything else you've ever done."

"Howard!"

"I'll bet you a car"—Billy cocks his head—"that I score better than half the dopes who take that stupid test."

"It's settled, then," Mom says, satisfied with the resolution.

"Believe me, I'm not too worried." Pop storms out of the room, red faced.

Later that night, Billy knocks on my door. "We're closed."

Billy steps into my room. All of my baseball cards that I keep in two Dutch Masters cigar boxes are on the floor, and I'm sorting through my favorite teams in order of preference. Tigers. Red Sox. Athletics. Reds. Orioles. "Can I borrow a hundred bucks?" he says.

The last time I gave Billy money was in the sixth grade, and the next thing I knew he'd gotten suspended from school for God knows what. "A *hundred* dollars?" Simple math tells me that's ten loops. "What the hell for?"

"I'm getting a tutor for this stupid SAT test. I need to cram four years of high school into thirty days." He hangs his head down, and I know he's thinking I'll fall for whatever stupid reason he gives me for coughing up my money just because he's my brother. "If you lend me the money, I'll give you a ride with my new car anywhere you want at any time. No questions asked. It'll be like you have your own set of wheels."

"You swear?"

He puts his hand up. "Scout's honor."

Billy had been thrown out of Boy Scout's for setting some fake plastic army men on fire. "Throw in your Ernie Banks card."

"My Ernie Banks?" Billy shakes his head. "No way. You know that's my most valuable card. How about Boog Powell's rookie card?"

I think of a smiling Ernie with his baseball bat on his shoulder in a pressed blue-and-white Chicago Cubs uniform. *The card from 1957 must be worth a pretty penny.* "Ernie Banks ... deal or no deal."

"Deal," he says and gives me a fake slow-motion punch in the jaw.

Billy's brilliance will surely show through on the test. Even if he scores pretty average on the test, he could get into some college, and that would shut Pop up. I can't imagine Billy still living at home while I go to high school and the two of them bickering about whatever. Once I reach eighteen, I plan to get out of Dodge as fast as possible.

I go downstairs that night to circle the date on the calendar for Billy's SAT test. Virginia has beaten me to the punch, circling the date in red and writing next to the date a quote from Osmond P. Peabody: "Don't hold yourself back in life! Take courage and leap forward, for greatness might await you just around the corner!" I stare at those words and wonder if those are really for Virginia, not Billy. Poor Mom. She tries to rub some of her positive potion onto Billy's oily skin. I don't have the heart to tell her the truth, but if I had to spout a bit of philosophy of my own, I'd scribe this in my lost spiral poetry notebook:

> And stoners are dreamers,
> not doers,
> And grinders are doers
> not thinkers,
> But thinkers that tinker,

End up driving gull-winged DeLoreans.
Stuff that in your self-help pipe and
smoke it, OPP.

∎ ∎ ∎

With Cleo undergoing round-the-clock medical exams,
I hunker down at the club, waiting for her healthy and
happy return. My life becomes one big hamster wheel
or an all-day pass on the Corkscrew at Cedar Point—a
loop-the-loop. Get up, caddy thirty-six holes, gulp down
chocolate milk and gobble tasty Myrtle dogs, fall asleep
exhausted, rinse and repeat. My shoulders become as
hard as an iron manhole, my thigh muscles toned taut,
my light brown hair bleached streaky blond. Three
straight weeks of nothing but caddying and endless golf
on my Mondays off. I'm becoming one of the reliable
troops among the Green Shirts.

Once you're used to carrying a bag and marching
and up and down hills all day, you can relax and actually
notice your surroundings. Like the different hues grass
can take on depending upon the weather, the time of
day, or even the length of the cut by the grounds crew.
Short grass on the greens is the color of caterpillars or
green apples, the fairway a praying mantis, the longer
rough a turtle shell.

A golf course has its own ecosystem, like an island or the surface of a planet or a zoo without cages. A narrow creek crisscrosses the course filled with trout, sandy craters scattered about, muskrats, willows and maples, oaks, and pine trees, all species of butterflies, including black swallowtails, goldfish, and box turtles in the pond on sixteen. Frogs, birds, geese, squirrels, rabbits, the fox den next to the woods on Number 5, gophers you never see except for their holes, garter snakes, red-shouldered hawks, woodpeckers, slugs, worms, beetles, ants, and every flying insect you can think of like dragonflies, bees, and Tiger moths.

One Friday, I cash my two caddy stubs, ready to go home and spin records and hope to stay awake long enough with Rocket to watch the Friday evening shows—*Benson, The Dukes of Hazard, Dallas*. Bobby Walton signals me with a snap of his fingers. "Hey, Ford, do you want to do a nine-hole double?" The golfers I caddied for didn't spray the ball too much, so my legs feel strong enough, and by now nine holes is practically nothing. "Sure."

By the end of the round, my ankles hurt from the bag scraping them as I lugged them around. But I make it just the same and began to enjoy working at Kensington Country Club. Virginia's proselytizing about the virtues of hard work and habit turn out to be true. The more you do something, the easier it gets.

14

Given Tuesday afternoons means Ladies Day at the club, Owen Rooney and I agree to skip out on a second loop. (Ladies play slow as syrup.)

We arrive at my house, and Owen combs through my record collection. "You don't have many albums. Nuthin' mod at all. Mods're s'posed to hate rock, but I like it all."

So would that make you a Mocker? I keep my little joke to myself.

"No one 'round 'ere cares anyway, everyone playing that silly post-punk post-disco synthesized mishmash."

"I don't have the money to buy new records every day." I have pretty decent music taste compared to most kids, but Owen's ahead of the curve because almost all of the great music travels to America via England.

"Why don't you just ask your old man for some money?" He scans through some more albums. "No Bowie? The Clash? The Kinks?"

"He's not exactly into funding my music tastes." No one gets it. I want to tell him not every kid in the Hills can afford to buy albums every day. I get most of my music from J.J. and the Morning Crew and Arthur P on 101 WRIF—my radio heaven. That's why we have music stations on the radio. I do have something to show off, though. "I just got a cassette tape player. A Sony."

He bends down and pushes the bass boost button. "That's mint." I rip out two live albums to impress him with my musical tastes. *Foghat Live* and KISS *Alive!* "Jesus. I got some work to do." He stands straight and drags his fingers through his thick black hair. "Springsteen. Okay. I can live with that."

Good.

He stops at a Cars album. "How much did you pay for this album?"

"'Round eight bucks."

"Rip-off." He pretend throws the Cars disc out the window and returns the vinyl to its jacket. "I know a place where you can get records for practically nuthin'. It'll blow your mind. Let's go."

We ride the bus to Sam's Jams, not far from the Palms, but to Hills kids it might as well be the world's end. On the trip down, Owen writes up a list of bands for me to find in the store. An ocean of records greets me in Sam's, and it's like I've gone to vinyl heaven. Owen tells me Chrysler used to make motor boats here.

We hunt through the stacks of records for gems, coaxing the vinyl records out of their plastic jackets to inspect for scratches. Records with deep nicks might as well be Frisbees. Faint spiderweb scratches don't skip. A decent Who or Zeppelin disc is impossible to find unless you're willing to shell out $10. If that's the case, I might as well just buy it brand new uptown at Vinny's Hi-Fi.

I pluck Owen's number-one pick, "The Kids Are Alright" by The Who, from a sale shelf labeled Greatest Hits Albums. A steal at only $4. I finger the disc from its wrapper and notice a light scratch curving across songs four and five—"Magic Bus" and "Long Live Rock." After selecting a few more albums from Owen's list, I hunt in a colony of 45s and notice through the donut hole of "Teenagers from Mars" by the Misfits, a green country club mesh shirt covering a pointed white bra.

That pinball girl. Gigi Arnold.

The front of her shirt is tied short at the bottom, exposing her belly button. I pretend to scrutinize the vinyl quality, but then she notices I'm ogling her innie with my eyeballs peering over the edge of the record at her.

"Are you staring at me, pervert?" My veins became Minute Maid frozen lemonade. "Are you a mute?"

I raise my chin and cough out a nervous laugh. "No, I can talk."

"Do I *know* you from somewhere?"

"I've seen you at Kensington Hills."

"Yeah, I switched over from Rottenville." Owen had told me Roddenville Country Club is chopped liver compared to Kensington Hills Country Club, and the course isn't even on the Evans scholarship list. "They're real cheap bastards over there. Only three-fifty for eighteen. I ain't nobody's slave." She carries a hard, tough edge to her, like she's itching for a fight.

"They sound like jerks."

"Completely. And the course sucks." She raises her thumb high in the air, then slowly turns it down to the ground. "They put sand on the greens and only water the fairways twice a week." She looks me up and down. "Let me guess, you're a member at Kensington? Why are you hanging out *this* far down Woodward?"

I shake my head. "No. I live in Kensington but caddy at the country club, too. Only five more loops and I get my captain's badge."

"Good for you," she says in a mocking tone, "but I'm already a captain."

Her flat blonde hair isn't sprayed and curled up high at the ends like a typical Hills girl. She comes around to my side of the aisle, inspecting the five albums I've discovered from Owen's pick list: *Quadrophenia* (Owen's a black-haired dead ringer for the mod motorcycle rider Ace Face in the movie), *The Kids Are Alright*, two Bowie albums: *Space Oddity* and *The Rise and Fall of Ziggy Stardust and the Spiders from Mars*, and The Kinks' self-titled debut album. I turn over a Bowie album and notice the song "Moonage Daydream." *Space music.* I can dig that.

She holds out her hand. "Let me see what you got there."

I hand over the albums.

"Bowie's ace," she says. "I'd looove to meet him. Do you think he's bi? That's what I heard."

"Probably." *Don't know or care.*

We exchange names but not phone numbers. Like a dork, I stick my hand out for her to shake. She offers her small, soft hand in return. Her skin is smooth compared to her gruff voice, and she has thick, pouty lips that are irresistible. Owen comes over holding a stack of records, including ones by The Doors and Small Faces, and shakes my arm. "Let go of 'er before her hand falls off."

She shakes out the vinyl from the *Space Oddity* jacket. "It's in great shape." Her eyes light up and fixate on Owen. "Hey, do you guys want to go to my house and listen to these records?"

Lucky Brit. I hate being the third wheel.

Owen speaks up for both of us in his most noble fake King's English. "It'd be our pleasure"—he sweeps his hand in front of himself and curtsies—"to accompany such a fine lady to her castle for an evening of song with Mr. Morrison."

"I have a friend for you at home," Gigi says, nodding to me.

Don't care about any girl but Cleo.

We wander a few streets from Sam's to a row of bungalow houses all stacked next to each other, sharing driveways on small square lots. Next door, a tire swing hanging from a large oak tree drifts in the wind. A junked car sits in the backyard with its hood open.

A girl with knobby knees and cut-off jeans eats a Twinkie on the concrete porch. "Thought you'd never get here." The girl, skinny as a pole with frizzy brown hair and thin lips above a pointed chin, stands and shoves the last of the Twinkie into her mouth.

"This here's Betsy." We enter the house through the front door and its peeling white paint. Loud, throbbing music booms upstairs. "I'll take these guys downstairs. Betz, go grab some weed from my brother upstairs."

Smoking cigs is one thing, but I'll be out of my element with pot. I read *Helter Skelter* last summer and know getting high can lead to mass murder, or in Billy's case, a whole lot of nothing.

The bass guitar from upstairs thumps down into the basement. Gigi stretches her tan legs out on the length of a brown couch and throws her long hair back out of her face. I wonder how many guys she's taken down to the basement. The walls are painted purple. A velvet Ted Nugent poster hangs crookedly from a nail.

"Where's your mum at?" Owen asks.

"She's working at the Gas 'N Go over on Ten Mile." She picks up the Doors album Owen bought and places it on her turntable. The room fills with the haunting voice of Jim Morrison, which skips every few seconds to "Light my Fire."

Betsy comes down the stairs with a plastic baggy in her hand. Gigi slides to the floor. Her blue jean shorts push up to reveal a small brown mole on the inside of her thigh. We form a circle while Betsy rolls a joint as casually as a wet burrito.

"Who's got a light?" she asks.

Owen clicks off a flame from his Bic for Betsy. He's one of those survival kids who always carries things in his pocket—a Swiss Army knife for cleaning golf club grooves and fixing divots on the green or a white rabbit's foot clipped to his belt loop, which he rubs for good luck.

Betsy sucks in, and the tip glows red. "How'd ya get that cut on your neck?"

Owen arches his neck, and you can tell he wears the scar proudly, like one of the mod pins on his parka. "Just a dust-up with some manky rockers back home." Owen had confided in me that he's from a rough neighborhood near London where they fought the rockers or teddy boys every other day like the rival gangs you hear about in New York. Cuts, bruises, and brawls are nothing to him.

Betsy passes the joint to Gigi who inhales smoke, holding her lips tight and crossing her eyes. Her anxious face melts away, leaving a relaxed smile, and her head sways to the pulsating rhythm of the music. My turn. I've never smoked a thing, not even a cigarette, let alone a joint, but I don't want Gigi and Owen to think I'm a total nerd, so I inhale, and the smoke forces its way back out of my throat.

Gigi laughs and squeezes closer to Owen while holding the joint in my mouth. "Breathe in really deep, like you're holding your breath underwater."

The smoke pierces my lungs. I pass the joint to Owen.

After the joint comes around a second time, Owen puts his hand on the inside of Gigi's thigh. The combination of the carnival-like music of The Doors and the pot makes me feel drowsy and nauseous. Gigi and Owen loop their fingers together, and the joint comes around again.

"This thing's spent," Gigi says, eyeing the withered joint. "Roll another one, Betz."

"We need more paper."

"Go ask Terry upstairs." She google-eyes Owen. "And take Ford with you." Gigi unhinges her fingers from Owen's, gets up, and flips the record on the turntable. The basement's submerged with the sound of an approaching thunderstorm: "Riders on the Storm."

By the time I reach the top of the stairs, Gigi has switched the lights off, because the basement goes coffin black. Lucky for Owen.

"Stay here," says Betsy. "Terry gets pissed when he's stoned."

The kitchen sink is full of piled, rotting dishes. The music ceases upstairs between songs. A phone rings on the kitchen wall. Four rings. Nothing. Seconds later, Betsy's footsteps come pounding down the stairs. "Red's coming over. We gotta get you guys out of here."

"Who's Red?"

"Gigi's old man." We stumble down the dark stairs, and Betsy flicks the light on in the basement. Gigi and Owen have become one soft SuperPretzel of limbs on the couch.

"Red's on his way."

"Shit," Gigi says and shoves Owen off her lap. She drags us by the elbows upstairs and pushes us out the door into the blinding sunlight.

The northbound bus comes steaming up Woodward Avenue. I spot Gigi racing toward us. "You forgot these, Ford." She hands me an armload of albums. "I'll see you guys later." I watch her strut back down the sidewalk.

"Snap out of it, Quinn. She's mine." A red welt has grown on the side of Owen's neck.

"Owen, Gigi pasted a raspberry on your neck."

He pulls off his silver belt buckle and eyes the reflection of his hickey. "Her lips're like a toilet plunger."

I give his neck closer scrutiny. "Your mom might notice."

"Mum? She's too tired from scrubbin' bubbles in motel room toilet bowls to keep track of us after two o'clock." Owen peels off toward home.

I board the bus with seconds to spare, wobbling my way to the farthest back seat. The bus passes a row of ugly brick apartment buildings on Woodward Avenue. I think of rain showers and Gigi on that couch with her belly button showing below her green-mesh shirt. I wonder why even guys like Rocket and Owen make it with girls without even trying.

What do they have that I don't? Guts and guile, I suppose. Boy, I wish I could get a dose of whatever the hell it is they have, or I'll end up an old, lonely bitter pill like my uncle Fred, who had a huge falling out with Pop for some unknown reason before he died.

15

After what seems like eons, they finally release Cleo from the hospital. I'm dying to see her, but her mother doesn't want visitors. I figure her mom probably still hates my guts even though my dog practically saved her daughter's life. She's become untouchable to me, like the incubator boy in the movie *The Boy in the Plastic Bubble*, only she's a girl. A week later, I receive in the mail from Cleo the mixtape I'd given her along with a mixed message.

> *Dear Giff: Thank you for the tape. I've listened to this so many times that it reminds me of the hospital. (It makes me sick!! Just kidding!) They did things to me at the hospital that were quite shocking, but at least I'm better now. Anyway, thought you might*

want your tape back· Talk to you
when I can· Cleo·

No, I don't want the tape back. I just want to see you again, Cleo. My fingers pinch the tape from the plastic cassette, and I unfurl the ribbon before stuffing it into my garbage can.

∎ ∎ ∎

Torrential rains strike the Hills the following week, which forces the groundskeeper to close down the golf course—they can't risk ruining the course with the PGA Championship coming to town. Since I can't caddy at all, I just lay on the couch in the TV room all week, watching the *Phil Donohue Show* and loads and loads of drama at Johnny's pub in *Ryan's Hope*—Kate's precious soap.

By Friday, the dull rain stops, the clouds scatter, and the sun blazes hot. Theo and Kate are folded on the couch, watching *Ryan's Hope*, which makes me want to puke. I take my dog outside to get some fresh air in the backyard when Dr. Clark appears on my driveway. Chimney lifts a hind leg next to the big boulder in the corner of our lot.

Dr. Clark pulls her black cat-eye sunglasses down her nose. "Ford, I need to talk to you about Cleo."

Perhaps she wants to play match-maker. I ask her when I can see her.

"She's feeling better, but she's not quite fixed yet." What the hell does that mean? You fix a broken bike; you cure sick people. "She's in a very delicate mental state but doing well. We can't risk you upsetting her."

"I wouldn't upset her, trust me." Adults are fools if they trust teenagers, but she can trust me with regard to Cleo. She's the last person I'd upset.

Chimney sniffs Dr. Clark's sandals. "People like her think they are sick when they aren't. She doesn't think she is sick anymore. We have to keep it like that for her sake. Do you understand?"

No. "Okay."

"She's eating again. Everyone thinks Chimney saved her life, which is kind of true because she did find her skin cancer, but she's stilling feeling really down about herself."

Out of sheer desperation to see her again, I think of something to get Cleo out of her funk. "Hey, can you at least give her a present from me?"

"Sure, Ford." She smiles. "How thoughtful of you!"

"Wait here a minute."

She brushes Chimney's coat with the back of her hand while I run into my house and grab one of Virginia's well-worn self-help books written by Osmond P. Peabody. She has scores of his books littered around the house like Fluffy's hairballs. From a shelf in the den, I grab the paperback titled *Live Now! Take Charge of Your Life with Mensa-Netics*. Virginia's constantly harping that all you need is a better attitude in life rather than a psychologist's couch. Maybe that's all Cleo needs. Just a little motivational "kick in the arse" as Owen would say—or in her case, the cranium.

I give Dr. Clark the book. "Oh, are you sure you want to give her this? It's quite superficial." A sympathetic smile radiates fake from her lips, and I wonder if the doctor knows she's just insulted Virginia's gospel. "I suppose it can't hurt." With that, she disappears with the book around the hedge separating our two driveways.

I grab a football and kick it on top of our garage roof, pissed as hell I can't see Cleo. I know it's her mother's doing. *The hell with her!* Maybe there's another explanation for her depression. I reread Cleo's note to me, and a word sticks out like a comet shooting across the sky: shocking. Is it Cleo's way of sending me a hidden clue? I've heard about people getting shock therapy and wonder if they used the treatment on Cleo at the psych ward and she's afraid to tell anyone. I picture Cleo's hair standing on end, her fists banging on the lab door to get free like R.P. McMurphy in *One Flew Over the Cuckoo's Nest*. Perhaps these shock treatments have numbed her emotions, and she's forgotten her true feelings for me. If she had had any in the first place, that is.

Round fifteen loops later (counting days has turned into counting loops), I learn through the Hills grapevine that Cleo is telling everyone that Chimney found her melanoma just in the nick of time. That is true, because I've heard melanomas can grow like mushrooms after a hot summer rain and spread to your bloodstream faster than the Six Million Dollar Man jumping over a barbed-wire prison fence to save Jaime Sommers.

The dog-saving story spreads through town, and Chimney becomes the most famous hound in the Hills. Cleo enjoys a constant stream of visitors and new friends. And yet she won't see me? I can take a hint. Kate tells me Cleo has gone from a weird loner to the most popular girl overnight. I like the girl I first met at Stoner's Lake, not some popular Kensington Hills girl. I've been waiting a billion light-years but haven't heard diddly-squat from Cleo.

The *Kensington Hills Observer* runs Cleo's story, and not long after, *People* gets wind of it, and the magazine plans a photo shoot. A week later, Chimney sits proudly with her shampooed coat on the front lawn next to the cancer-dog trainer I'd met outside Olga's Kitchen. I don't go to the photo shoot or the TV station in Detroit later that week, on account of getting a serious bout of the summer flu. Kate goes with Chimney instead, which is fitting, I suppose, since she'd picked her out. I sweat out a fever alone on the couch at home and watch Kate, Chimney, and Cleo on *Good Morning America.*

I thought Cleo might at least say I'd saved her life, but she gives all the credit to Chimney and that stupid vest-wearing dog trainer. She doesn't even mention my name, but I don't really care. I just want to see her as soon as possible. I notice how brand new she looks now. She's lost her Egyptian bangs—now parting her hair in the middle—and gained weight so her jeans are no longer falling off her hips. She reminds me of a young Linda Ronstadt, only much better looking, if that's even possible.

The following week, I recover from the flu and call Cleo to tell her I'm no longer contagious. She says she'll call me in a few days if she has time to fit me into her "busy schedule." Before she hangs up, she says something that blows me away.

"That self-help book you gave me changed my way of thinking and my life."

Virginia's Mensa-Netics? Huh? Maybe the hospital forced her mom's pills down her throat, and she's numb to the world and can't think on her own.

Before I know it, Friday has arrived and nary a word from Cleo. After I watch *Fantasy Island* and *The Rockford Files* for the zillionth time that summer, I put a cassette tape into a new Sony Walkman that Rocket's dad brought back from a business trip to Japan. I listen to "Miss You" by the Stones over and over in bed with Chimney asleep on the floor next to me, hoping I never wake up.

I have a sour feeling in the pit of my stomach that my Cleo days are numbered, if not over. She's gone over to the cool-kid side of the line with a push from Mensa-Netics, while I teeter on the edge of obscurity. I still hold out a sliver of hope that I'll penetrate the Lund Gang. With my dumb luck, Nick Lund will start bragging about getting a raspberry on his neck from Cleo. If that ever happens, it'll confirm her psychotic diagnosis, and I'll jump into Stoner's Lake naked.

On Saturday, I stuff a message in a bottle and fling it into the ocean, hoping it lands on Cleo's shore sometime during my lifetime. On my way back from the corner mailbox, I notice a rare front-yard sighting across the street: Laney Carter. She's sitting on the front porch with her bare legs crossed, furiously scribbling notes in a book like she's trying to finish a school essay due this morning even though we're on summer break. I kick one of Chimney's foamy, drool-lathered tennis balls lying on the edge of our front sidewalk to vent some of my anger at losing Cleo, and the ball bounces down the middle of the shady street. Laney jerks her head up and quickly closes her book. Our eyes lock. She stands up in her short yellow sundress, lingering on the step for a moment like she wants to tell me something, before turning away and disappearing through a door to their screened-in porch.

Don't think I've spoken two syllables to her, even though we've lived across the street from each other our entire lives. Virginia once told me Laney's mother referred to her daughter as an "introvert." Mom said this as a nice way of saying she's painfully shy. I'd corrected Mom.

It just means you're not into small talk or dumb chitchat.

Dear Cleo — I've called your home a ton the past week, but I can't get through to you. I know your mom doesn't want me to see you. She told me not to _ever_ call you again and that you don't want to see me. I know that's not true, of course (?). For awhile there, I thought you might be dying. Thank God for Chimney. I think she'd like to see you again. Me too. Maybe I'll see you at the country club? I'm caddying almost every day and playing tons of golf. Do you play?

Stop off at my house if you want! We'll listen to some music. Have you ever heard of a band called The Talking Heads?

—Fondly, Giff

16

I n late July, Bobby Walton calls me up from the caddy-shack bullpen while I'm busy hitting Farrah's belt
buckle with a pinball, even though my name's near the
bottom of the looper list because I overslept. I descend
the bridge and see Owen hand a driver to Bobby. Next
to him stands the caddy master. A vertical Bogart is as
rare as a double eagle in golf. Something isn't right.

"You're caddying today for Mr. Bogart," Bobby says,
"and we're starting on the back nine." Given I earned
my captain's badge weeks earlier, I'm not nervous about
caddying for Bogart. By my last count I have sixty-seven
loops; they add up quickly when you carry two rounds
in one day.

I drag Bogart's black bag next to Owen's. "Are we
in the soup?"

"A member must've complained 'bout our caddying." Owen breaks out his knife and carves the sharp tip back and forth through the groove of a wedge, even though there's not a speck of dirt on the club. "Jake told me if you ever caddy for Bogart it means you're in deep shit, and he'll give you a flunk test. If you flunk, you're fired."

"Who do you think blabbed?" I can't think of one member I've royally pissed off. All of my summer plans are coming to a dreadful, dreary end. Lost Cleo, about to lose the caddy scholarship.

"It was probably Toad Fart. Remember him and his guest who couldn't find the bloody dance floor if they tried to walk to it?" Golfers and caddies have their own language for everything—the dance floor, or carpet, means the putting green. "Or maybe Bogart's just been on an all-day binger."

I shake my head, thinking of that round. "We shouldn't have given his guest the wrong yardage on five."

Owen grins, showing the crooked teeth in his large mouth. "He musta plunked six balls in the creek."

Toad Fart is Mr. Toadrey. He suffers from a skin disease where pimples fester on his face. If you blow up a golf ball to the size of a pumpkin and paint it red, that's Toad Fart's face. Caddies consider him the worst loop at the club. His normal tip is $1.50 (average is $3, a decent tip is $4, $5 and above is ace), and he has a bad case of flatulence caused by the skin medicine he keeps in an orange vial in the front pocket of his golf bag. Jake Withers once stole a Toad pill, ground it up, and deposited the medicine into Chip's chocolate milk on the tenth tee. Chip blew raspberry tarts (that's what Owen and Jake call farts) at Jake the whole back nine. When caddying for Toad Fart, we'd throw grass in the air to test the direction of *his* wind.

Caddies can wreak revenge on nasty members or guests, and they'll never catch on. Giving wrong yardage over a water hazard is the easiest way. Say it takes a 3-iron to get over the creek on Number 5. You'd tell 'em to hit a 5-iron. Then you return after the round and fish the balls out of the creek. Chip told me Lou Ballantine collected over one hundred balls last year by underclubbing his golfers. He sells them on the black market for two bucks apiece.

You can do other bogue things to golfers like reading the putt the wrong way or smearing Vaseline on the clubs, which causes the ball to shank off the face. Nothing pisses off caddies more than not stopping after the front nine for one of Myrtle's dogs bathed in greasy butter. In that case, you push microscopic pin holes into their golf balls, dropping the compression from the normal ninety to about sixty-five—caddies call it giving them a flat tire.

Owen and I figure we'll be getting canned for sure. Why else would we be caddying for Bogart and Walton?

"Mum and Dad are going to strangle me," Owen says, shaking his head. Caddying's a Rooney family tradition, like floating on the high wire is to the Flying Wallendas. Owen's mom's a MacGregor. According to Rooney family lore, her grandfather caddied until he was eighty-seven at the famed Old Course at St. Andrews in Scotland, where they invented golf. Owen'll be lucky if he makes it to age fifteen. Plus, he'll miss out on working at the upcoming PGA Championship.

Bogart pesters me with a slew of questions during the round, like every hole is a contestant on *What's My Line?* Distance to the pin, 5 or 6-iron? 3-wood or driver? Read this putt.

I reply, "All putts break toward Kensington Road … place her a foot outside the hole … give it a firm stroke."

A gold sun lowers below a row of tall pines in the left rough, casting a Roman legion of shadows on the eighteenth fairway. A gun fires to start a swim meet race. I run my fingers along my chest to check for bloody holes. Perhaps Bogart's plan all along is to execute us with a firing squad. I imagine Bobby Walton burying us in the deep pot bunker in the middle of the eighteenth fairway. Human yardage markers.

"It's 235 to the middle of the carpet from Ford Quinn's occipital bone."

The crowd claps, and a mother crows her kid to victory. The announcer barks the winners of the Thursday night 50-meter breaststroke relay: "Royal Surrey, first; East Devon Hunt Club, second; Kimblewick Lake, third; Kensington Hills, fourth."

The pool or tennis courts or root beer floats that the member kids enjoy inside the clubhouse don't make me bitterly jealous. Public kids have access to all those things. It's that swim meet sound—an excited, electric buzz vibrating from inside the exclusive pearly pool gates. The sound reminds me of everything I don't have and everything I want—hanging with the Lund Gang, watching girls in Speedos and swim caps who'd consider dropping a raspberry on my neck, wearing a white Polo shirt with the collar popped up and sipping on a peach daiquiri poolside in my white-soled topsiders. Coming up on the last hole, Bogart asks me how far the middle fairway bunker is from the tee.

"Two hundred and eighty-seven yards," I spit back.

After we finish up the round, Owen and I exchange frightful glances, thinking this is the last caddy show. *Screw you, Kensington Hills Country Club.*

"Meet me inside my house," he says. We follow Bogart as he limps his overweight stocky frame to his lair, and my stomach juices roll and froth like the waves of the Atlantic Ocean. It occurs to me that my last link to Cleo is the country club, and that's about to end.

"We're toast," I whisper to Owen.

"Let's hope he's all piss and wind, and we didn't cock up."

Inside the caddy master's shack, I eye photographs of Gary Player and Ben Hogan, winners of major championships at Kensington Hills, hanging on the wall. Bogart turns his grim, fleshy, pock-marked face toward us, and I know the news won't be good. He holds out his sweaty palm.

"Hand over your badges, boys."

Owen's eyes flood. I take the badge off my shirt, surrendering it to Bogart, the sheriff of this shire known as Kensington Hills Country Club. I think Owen might refuse, but he removes his, too, leaving two pin holes in his green shirt.

I want to shout at Bogart, *Why don't you take the shirt off my back, too, so I can ride home half naked and humiliated?* Bobby Walton doesn't come to my aid, just stands expressionless. So much for my Hills connections. At some point I'll have to tell Pop why I'm no longer caddying; perhaps I'll tell him the bubonic plague has struck Kensington Hills, spread by an infected rat.

While I'm thinking of other excuses, Bogart spins around in his chair and opens a desk drawer. Our blue badges clang along with the names of other fired plebes. I consider turning around to leave, thinking to hell with 'em all, but then the caddy master swings his chair back to face us.

"Congratulations, boys!" He flashes two shiny red badges. "You're both honor caddies now." Tension drains from my pores and forms a lake on the concrete floor.

Bogart holds out his right hand, and I give it a firm shake. The caddy master musters a proud smile. We pin our new honor badges on each other's chests. At that moment, I think of all the poor plebes who hadn't made it this far, running away scared from King's antics or the hard labor of the bag, and suddenly I feel pretty goddamn proud of myself.

"One more thing." Bogart fixes his eyes on Owen.

"Yes, sir?"

"Keep your hands out of Gigi's pants."

Why in the hell does Bogart care about Gigi Arnold? I shrug it off.

On my way home, I glide my Schwinn down Dot Ave, and I'm almost run over by a blue car. A girl ducks down in the front passenger seat.

Who the hell was that? I head home to find the car's parked and empty at the end of the driveway. It doesn't dawn on me until after I grab two pints out of the milk chute that Billy's test scores have arrived. They must've been totally ace. I rush into the back door and see the SAT envelope on the kitchen table. Virginia beams in front of Fluffy's litter box. Pop's jawing into the phone to Grandpa Quinn.

"Yeah, the kid's got your brains after all. I knew that boy was smart. Not book smart, but smart just the same." Pop nods into the phone. "Engineer? Hell, with those scores he can do just about anything he wants. Maybe nuclear medicine. Those guys make a fortune."

Mom tacks Billy's scores on the fridge with a magnet next to her daily self-help phrase from Osmond P. Peabody: "Flick the little No-Man off your shoulder. Say to yourself, yes—I'm going to do something positive today!" (You always know Virginia is in her do-something mode when she starts the day flicking imaginary little No-Man off her shoulder.)

Billy scored off the charts in both math and verbal. 1529 out of a total of 1600. The odd thing is he scored the lowest on the spatial reasoning part of the exam—his strongest area based on his performance with Rubik's Cube. I'm not about to question Billy's winning moment. Besides, he'll be my personal chauffeur for the rest of the summer. Things are looking up in the Quinn household. I've been promoted to honor caddy, it appears Billy's going to college. Maybe Kate'll make the varsity tennis team. Everyone knows good things happen in threes. Virginia can finally have something to brag about at bridge club. Well done, Billy.

17

Foul weather normally wastes a good summer day and forces me to spend the day in the basement, roller skating to records or watching Rocket light his farts on fire. But when you have to follow a pair of polyester pants around for hours on end while lugging a bag, rain sometimes proves a Godsend.

As soon as Billy drops me off at the country club in his new SAT LeSabre, a rain blitz assaults the roof of the caddy shack. The Green Shirt brigade retreats to the tin bomb shelter. I decide to call Virginia to pick me up after realizing getting a loop is wonderfully hopeless with the lousy weather. Another caddy is on the pay-phone calling home for a ride, so I wait my turn behind three other loopers.

King rings his bell and barks out an order: "No one's leaving, the course will eventually reopen." He comes through the door and disconnects the silver cord from the box.

Lightning flashes outside, and I can hear the club's warning siren sound, calling in the golfers from the closed course. With my plans to leave dashed, I squat outside while rainwater drips off the awning and soaks my head. Rain stops time when you're a kid. I notice that King has posted guards with umbrellas at the foot of the bridge to block the escape route. In the middle of the bridge, Gandy wears a yellow rain slicker under his cowboy hat.

A familiar face leans up against the building. Owen. He tosses into the air a purple rubber parachute man and shoots it down with his imaginary handgun. Owen notices me and shoves the kid toy into his pocket.

"I guess we're kind of screwed today," he says. "I'll never get a loop in, and I could sure use some Crosby." Crosby equals cash in Owen's old world.

"I want to get the hell out of here." Caddying is kind of like that for me; I'll be eager to show up, but the minute I get there I want to hit the road.

"We can play pinball." I have the impression Owen doesn't want to go home to his motel room. I've developed calluses on my fingertips from playing a ton of pinball this summer. Something rustles in the bushes by the fence. Smoke signals float to space from a makeshift teepee up the fence line.

"Did you see that?" I ask Owen, who peers down the fence line.

"Yeah. Something in the bushes over by the fence."

"Smoke."

We run through the raindrops about fifteen yards from the shack. Three older boys squat in the bushes under a blue shelter tarp, which Owen lifts up from the ground.

"Get the hell out of here, dickweeds," a caddy in white overalls says.

"It's cool. He's a Rooney," a caddy named Pimples says. "Jake's little bro. Get in here fast."

We duck into the makeshift fort. Pimples holds a smoldering cigar in his hands. He offers us a toke, and I inhale a deep breath, letting out a loud cough of smoke.

"Keep it down, Wookiee."

I learn later that Pimples is a *Star Wars* fanatic, and the country club is like his own little cosmos. I pass the cigar to Owen. We all crouch down like we're surrounding a campfire, roasting marshmallows; it's too wet to sit down without getting your pants wet.

"Jesus, you two scared the hell out of us," one of the boys says.

"This is bullshit. Let's get out of here," another boy says.

"We can't leave." Owen points at the bridge. "Commandant King's got guards positioned all over the place."

Pimples makes an opening through the bushes with a smoldering stick for a better view. "Screw King, there's a hole in the fence just past the bridge. You guys want to do a little bowling?"

"I'll try," I volunteer.

"Do, or do not. There is no—"

We bolt out of the tall bushes behind Pimples and up along the fence line. I can see Gandy's umbrella near the middle of the bridge, hanging low over the east side, not the west side toward the Thunder Bowl. We reach the opening in the fence.

Pimples whispers loudly, "May the farce be with you." One after another, we slither through the fence. I hesitate for a second before slipping through the opening, following Owen into the outside world. A feeling of freedom wells up inside of me like it's the last day of school before summer vacation. I follow four green shirts hauling ass up Kensington Road, kicking up mud from their heels.

At the Thunder Bowl, I notice we aren't the only ones to make a brave escape. Each alley is filled with flashing white pants and caddy-issued shirts. The man at the counter hands me a pair of red-and-black bowling shoes. I pull off my wet socks, and along with my shoes, set them to dry on top of a hand blower on the empty lane next to ours. Besides golf, Pop excels at bowling, always bragging about the near-perfect score he'd thrown during his Korean army days in Alaska. After a long day of testing tanks in the bitter cold, he'd drawn a crowd before admittedly choking in the last frame. Bowling isn't too bad—at least you're trying to knock something down.

I roll and bounce three full-throttle games of gutter ball that afternoon. During the fourth game, I bring my hands together as if in prayer and aim for a makeable spare, but Owen interrupts my laser focus.

"C'mon," he says, tugging on my arm.

I fend him off. "Get lost."

"Gandy's comin', Gandy's comin'," Owen announces in his loudest Paul Revere. "It's a raid. We gotta get the hell out of here."

I turn around to see Gandy clutching a frightened looper by his shirt and yelling, "You little shit traitor." The shocked kid drops his brown bag of popcorn, which explodes on the floor. Gandy shifts his gaze toward my lane. I hurry off behind Owen and Pimples toward the back exit of the building.

As soon as we hit the outside air, I realize the reason for the panic. The sun blazes pot-pie hot on the steaming parking lot pavement above a scattered blue-and-white sky. Bogart will soon need a new bumper crop of caddies for the players huddled in the pro shop, dying for a round on the links. We scurry like scared rodents back down Kensington Road and slip through the gate. One of the older boys doesn't go back, instead turning left on Swan Lake Road for home. The smart caddies park their bikes *outside* the club fence just for this type of an emergency.

Owen and I sit inside the shack, motionless, holding our towels between our knees. Only a handful of kids mill around the shack as Gandy returns and shouts off a new round of names to cross the bridge. Owen checks the list, and our names haven't been called yet. We're safe. A few minutes later, King rings his bell behind the counter. Gandy steps out and raises the tip of his cowboy hat above his eyes.

"All loopers report to the back of the shack."

"That's us," Owen whispers. "We're dead meat."

"I don't think he saw us." I felt like knocking Gandy's cowboy hat off his head and tossing it on the roof of the shack. Where's Rocket when you need him? Ten of us stand in the tall weeds behind the caddy shack, littered with junk golf carts and old tires. A group of players and their solemn-faced caddies march toward the first hole on the north course. Gandy tells us to line up in two rows. After we're in place, he flashes a wide grin at us, showing a missing front tooth.

"What's the deal?" one looper says.

"This is bullshit," another says.

"Shut up. No talking." Gandy steps forward in his cowboy boots. If I had a lasso I'd hog-tie him and throw him off the bridge.

"Eat me," escapes from the back row.

Gandy realizes he could soon face a rebellion. "Don't any of you move an inch. I'll be right back." A minute later, Gandy returns with his grin and King, who takes long, loping strides. His large head tilts to one side like it's too heavy for his neck to keep upright.

"Okay, boys, I know it was raining," King says calmly, "but you're gonna need to tell me who left the club." He fixes his gaze on me. "I know who you are, so don't dare lie."

"Step forward!" Gandy yells. Five boys are dumb enough to obey. Owen and I don't flinch. King patrols up and down between the rows of boys, staring into their faces. He stops in front of me and looks down toward the ground. "Now, Quinn you wouldn't have tried to leave and risk getting demoted to captain, would ya?"

"No."

"No, sir, you mean?"

"No, sir." I say no because it'd be a disgrace to get demoted right after earning my honor badge. If that happens, I might as well just throw in the caddy towel and join the Mix-Fare Federation.

King drops his chin toward my feet. "You always wear bowling shoes to caddy in?" A couple of boys chuckle. My red-and-black bowling shoes stare back at me. Damn. I've forgotten. King's eyes bulge.

"No."

"You just thought you'd wear them today, did you?"

I mumble something.

"I didn't hear you."

"I don't know."

"You picked the wrong person to mess with, Quinn."

King dismisses all the other boys, including Owen, except for me and the five boys who had stepped forward. He herds us into one line. "Okay, you guys want to disobey my orders? You're all going to wish you were dead, plebes."

The six of us shake, like his voice is a train rattling the windows of a nearby house.

"Now, drop and give me thirty push-ups."

One boy with a crew cut drops first and starts his push-ups. Like dominoes, we all fall. Gandy counts for us. *One, two, three ...* The ground is swampy, and my hands sink into the mud. Push-ups aren't too hard for me because our gym teacher at Holy Redeemer made us do them all class long while he sat in the bleachers eating roasted pork rinds. A skinny boy with large curls can't go any further than fifteen. Gandy gets in his face and screams, but the boy can't move, his chest flat in the mud, his arms quivering like flagpoles in a hurricane. King steps on his back with his large duck boot, and the boy's entire body sinks into the mud. For a second I think he might disappear. The boy starts whimpering.

"Get up now, plebe, and go cry to your momma."

"What?" the boy says, his face peering up from the mud.

"I don't want to see your face anymore, now go home and cry to your mommy. They take babies like you over at the Roddenville Country Club. Go cry over there, baby."

The kid sprints away, leaving his green-striped towel behind in the mud next to his body print. I can see what King is up to now. He's going to force us to quit.

Isn't the caddy master the only person with authority to fire a caddy? I should bolt right now, but I don't want to give King the satisfaction, so I grab my towel and wipe the mud off my face and hands.

"Gandy, get their towels." Gandy rips the towel from my dirty hands and gathers up all the other towels. He throws them against an old abandoned golf cart.

"Fifty more," King yells into our ears.

We drop again. The boy next to me is a whopper of a kid and appears strong, but he has trouble getting past the first five. I whisper encouragement to him. "You can do it. Don't let him beat you."

The boy falls into the swampy mess. King picks him up by the armpits and drops him back down. Another caddy at the far end of the line quits at twenty. King pounces on him.

"You big piece of crap. You're pathetic. What makes you think you can caddy at this club? You're an embarrassment to all loopers, pleon. Now get out of here. I don't want to see your pathetic fat face at this club again, do you hear me?"

The kid picks himself off the ground and slinks away. King's snowshoe-size feet clump back toward me. I've nothing left in my arms, which have become useless wet noodles.

"You got ten left. If you can't manage that, you don't deserve to wear the Kensington Hills Country Club crest."

"I think we've done enough," I say.

"I'm sorry. I didn't hear you? What was that, Quinn?"

Something shifts deep down inside of me. I'm sick of King bullying weaker kids because he's on top of the nerd-pile hierarchy. Teachers, parents, and invading armies can keep you prisoner, not some caddy-shack oaf. I refuse to let King make me quit. Besides, I enjoy rubbing elbows with members like Mr. Valentine and meeting new friends from all around the county like Owen and Chip. Hell, I'm an honor caddy now, breathing rarefied caddy air, not some plebe or pleon. King gnaws on some raw bone in my central nervous system. I recall missing Springsteen because of King, and a beast rises from my trembling veins.

I crawl to my knees, eyes trained on King's shinbones. My back arches, much like a threatened cat's. King raises his duck boot into the air to press my back down into the swampy mud. I lurch forward, grab and twist his boot while at the same time driving my shoulder up and through King's left knee. Caught off balance, King collapses onto his back, and I drive him into the mud. I flail my fists at King's face, and blood gushes from his nose. He lands a lame punch on my mouth.

"Stop," a voice says from behind me. Two arms pull me off King. My body goes limp. I give up, falling back into the mud. King rises but makes no attempt to come after me. With the madness over, I see the boy who pulled me off King. He isn't a boy at all, but a thick pint-sized man with a beard and handlebar mustache below a bald head.

"I don't need your help, Rat."

Rat throws King a towel to wipe the blood and dirt from his face. "Yeah, I can see everything is under control here. Bogart sent me over here, says no one's answering his calls at the shack. I guess the rain scared most of them off. I need to recruit two loopers to join me. If you don't find me two, you're going to have to carry, King."

"Hell if I'm going to caddy." King points at the crew-cut kid and me.

"But I have to get my shoes."

Rat looks at my bowling shoes and shakes his head. "No chance, kid. The players are on the first tee. You guys look like crap. Bogart's gonna be pissed as hell."

"Wash your dirty faces out in the faucet," King says, wiping his nose.

"Screw off," the crew-cut boy says.

"You heard him," Rat retorts.

King wipes his bloody face with the back of his hand. My lower lip's got a slight bruise. After finding our towels, we follow Rat across the bridge in our soaked shirts and dirty white pants. I figure King will rat me out to Bogart, and I'll be fired for sure. Crossing the bridge, I wonder again how I'll tell Virginia that I lost her Chick Evans Pipe-Dream Scholarship.

Rat puts on a denim blue jean patchwork flat cap over his bronze dome. "You got Father Steve."

"A priest?" How can they afford it here? "They can play golf here?"

"Yeah, they're people, too, you know." He pulls his cap down tight. "Plus, he's a pretty good tipper as long as you're not a Jew."

"Are you serious?"

"I'm just kidding, kid. Relax." He reshuffles the irons in his bag so they're in numerical order and in the correct slots: woods and putter in front, low to middle irons in the center, 7 through SW in the back.

I do the same to show him I'm on top of my caddy game, not just some punk looking for a fight. I've had a few scrapes along the way, but that one with King was my first real fight. "I'm Catholic anyway."

He clenches his fist in "right-on" style. "Then you have something in common."

Father Steve appears in white collar and black golf pants and shakes my hand. "Forgot to take my collar off again. It's a bad habit, but don't tell Sister Margaret." His shoulders shake with laughter. The collar goes in the bag. He pulls out his driver, removes the cover, and tosses me the head of Pope John Paul II. "Time to let the Big Dog eat."

He runs his fingers through his thin black hair and waddles like a penguin toward his ball on the first tee. A sign of the cross before a swing of the club. God plays no favorites in this game; his tee shot slices into the right rough.

"Wind took that one. Grab my windbreaker out the bag, please."

On the fairway, the priest doesn't ask me a thing about Catholicism, only commenting briefly on how as a young priest he had first started out at Holy Redeemer before being transferred to Shrine Academy, Holy Redeemer's hated league rival. I don't tell him we despise Shrine's holy guts. "You look like you got in a fight with a pig and lost," Father says, looking over my filthy trousers and mangled hair.

"It was nothing." I hand him his wedge as he waddles down into a sand trap on Number 2.

"That means it was something." He throws me a rake from the trap. "Why don't you tell me what happened?" He settles his feet into the sand and swings. The ball pops up on the dance floor along with a showering hail of sand, like he's baptized the hole. I can't refuse to answer a question from a priest. I might as well have been sitting in the confessional box in my blue shirt and navy clip-on tie waiting to answer Father O'Brien's question: "Tell me, son, how have you sinned this year?"

Sinful thoughts 'bout Gigi, accessory to a grocery store robbery, the desire to murder my sister for stealing my poetry notebook.

Father Steve waits for my answer.

"It was nothing, really."

"Then why does your fellow caddy over there have the same dirty markings?"

Realizing he figures the crew-cut boy and I have been in a wrestling match, I have to confess to this collarless priest in golf spikes and a yellow windbreaker the complete story about the daring prison escape and the ordeal with Commandant King. He listens as we trek up to the green, Rat having already grabbed the pin. I ready for the sermon. The wind whips my hair atop the carpet perched on a hill.

"Violence never solves a thing, Ford. Jesus did turn over those tables in the temple, but that was because he considered it a sacred place. I feel the same way about this golf course. Mend fences with King, if you can. Now, help me read this putt, will you?" Father Steve sinks one of his few putts of the day. Smiling, he hands me his putter and says, "What did I tell you?"

The golfing priest never mentions the incident again, and I trust he won't say anything to Bogart, but he's right in a way. King had to report to Bogart about how he had no caddies left in the shack. I figure Bogart reamed King a new one.

Since the second hole, the hard leather of the bowling shoes has been scraping at the back of my heels. The shoes narrow at the tips; my toes turn inward, causing my toenail to dig into the flesh of my middle toe. By the eighth hole, I walk on my heels to take the pressure off. During a break on the tee, I take off my shoes. My heels are chapped and red, the middle toe on my left foot oozes drops of blood. I turn over my hands to see my palms, thinking God has led me to this point; perhaps Father Steve's my John the Baptist, Rat my Lazarus, and King my Pontius Pilate. Or I'm enduring the ultimate sacrifice for all those tortured loopers who've been cursed by the ghost of Chick Evans, roaming the grassy knolls of Kensington Hills Country Club.

At the turn, one of the golfers utters the words that makes every caddy cringe more than the sound of Bogart's voice: "Let's not stop at the turn. It looks like it might rain again."

I'd planned to skip my usual hotdog at the shack from Myrtle and run to the bowling alley to get my high-tops and socks because I'll never make it another nine holes in these bloody bowling shoes.

Father Steve holds his chin up to the sky like I imagine he does daily during the Eucharist. "The hell we're stopping. I need a drink after that lousy nine."

God bless you, Father.

At the end of the round, I decide to test my fate with Commandant King. I'd sooner be fired than be seen as a coward and a quitter, and I figure at worst I'll get shithouse detail for the rest of the summer. I trudge into the caddy shack and hand solemn-faced King my pay stub. He slides the cash under the plastic chute. I take the money and turn to leave.

"Hey." I turn back around to King and see an embarrassed look on his face. "What happened earlier is between you and me. Got it?"

I try to remember that word my history teacher used to describe our relations with the Soviets. Oh yeah, détente. "Got it."

A bone-tired limp back over the bridge. This has been the longest day of my life. The sun emerges from the clouds, casting a Tang-orange glow across the clearing sky as it begins to set behind the tall pines that border the course. I descend the bridge with the cars rumbling beneath my feet along Kensington Road when a caddy shirt brushes past my shoulder.

Gigi Arnold.

"Where are you're going?" She says this like she wants to tag along.

"Home."

"Where do you live?" I tell her. "Oh yeah. The Hills." She writes down my address on a caddy pay stub.

I turn around and watch her skip across the bridge, her white towel dragging behind her like a tail on a doe. Why's Gigi so curious about where I live?

18

One lonesome Friday, no one's around to hang out with tonight. Rocket's gone to his cousins' cottage in Marquette for the weekend, and Owen's missing in action. Playful voices from the neighborhood echo through the window screens of my house, and I feel like everyone's having the time of their life this summer but me. This feeling works up the nerve in me to call Jack Lott and ask him if he wants to ride our bikes to the Kensington Royal Knights' minor-league baseball game. Jack's uncle, Leon Lott, played catcher for the Royal Knights ages ago.

Normally, you'd never call a kid like Jack out of the blue. You wait until he phones you. For me that'd be forever. When I speak to Jack on the phone, he tells me he's already going with a gang of other kids from my class, so he tells me to meet him at the game. That isn't the idea.

I could've done that anyway. You want to show up *with* one of the Lund Gang, not run into them in public.

I settle down in the kitchen and play round after round of Solitaire, and the phone rings and rings. I ignore it because I know it's for Kate.

Virginia pokes her head into the kitchen, annoyed. "Ford ... the phone is ringing off the hook. Why don't you answer it?"

"I don't hear a thing." *I'm not Kate's personal secretary.*

"How could you not hear that? Never mind." She grabs the phone off the wall, and I go back to my card game.

"It's for Kate. Go get your sister upstairs. Tell her Theo's on the phone." It's the Summer Solstice Dance night at the high school, and Kate's getting ready for the bash. Theo's her date, of course, and they're double-dating with Vicky Fontaine and her boyfriend, Max Northrup.

"Jesus, Virginia, I'm not your slave."

"Don't push me, Ford! I'm in no mood."

Fine. Twenty leaps up the stairs. A blow dryer rages at full volume. "KATE!"

She switches the hair dryer to a low buzz. "Get out, creep!" She arms her free hand with hairspray and aims it at my face like mace.

I yank the cord out of the wall socket. "Vomit's on the phone."

She smiles smugly in the foggy mirror, primps her fluffy hair, and says in a sweet tone. "Tell him I'll be right there."

I don't think so; he can wait in dead silence. When she finally appears in the kitchen, wearing a yellow dress with ruffles adorning the wrists, I'm frustrated as hell because I have all four aces out, but I'm stuck with no move. Game over. I shuffle the deck and deal a new game. Kate stretches the phone cord out of the kitchen and down the block. She does this every time she's on the phone, even if it's one of her flaky friends. God forbid I overhear her conversation about something stupid like who's dating Leif Garrett. The den door slams with a bang, and my cards jump out of their suits. A sobbing, howling Kate shakes the house.

"What's wrong?" Virginia asks me, coming in from the mudroom with a box of Mix-Fare milkshake containers.

"Can't you tell?" I smack my hand on the table. "I need the Queen of Spades to turn up or I'm done for."

"Not *you*, Kate."

"How should I know?" *Or care.*

It turns out Theo dumped her at the last second, and Kate will be going solo to the dance, if she goes at all. She spent a quarter of her summer savings on a dress only to get blown off by Theo. Maybe she'll realize now she's wasted six months of her life on that dope. I normally couldn't care less, but I can't be totally heartless to my loser freak of a sister. So I collect my cards from the table and find Kate moping in the den. She inserts an old 8-track, and the Cher song "Cherokee Woman" fills the room. Perhaps Kate will don some war paint and shoot Theo in the heart with a bow and arrow like he's done to her. I wouldn't blame her one bit. For a second, I consider offering to go with her to the dance, but that would be weird and awkward.

When we were little kids, we played a game whenever one of us got depressed for whatever kid reason. It worked like this: We'd pretend we were married, and I was the lord of the manor, and she was the lady. Kate would make tea. I'd make crumpets out of rolled-up Wonder Bread with Peter Pan peanut butter spread. We'd sit outside on the patio and pretend the whole block was our estate, and the people that lived there were our servants. Virginia and Pop were the maid and butler, respectively. Billy the court jester. We haven't played that game in years, of course, but it occurs to me now how close we used to be. We never once fought until we hit our teens, which might sound weird for siblings close in age. To me, Kate has been the calm port in the Quinn storm.

So I open up the den door and see Kate in her pajamas, her dress crumpled on the chair. "Forget about the stupid dance," I say.

"Don't worry, Ford, I'm okay." Moist Kleenex is piled high in her lap. "Really."

Usually it's the other way around. Kate was the one who protected me. For example, when I was about ten, our family spent our summer vacation at Walloon Lake. Uncle Mitt was there with his family and my cousin, Mitt Jr., who has always been called Mitty.

Mitty and I ventured down to the gas station to buy night crawlers to fish with that day. A local boy no more than eleven came by in a wife beater T-shirt and the biggest muscles I'd ever seen on a kid. He wasn't a big kid with big muscles; he was skinny but ripped. He wore a crew cut and didn't mince words to Mitty.

"I'm going to beat the crap out of you if you don't give me those worms." Mitty handed over his night crawlers without blinking. "You too, weasel dung."

He shoved me in the chest, and I stumbled back. I wanted to give him my worms, but fear paralyzed my arms. I saw a fist coming toward my face in slow motion.

Out of nowhere, a hand blocked the bully's punch. A hand flew into the kid's face, slapping him square in the nose. Mitty's muddy worms splattered on the concrete. The boy fell down in a heap, clutching his bloodied nostrils. Kate pulled the kid up by the hair, and while blood dripped from his nose, she said, "Get lost." The kid looked up, realized he'd been popped by a girl, and ran off down the street.

"Do you remember the game we used to play? So you'd make us feel better?" I ask Kate.

"Lord and Lady Kensington."

"Yeah. I guess we're too old for that now."

"It's okay, Ford. I hate dances anyway." Her eyes are dry now, and the 8-track player clicks to Sonny and Cher's "I Got You Babe." "And everyone is so fake in this town, anyway."

You mean heartless. I'm about to say "I'll take you to the dance" when the doorbell rings. A moment later Virginia strolls into the den, shuts the door, and whispers. "There's a boy at the door for you. You need to tell him you have plans."

Good for you, Virginia.

"Who is it?" Kate asks. I know she's hoping it's Theo. He can screw off if the cad thinks he can crawl back to my sister.

"Why are you whispering?" I ask Mom.

"It doesn't matter who it is, you can't go with *him*." Theo's got Mom convinced he's Elvis reincarnated, so I'm confused.

"Go where?" Kate asks in an exasperated tone. "The dance?"

"Forget it, Kate." She turns around to leave. "I'll just tell him you're not home."

"Jesus, Mother." Kate pushes past Virginia, and I follow.

"Kate, come back here!"

A familiar boy appears in the living room, holding a white corsage. At first I don't recognize him in clothes, let alone in an ill-fitting blue tuxedo. Pauley Clark from next door rises from the couch and bows.

"I'd be honored to take you to the Summer Solstice Dance tonight, Ms. Kate Quinn, if you're so inclined to accompany me."

Seems Pauley's had a crush on Kate.

Kate's face turns from Coppertone brown to bright red before a smile emerges from her lips. "No … it would be *my* honor to go with you, Mr. Pauley Clark."

He holds out his arm to escort Kate out the door. I pull the front door open, bow, and wave them through with a royal gesture, knowing very well Kate's not going anywhere just yet. "I have to change into my dress, Pauley."

He pulls his lapels tight. "No, you're very fine the way you are."

"*Pauley*, I can't go in my pajamas." She holds her index finger in the air. "Just wait here a sec. I'll be right back."

As Kate gets dressed, I'm tempted to hug Pauley, who I normally only hear playing the same Emerson, Lake & Palmer songs from their *Brain Salad Surgery* album on his ukulele out his open bedroom window. Or that time I caught him attempting odd, clumsy yoga poses. Mom once told me Dr. Clark follows some fringe liberation "unschooling" movement, which espouses parents teaching kids at home, which I've never heard of and sounds like some version of hell. Anyway, Pauley and I stare at each other for a few moments when he bends over and utters to me, "Billy."

I reach down and untuck Pauley's pants leg, which is caught in his sock. "Billy's not home."

"I know."

I'm not sure how Billy figures into all of this, if at all, because he could care two wits about our sister, but Kate comes in just then with her yellow prom dress on and her face radiating happiness beams. I imagine them slow dancing to the Bay City Rollers at the Misfit Prom.

Pauley doesn't drive, so Kate drives them to the dance in Pop's Impala. I wonder how Pauley knew to come at just the right time to save Kate. There's only two ways Pauley could have known. He either tapped *our* phone, or it had something to do with Billy, as Pauley seemed to hint at.

After they leave, I return Kate's diary to the drawer in her nightstand. She'll have something new to write about tonight. I don't think she stole my poetry notebook because she would have weaponized the information by now. As far as sisters go, Kate's annoying, but not half bad.

I decide to bike alone to the baseball game after all, and I meet up with Jack Lott and a bunch of kids on bikes milling around the fence next to the bleachers. My front tire nudges into the circle, and I say hello to Jack. The boys' handlebars are pointed toward Jack and Nick Lund as the leaders of the pack. Nick Lund shakes his pompadour cool and says, "Hey, Quinn, I saw you hanging out with that fake mod in the parka who thinks he's the second coming of Sting. What's his name? Nigel? Oliver?"

"Owen." I should have tracked down Rooney and headed to the arcade tonight. There's been some rumors of a dust-up between the Lund Gang and public schoolers at Stoner's Lake. Owen hasn't mentioned a thing to me about any turf war, but I noticed a faint shiner on him the other day that he wouldn't talk about other than mumbling something about "he'll get his arse warped."

"You both caddy. Pretty lame if you ask me." In Nick's world, "caddy" only translates to the luxury car brand. Lund turns his head to our fellow Holy Redeemers. "Hey, guys. You should get a load of Quinn's new mate." Nick laughs so hard he almost falls off his bike. Fat Albert shows a goofy grin. I feel my cheeks turn Jolly Rancher red, and I want to punch Nick in the face. Owen's a decent guy.

"Let's blow this pop stand," Jack Lott says.

They swing their front tires around to follow Jack's bike, and mine gets tangled with Nick's rim. I lose my balance, and my Schwinn collapses into the fence and on top of me. Lund laughs back at me and rides out of sight. He did it on purpose for sure. No one even notices as they ride to the other side of the field to find girls. I pick up my bike; the rim's bent, so I slink off to sit in the stands and watch the game alone.

The baseball players run onto the infield, creating a red dust storm, and the crowd rises to cheer them on.

I spot Pop in his usual seat. He rarely misses a Royal Knights game. I clang up the metal bleachers and perch next to him. "Hey, Pops."

"Hi, Fordo. Get yourself something to eat." Pop pulls a two-dollar bill and a Washington from his wallet and hands it over to me like old times. "The Royal Knights have their hands full tonight against the Polar Bears."

Jack and his friends circle like sharks below me under the stands. It's a long wait before they ride off into the night. At the concession stand I buy a box of Cracker Jack, a roll of Necco Wafers, and a Coke. To hell with Jack Lott and his buddies. I'd rather watch the game with Pop anyway tonight. We've been going to minor-league baseball games together as long as I can remember. Baseball is the one thing we both love. Golf is becoming a close second, though.

We laugh and clap the Royal Knights around the bases all night. He gets around to asking me about how my golf game's coming this summer. I tell him I've changed my grip (but don't tell him Mr. Valentine's role), and I'm playing pretty well. Broke 85 for the first time this past Monday, I tell him, which lifts one of his eyebrows and causes him to bob his chin in approval. That's as close to a compliment one is likely to get from Pop, but I'll take it.

During the seventh-inning stretch, he waxes nostalgic and tells me a story about how he and his two brothers, Uncle Mitt and Uncle Fred, had set a trap for guests during one of Grampa and Grandma Quinn's blowout parties at Cass Lake. They'd dug a deep pit, covered it with a blanket, and lured some of the drunk dads out the door to their demise. A burst of laughter from me causes the third-base coach to turn in his cleats.

Pop leaves in the bottom of the eighth inning to pick up Virginia from a bingo match at the church reception hall. Before he leaves, Pop tells me we should play golf together soon. That'd be nice—just Pop and I doing something we both enjoy together.

After the game ends, I drag my misshapen bike home alone and wonder when the neighborhood had suddenly changed. Growing up, the single block of Dorchester between the Masons and the Olivehammers seemed as big as a village. Back then, before Virginia rang the dinner bell, twenty kids aged eight to fifteen would play smiley ball. The Olivehammers' driveway served as home plate, the paved road the infield, and the Carters' side yard centerfield. A large green plastic ball with a smiling face was pitched underhand. I hadn't needed to phone a soul to find a friend.

A game of pickle or kick the can had been five yards from my front door. I'd simply step from our stoop into Dorchester Village. After supper, we'd play a game called prison in the humid, dark summer nights, hopping fences, trampling garden beds, hurtling box shrubs. We owned the street and the towering elm trees and everything in between. Every garage, tree fort, and front porch had been a potential hiding place.

When I get home, my street feels shorter and narrower, the yards private and small. Not a village at all. Now neighborhood kids pair off and form private alliances. When did this happen? Overnight, it seems.

19

The next weekend rolls around, and I can't find anything to do except play Frisbee fetch with my dog until nightfall because Rocket's grounded. (Every day is a Friday in the summer unless you have no friends. Then every night feels like a Monday school night, and you're left watching TV, wondering who shot J.R.)

Bored out of my gourd, I go upstairs to mope and find Rocket has left me two things: a note on my pillow to meet him at a public-school party (he must be planning an escape) and a fancy blue cotton sweater. He knows an older kid from his high school named Ned Hinkelmann who works at Jacobson's and has figured out an inventory-fixing scheme to steal summer sweaters. I pull on the thin V-neck sweater and head downstairs into the night air.

Cars are log jammed along the street, and kids are streaming toward the party house. A musclebound guy with a leather vest and a unibrow strides cockily out of the garage with a small posse following him onto the front lawn, and I stall out in front of him because the line to get into the party house snakes into the front yard. The guy's wearing a chain necklace with crossbones.

His buddy eyes his knuckles. "You hurt your hand on that guy's face?"

"Hell no." He flashes his fist, along with a gold ring on his finger. I gawk at the guy, thinking he should be playing bouncer at a biker bar, and he says to me. "What you lookin' at, asshole?"

I don't wait around to reply and push through the bodies and Brut fumes clogging the front door. I take a few laps around the first floor but can't find Rocket. They are mostly public-school kids, and I don't see a single Holy Redeemer.

A kid with a hairdo that curves into his sideburns stops me and says, "Did you know sloths eat a plant that makes them stoned all day?" He drifts off. I deposit that factoid in my memory bank and squeeze past kids bouncing quarters into a Detroit Lions coffee mug. The bass from the Cars tune "Let the Good Times Roll" thumps from the stereo speakers, and I wander out a back door and onto the patio.

"Fooord?" My sister Kate huddles next to two other girls, sipping from plastic beer cups. Her eyes are red and swollen, and at first I figure she forgot to turn off the sunlamp at home before realizing she's been crying her Quinn eyes out. Her two friends shoot radioactive laser beams across the pool patio bow. I follow the trail and see Theo Nichols groping a girl on a lounge chair. I feel both happy and sad for Kate. The last guy in the world she needs to date is Theo, particularly after getting dumped before the dance. The girls whisper in each other's ears. Vicky Fontaine, drunk as a wheelbarrow, grabs a plastic cup out of Kate's hand, strolls across the patio, pretends to trip, and spills a foamy beer on Theo's lap.

"What the hell, bitch?" He springs from the chair, revealing a dark, wet crotch to elephant laughter. He scurries inside, presumably toward the bathroom.

I log a few more laps around the party before landing back outside with Kate's girl-squad. "I was supposed to meet Rocket here. Have you seen him?"

"I guess I forgot to tell you." Kate crosses her arms, still simmering from getting played by Theo.

"Theo's a jerk anyway." *Get over him Kate.* "So? What did you forget to tell me?"

"Rocket got into a fight with Gorilla."

I thought of the jerk with the gold ring I'd run into upon arriving at the party. "Now you tell me?"

She hands me a drink, and I shove it out of the way.

"How the hell did he do?"

My sister holds her palms out in Kate-drama style. "There's a reason they call him Ga-Rill-A."

Great. Rocket might be lying dead somewhere in the Hills.

"Christ. I've got to find him." I knock over a hundred people and spill a gallon of beer exiting the front door. I sprint toward Dot Ave, hoping like hell Rocket's still breathing. I reach the Olivehammer house and find a collapsed tent on the backward lawn. A light would be on in the house if Rocket's been seriously injured, but it's vampire dark, so perhaps he's just got a bloody nose and a bruised ego. A spotlight beams on their in-ground trampoline from an early August moon. A quick check of the doors, but they've battened down the hatches for the night.

Rather than go home, I jump on the trampoline while worrying about whether Rocket's in one piece. JUMP! My head feels light and woozy as my body thrusts high and my eyes hover at the roofline of the Olivehammers' garage. A bat swoops across my hairline.

Bounce, booounce, booooounce.

Flip.

I land with two feet in the long jump pit. A frontward flip! I've never, *ever* done that before. After making the first one, the rest fall like dominoes. Six more flips, three perfect landings. Even a Soviet judge wouldn't deny me a perfect Nadia Comaneci-10.

A faint clap bubbles up from the ground. Rocket crawls out from beneath the flattened tent along with a bag of frozen peas in his hand. His right eye is swollen shut, his left a small slit. He lifts his battered red head and garbles from pufferfish lips: "Gorilla bot me, but I'll way him back wood." Translation: Gorilla got me, but I'll pay him back good.

"Why did you get into a fight?"

"I pinched some wooze from Joel Krickstein's wide."

"What's that got to do with Gorilla?"

"Joel is his vest fend."

I step closer, eyeing his wounded face. "You should be in the hospital. Shouldn't we wake your mom?"

"No. Just yelp me put this rent up." I raise the tent and secure the sides. "I need to well you some ..." Before he can finish his sentence, his head falls on the grass. I drag him by the legs into the tent and zip it closed behind me. *Goodnight, Rocket.*

I wonder what he wants to tell me, but it'll have to wait until tomorrow. I rumble toward home in the still-night glow. A katydid chorus sings from a secret hiding place. Katydid … Katydidn't … Katydid … Katydidn't … Katy…

At the edge of my front yard, a figure rushes past me along the hedge. A door bangs closed at the Clark house. Pauley? I tiptoe around the back of the house, entering through the mudroom. Lightbulb beams escape underneath the kitchen door. A rustling sound inside.

Who's up at this hour? Fluffy whines inside. Just the freaking cat. The quietest way to open our back door in the middle of the night is to turn the knob until it stops before opening the door. You never turn and open at the same time, or you'll wake the dead.

"Hey, Fluffy, knock off the noise, will … Mom?"

The cat rubs her spine against Virginia's right shin. A Pall Mall packet lays on the table next to a mountain of ash. "Sit down, Ford."

I'm in no mood for Virginia. "I couldn't sleep, so I went out for some fresh air." I wave my hand through smoky Pall Mall air.

She points to the kitchen table chair. "Ford, take a seat."

I make a futile excuse. "Thanks, but I have to get some sleep. Early loop in the wee mornin'."

She crosses her legs beneath her long white nightgown and takes another slow drag on a stubby cigarette. "I need to tell you a couple of things."

"Do you have to smoke in the house, Virginia?" I don't need any lecture or self-help spin after tonight.

"You're not my mother, Ford."

Fluffy whines again, so I open a can of Purina. The cat growls, groping my knees with her paws at the sound of her snack bell. I shuffle the tin across the linoleum floor with my foot. Fluffy pounces.

"Sit down, will you?" Mom pleads.

The front door opens and slams. Must be broken-hearted Kate or an early night for Billy. I ask Virginia why she isn't in bed at this late hour.

"You know I have terminal insomnia." She pauses. "I could ask you the same question."

"Already told ya."

"Listen." She sighs, flicking ash off her cigarette. "The Olivehammers are moving to Australia for a year ... Mr. Olivehammer's been transferred there for his job."

I take two wobbly steps toward the sink, feeling like I might puke, before turning to face Virginia. "Don't tell me Rocket's leaving, too?"

She shakes out a new Pall Mall, tries to ignite it with an empty Bic lighter to no avail. "Shit." I grab a match from a matchbook with a cover featuring the Village Women's Club and light Virginia's cigarette. She inhales nicotine. "Everyone, except for Mrs. Olivehammer."

At least *Virginia's* closest friend is staying—good for her. I throw the matchbook on the kitchen table. "Why isn't she going?"

"She's decided to look after the house." Right.

"Are they getting divorced?" I think of Mrs. Olivehammer's therapy session with Dr. Clark. Don't think it worked so well.

Her voice lowers an octave. "Sometimes couples just need time apart."

Parent translation: They're divorcing. I hear Kate sobbing upstairs in her bedroom, which is right above the kitchen. *Theo's not worth an ounce of tears, Kate.*

An ancient memory bolts through my head: Rocket's freckly face at the door when I was no more than four, barging his way into my new house, taking off to roam the house like it was his own. "When are they leaving?"

Virginia hangs her head, staring at the floor like she's thinking of something besides the Olivehammers' move to Australia. "Soon."

"Why can't Rocket stay behind with his mom?"

She shakes her head and taps cigarette ashes into a blue crescent-shaped ashtray. "I've already asked, honey. His dad's making him go, along with Basil."

In the land of hopping kangaroos and extinct Tasmanian devils, the seasons are reversed. Rocket will be able to enjoy two summer vacations in a row. Just his good luck. But I'm pretty sure his parents are splitting up, and that isn't so lucky. Poor Rocket. Perhaps I should say something to him, but what would I say?

"One more thing." Virginia blows an O-Ring to Venus, and her eyes seem a million years away. "Sit down, Ford."

"There's more?" I'm losing my only good friend who's never let me down. What if Rocket's mom ends up moving to Australia, too? He'll have no family con-nection left in the Hills and no reason to return. Who would I hang out with besides Owen? There's still an outside chance I could throw a Hail Mary and penetrate the Lund Gang. Jason is hip, Jack Lott is mythical, but Rocket's like a brother to me.

She pushes out a chair and pats the seat. I sit down and notice a milky wet film to her eyes. The same shade as those tiny square Kodachrome slides she pulls out of the filing cabinet in the laundry room whenever our Ohio relatives visit and starts clicking her way around the humming Carousel projector. Grainy color photos projected on the dining room wall of a young, hopeful Virginia in the late fifties, riding cool in her convertible with her friends while wearing pointed white sunglasses and a red crew neck cardigan. Then toward the end of the Carousel ride down memory lane, a young Clark Gable look-alike in a fancy light-blue sport coat is chasing Billy around in his diaper in the early sixties on the front lawn of the old red-brick ranch on Lincolnshire Lane before the family moved to Dorchester. Pop in his prime, grinning for the camera.

Virginia clicks her own moist eyelids and snaps me back to reality. She takes one long drag on a Pall Mall cig before detonating a Soviet hydrogen bomb on my world. "We're selling the house … We can't afford the real estate taxes." She extinguishes her cig along with my former life in an ashtray and pops a Tic Tac.

I want to yell and scream at Virginia, but I know it's not her fault. No one's tried harder than her to keep our house boat floating in the Kensington Sea. So I just say to myself, *Damnit, Pop.*

I bolt upstairs, slam the door shut, and cry in my bed next to Chimney. After an hour of fitful tossing and turning, I pull out my telescope, point it out the window, and spot nothing in the night sky because of the full moon.

How am I supposed to survive in this stupid, messed-up world now? After plugging my headphones into my stereo, I turn the volume to high infinity to drown out Kate's sobs and my own muffled cries. I feel sorry for myself, but more than anything I feel awful for that young, awkward, happy smiling lady in the fuzzy Kodachrome images, oblivious to what her future holds. Maybe I could make her happy again by getting that caddy scholarship. At least I'd make her proud.

"Live and let die," I say to the room that will soon be someone else's.

20

I check up on Rocket's condition the next afternoon, and the bruising on his face has gone from peach to prune. He tells me what led to his face getting pulverized. He had mouthed off to his dad after Mr. Olivehammer told him he had to move to Australia, but what got him mad was he begged to let *me* go with them, but his dad had refused. He'd been grounded but snuck out that afternoon to leave me the note to meet him at the party later that night. He'd turned his lights off in his bedroom, stuffed rolled-up blankets under his bed cover, and after his parents had left for dinner at the Sign of the Beefcarver, snuck out into the night. He stole the alcohol from Gorilla's friend's car so the two of us could drown our sorrows together on the news we wouldn't be hanging out with each other for a year.

I wonder whether Mr. Olivehammer doesn't want me to go with them, or if he asked Mom or Pop and they'd said hell no. If I'd been asked, I would have had to think real hard because of Cleo and the Evans scholarship, and I wouldn't tell any of them this, but I think I'd miss my family, too.

■ ■ ■

A lunar phase later, I drown Cheerios around an Annie Oakley souvenir breakfast bowl for dinner and try not to think about Rocket moving halfway around the globe. He'd come home next year, trespass through the back door, and find a new family eating at the kitchen table. Probably a new best friend, too.

Life sucks. Big time.

A knock comes at the mudroom door. I ignore it—probably one of Kate's friends to console her from the Theo nuclear fallout—but the pestering raps keep coming. I yank open the door to Gigi Arnold standing in our mudroom.

"I need to talk to you." She barges past me and sulks at the kitchen table. I ask her what's wrong. We know each other well through the country club, but of course she's Owen's girl. She pulls a pack of Marlboros from the back pocket of her jeans. "Every-fucking-thing."

"Join the club."

This garners a slight smile from her. "You, too, huh?"

"Forget about me."

Gigi takes a long, sad drag on her cigarette. *Why does everyone mope and smoke in this dreary ugly yellow wallpapered kitchen?*

"You can't smoke in the house." Virginia can smell the scent of any foreign brand. "Follow me." I lead her back through the mudroom and outside onto the patio. Clear sky, brilliant stars. Some people like oceans or lakes or mountain views. I love the night sky. Gigi hands me her Bic lighter, and I light the tip of her cigarette. She passes it to me, and I inhale. Smoke singes my lungs. We sit for a while without saying a thing as Gigi tilts her chin up and blows tiny, misshapen smoke rings at the sky. In another lifetime, Gigi and Virginia would be best buds. "What's up, Gigi?"

She taps her nervy foot on the wrought iron table. "My mom ... that's what's up. She lost her job at the Gas 'N Go."

Below a bright moon, the golden planet Saturn shines down on the patio bricks from the constellation Scorpius.

"Sorry." If I grab my telescope, Saturn's ring might come into focus.

"We're being thrown out of our house," she says casually between blow rings. "And that's not all." She shifts her tight jeans on the rubber-lined seat. A Clark cat sneaks between my legs, rubs its torso against my calf before slinking onto the driveway toward home.

"There's more?" *Didn't I just have this conversation with Virginia?* Perhaps the whole world's disintegrating, and if they make it out alive, the Iranian hostages will be returning to an arid wasteland of teenage zombies ruined by their parents' poor decisions.

Gigi gets up and sits next to me; our knees touch, electricity sparks. "Mom's threatening to move us in with Bogart."

"Bogart? As in the caddy master?"

She reclines back and exhales to Saturn. "They've been kinda seein' each other."

A firefly turns her lamp on and off. Suitors swarm.

"Jesus, Gigi. Bogart?"

"Why do you think I hardly have to wait for a loop at the club? I can't imagine living with him." She tosses a butt end into the fake charcoal of our gas grill and shakes out another cig. "You know how he looks at me."

No, I didn't quite notice that, but then I remember the comment he made to Owen after we'd passed our honor's test.

"What does Owen say?" She should be confiding in her boyfriend.

"I'm not sure he gives a flying turd." Her eyes follow a puff of smoke. "Hey, let me ask you something, Ford." She slides her ass closer to mine. "Can I move in with you guys?"

Now I know why she's taken a sudden interest in me. "We don't have any extra rooms."

We night-dream into an ocean of a milky sky for an epoch.

"Hmm, I know." Gigi presses her leg against mine. Conjoined twins now. "What if I slept in the basement or bunked in with your sister?"

Horny fireflies spark, dart, and date.

"My mom would have a cow, Gigi." I'm sure the Palms Motel has a vacancy.

"I thought I'd ask with your house being so big and all."

I can smell her fresh lemony scent, and consider for a second how I'd convince Virginia to take on a new guest with a penchant for pouting. I don't see Kate sharing her bathroom with Gigi. "Sorry, Gigi, but my mom never takes on boarders."

Mom's talked about renting out the basement for extra income. She figured it would have covered half the real estate taxes. But with Pop barely working, she feared the new tenants would leak the news and ruin her upscale reputation with the Hills bridge crowd. I don't feel like telling Gigi the truth—the Quinns are on their way out of Kensington Hills.

I ask Gigi where she's going to live. There's no way she can live with Bogart, can she? It'd be like opening Dracula's coffin lid. She shakes her head and tucks a strand of blonde hair behind her ear. She reaches into her pocket and pulls out some lip gloss, twisting off the top. "Maybe I'll just move in with my brother." She wipes glistening gloss across her lips. "At least I could score some weed from him. He's a total dope fiend."

I struggle for something encouraging to say to her. *Why don't you just tell her you won't have any place to live if Virginia gets her way?* Maybe I'll end up asking her if I can move in with the Bogart Bunch family. "Don't worry. He can't be that bad. I've never had a beef with Bogart."

A smile grows above her lovely dimpled chin. "You're not so bad, Ford Quinn." She holds my hand. I hold my breath. She gently pulls me toward her.

"Gigi, stop." I push her away.

She lets out a laugh. "You saved my life for just talking to me tonight. I owe you something now."

What's she mean by "something"? "Owen's my friend."

"He won't know a thing. I promise." She lets go of my hand, kissing my cheek instead, and disappears into the night. Two minutes later, a car roars off down the street. I sit for an eternity, contemplating life without Rocket and Gigi fouling up my life at the country club. I wish I was a zillion miles from the Hills.

· · ·

Two days later, Virginia gathers us kids around the living room table. Pop's out somewhere, perhaps Finney's Pub, the nineteenth hole for the public-course golfing crowd. I stand in front of the huge glass window in the living room, staring out at our patio and backyard. Pop had installed a gas lamp pole when the patio was built years ago, which glows bright all day long, and I wonder if the new owners will keep it. Perhaps they'll tear out the patio and build a pool. Kate pesters my parents every summer for an in-ground pool.

What dumb planet has been she living on? They cost a small fortune. Anyway, she can forget that now. Rocket has a hand-drawn map of all the pools within a four-block radius of Dorchester—the Babcocks over on Berkshire were smart enough to invest in an electric pool cover you can't get operate without a key—and we used it to pool crash any house with newspapers piled high on the porch. I notice a robin sipping from our pedestal bird bath, and then it soars into a tree. Chimney presses her nose against the glass.

Virginia snaps her fingers in front of my nose to get my attention. "I'm getting a job," she announces. "Full time at a bank in Detroit."

"We're moving to downtown Detroit?" Kate shrieks.

"Yeah, Kate," Billy says, "like Pop would ever move to Detroit."

Virginia groans. "Just stop, you two."

"You're going to drive all the way to Detroit every day?" Kate asks.

"No, I'm taking the bus. It drops me off right in front on the First National Building downtown."

"Does this mean we're not selling the house?" My hopes soar before quickly plummeting.

"'Fraid not, Ford."

Kate scrunches her face. "Where are we going to live?"

Virginia slowly closes her eyes, bracing for our reaction. "We'll get an apartment before we find a new house somewhere."

Kate screams. "Noooooooooooo ... How I am supposed to have any friends over?"

That sums up the situation, Kate. Geez.

A full-time job is a huge deal for Virginia. She hasn't worked at a real one since she was a substitute teacher in my kindergarten class. She quit her Mix-Fare distributorship due to sluggish sales. We've housed enough boxes of Mix-Fare chocolate mix and Super-V to feed the entire state of Michigan and clean I-75 from Cheboygan to the Ohio border.

All three of us sit on the couch like we're in a church pew, contemplating our fates while two black squirrels play tag outside. Grand Canyon silence. There is the unspoken word that the fault line under our family's feet is about to crack wide open. Pop's anger and unhappiness is always an unsettling tremor. Mom's the glue that holds the family together. If she cracks, we'll have an earthquake on our hands. I've never seen her this close to the brink. It's now that I harden my resolve: Evans scholarship or bust.

. . .

After skateboarding up and down my driveway, I head uptown and board a southbound bus toward Sam's Jams. I want to both get away from home before I murder someone and buy an album to calm my nerves. After hunting through old albums for over an hour, I luck upon a used Jethro Tull album titled *Thick As A Brick* in pristine condition; a bargain at only $3.75. I know nothing about him, but Owen's been raving about the music. The title describes me perfectly.

Instead of returning to the bus stop, I continue toward the Palms Motel to find Owen. Perhaps the Quinns can stay at the Palms while Pop scouts for new digs. Wouldn't that be interesting: the Rooneys, Quinns, and Gigi Arnold living under one roof.

Owen's not around at the Palms. With nowhere to go, I play *Space Invaders* at the motel lobby arcade. I haven't broken 2,000 for centuries. Four quarters in my pocket, good for four games. My eyes lock in, and soon I'm destroying incoming aliens and missing their blasters. I pass 1,000, my heart pounds, and I still have all four alien blockers intact. 1,700. One blocker down. Falling aliens. 2,000. Two blockers down. Misfire. Damn. Two alien space blockers destroyed. Game over. My initials pop electric on the screen—I just crack the top ten at number 9. 2,698. New personal record. I've learned trampoline front flips, earned honor rank at the club, and now I'm an ace at *Space Invaders*. But who the flip cares? I haven't a soul to share the news with now.

I think that perhaps Owen's over at Gigi's, so I head to her house. Woodward Avenue pulsates with over-heated cars, box trucks, and buses vomiting fumes into the noon-time air sweat. Fresh country-club air seems like a dream right now.

Gigi Arnold's family hasn't moved out yet. There's a car in the driveway, and "Wango Tango" screeches from the open upstairs window. I knock. After a minute, the door opens, and Gigi stands on the threshold with wet hair, wearing a pink bathrobe. "Ford? What are you doing here?"

"I'm looking for Owen. Is he here?" *No? I'll be on my way now.*

"I know you came to see me." She tightens the belt on her robe and wags her finger. "Don't lie."

"No, really. I want to show him this record." I turn around to leave, but she grabs my hand and yanks me through the door.

"Hey, what album did you get?"

"I probably should go." She takes the Jethro Tull album from my hand. "Do you know where Owen is?" I ask.

She gives me a who-the-hell-cares shrug. "Pretty sure he's caddying. Where else? Come on in." She trails her finger along the album's cover. A Brit newspaper showing a bald man handing a kid first prize in a nationwide poetry contest. "I can't live without music."

"Me, too." I try to tell myself, *Maybe Owens found a fellow mod girl and has ditched Gigi.*

"See?" A sly smile and a sexy wink. "We have lots in common."

I follow her upstairs and into her room, and she shuts the door behind us. I plop down on a yellow beanbag. This is a first for me—alone in a girl's bedroom.

Gigi shakes the record out of its jacket. "You know, it's okay you didn't let me move in with you. Your mom would have been nuts to let that happen."

"Why?" I suppose that thought did occur to me.

"You know why." She stands and scans the record for scratches. Her blonde hair loops around her creamy earlobes. "It's in great shape. I'm going downstairs to grab some ice. Why don't you put the album on?"

I place the record on the turntable, wondering what the hell I'm getting into. From reading the album jacket, I learn that the lyrics of the song "Thick As A Brick" describe a psychologically disturbed literary prodigy, and Jethro Tull is not a person but the name of a band.

Gigi returns with a tray full of ice. She drops two cubes in a cup filled with Lipton tea, applies watermelon lip balm, and turns the volume knob up. "I bet your fridge has one of those ice-making machines."

"Yeah, we have one of those. You can get cubes or crushed ice." I hope we'll take the fridge to our new home along with our birdbath.

"I should have known." *Huh?* She turns the music down. "That you'd have one, I mean."

An ice-cube-making machine? "No, it's not really like that."

She flips the volume knob *way* up and swings her hips back and forth. *Gigi-gravity pulling me into her orbit.* "YOU'RE LUCKY."

"HOW SO?"

She turns the music back down. "Where you live—in The Hills—you have parents who actually give a crap where you are at night."

I think of Virginia and her sleepless nights. Maybe she's just worried about the three of us kids. "Your parents care," I say. "You said your dad wanted to kill us if he caught us in your house."

A loud Ha! escapes from her mouth. "He doesn't want me to get knocked up. You wouldn't get it."

"You might be surprised."

"Really?" she says, turning to face me. "How so?"

I resist the urge to tell her, tell someone: The Quinns are not long for life in the Hills, still living with a faint hope we'll somehow stay on Dot Ave. I simply say, "Everything's not exactly perfect at my house."

"Yeah, but at least you don't have to worry about money. I mean, look at the house you live in."

I want to tell her "why do you think I caddy?" or "we're selling the house because we can't afford the bills in the Hills." But I simply agree. "I guess you're right."

Her face relaxes, radiating a soft expression I've never seen in her before. "That's what I like about you, Ford."

Gigi-gravity pulls my red Wrangler jeans completely into her orbital sphere. Warning bells sound and red lights pulsate at Mission Control.

"What's that?" I shift uneasily with no ready exit strategy.

She bends over, cups her hands around me ear, and whispers, "You're so humble." Gigi spins, flips open the nightstand, and removes a brush, dragging it through her wavy blonde hair over and over and over. I try hard to think of Owen and our friendship, and even Cleo, but my willpower is wilting by the second as Gigi keeps brushing her hair, tapping her bare foot slowly to the music. *Caught in Gigi's orbit.* "Yeah. I like this album. You have decent taste."

I remember something Owen told me about the record. "There's just one song on the whole record."

"It just keeps going without any breaks?"

"Yeah. No breaks." There's no way it'll ever get radio play on WRIF. "One long song on each side."

She coaxes me onto the bed. "Okay, then, I'll let you leave when this song is over."

We play fifteen rounds of gum swapping. Then the song ends with a deafening SHOUT. I hurry down the stairs, and she yells after me. "Call me tomorrow, okay? Okay? Ford? You better call me! WAIT!"

She catches up with me at the foot of the stairs and hands me a ripped page from a notebook. "Here, take this. It's my new phone number. My own private line. Only three dollars a month extra."

Commissioner Bogart won't be answering Batgirl's phone. I shove the paper into my pocket, leap out the front door into a sweltering summer gale, and slump along on Woodward Avenue toward the bus stop while cars honk, and their exhaust chokes the air. A quick glimpse of a Seagram's V.O. Canadian "Smoooooth" billboard sign on stilts before I step onto the slow cooker on wheels. As the bus jolts forward, I realize I've forgotten *Thick As A Brick*. Damn.

A girl on the bus flicks her ponytail. Cleo? Nope. I wonder what I should do about Gigi—*Does she think we're dating?*—and Owen. Gigi expects me to call her.

What a thorny mess I've made of my life.

. . .

Back home, I learn Billy's jig is up. He's under indictment by the SAT police. Another kid from his school, and with grades just as poor as Billy, also scored better than almost every kid in the country after he took the test six months before my brother had. He also happens to be one of Billy's friends, Pierre Lennon. According to Billy, Pierre is such an idiot he once copied his classmate's answers on a geography quiz and mistakenly wrote Nancy Wineholdt under the line for his name. Pop's sold Billy's LeSabre for $500. He'll have to retake the SAT to prove his innocence.

Even though he cheated and stole my money, I still feel sorry for Billy because I know he's a genius in things tests don't measure. I tell this to Mom while she's polishing my late grandmother's silver.

"Funny you say that, Ford. One of those school test investigators combed through every one of Billy's report cards and IQ tests since kindergarten."

"And?"

She stops and squeezes out a glob of silver polish on her rag. "She said the only courses he got As in were Geometry I and II and shop class. That kid who took his SAT test missed the only three geometry questions on the exam. She said his IQ tests all showed he's off the charts in one area."

"Pray tell?"

"Something totally worthless." She returns to polishing. "Abstractions."

Not sure that's a word. "Abstract reasoning?"

"That's it. 'Theoretical' is what that the man called it. Billy's going to get a dose of abstract reality when he ends up working at the Chrysler plant." She raises Grandma's silver teapot. "How's this look?"

Word in the Hills is that my hundred bucks funded Barry Greenblatt's keg party. Barry started as a tight end for the football team and is headed to Princeton on a full ride on account of his brawn and brains, so he planned one last summer blowout before college started. If Billy or Pierre confesses, then Barry could lose his scholarship. Pierre Lennon skipped town. Billy would have sooner shaved his head than give up Barry. My brother says he won't retake the SAT. Sad thing is, I know Billy can win that bet with Pop if he only tries.

Three days later, under a grim, muddy-streaked sky, I say goodbye to Rocket. It's kind of awkward and weird because guys don't know how to say goodbye to each other. We just punch each other in the shoulder and give each other a half hug and lame handshake. He promises to send me pictures and says he'll bring me home something from Australia. I help him carry one of his suitcases to the car.

Mrs. Olivehammer stands inside the doorway, dabbing her eyes with a Kleenex while holding a drink in her other hand. The car honks, and they drive off down the street. A memory kicks in of playing pickle in the middle of Dorchester. We both love to play that simple game. You only need three guys to play, but sometimes we'd have all the kids on the street join in. Rocket had always been the one who organized the games. He'd round up every available kid on the block to play, never caring what kind of kid played—athletic, tall, small, or slow. He just wanted to play the game of pickle in our tiny hamlet of a street, and he always asked me to play first.

PLAY~OFF

21

The PGA Championship is the last of the four major golf tournaments of the year after the Masters, the U.S. Open, and the British Open. To pro golfers, winning a major is like taking home an Oscar for actors, for caddies, best key grip. If you land a big-name bag, you might be seen on ABC's *Wide World of Sports*. Many of the professionals lodge in the houses near the Kensington Hills golf course. Jason Sanders's parents are hosting two-time major champ Johnny Miller. Mom tried to have a player bunk in our house for the extra money, desperate enough to break her no-boarders rule, but you have to be a member to host a player. I overheard her on the phone saying, "But my son's an honor caddy there!"

The club imported fine white Caribbean sand to fill the traps and bunkers. What a farce. If you don't like our sand here, go play in Saint Lucia, for Christ's sake.

Of course, the grass is from Bermuda. I don't expect a bag, but there are other jobs to fill, like carrying a group's scoreboard high above the crowd or being a ball marker for errant shots into the rough.

The well-known players arrived with their own personal caddies in tow, but a lot of the golfers aren't such big shots. The Professional Golf Association gives special invitations to the tournament to its member club pros throughout the country. Each country club has its own club pro, who gives lessons and promenades around the course like a headmaster at a private school. The member pros don't have the luxury or the money to hire professional caddies, but some like to hire local caddies who know the contours of the greens and the blind hazards to avoid.

Owen Rooney and I arrive at the crowded caddy shack to hear Bobby Walton announce the PGA assignments. As soon as I pass through the door, King asks, "What are you jokers doing here?"

I can't answer that question—just hoping to get a chance to do something at the tournament. Most of the volunteers came from the club itself, with lots of the members' kids getting choice positions like raking traps around the holes or handing out drinks in the various beverage tents. I don't think it's fair; most of them have never even raked a trap, let alone set foot in one. Raking isn't just a mindless task like it sounds. You have to rake it smooth like jelly on toast, and usually away from the dance floor to avoid any so-called fried eggs—the most impossible shot in golf.

Owen's brother, Jake, is the first name picked for a bag. Chip lands Danny Molitor, a decent tour player. Rat nabs one of the most famous tour players, Chi-Chi Rodriguez. Chi-Chi rarely misses a cut; Rat will be caddying on the weekend for sure. Owen nudges me and whispers in my ear. "Caddies can get ten percent of the purse if the golfer isn't a jerk. A top-twenty finish in the PGA Championship means at least twenty grand. Can you believe that?"

The money hadn't dawned on me. Just the excitement of hanging around the top players in the world kills me. I'd gladly caddy for free. But $20,000? I won't need any Evans scholarship with that kind of dough.

Near the end of the cattle call, Bobby Walton shouts out a name. Pimples elbows me. "Quinn, he called your name." The next words spilling out of Bobby's mouth are "Winston Somerset, Nashua Country Club."

Damn if I didn't get one! How epic is that? Dream come true. Owen's turn has to be next for sure. I see him pinch his eyes closed, furiously rubbing his rabbit's foot, hoping he'll punch that golden ticket to the Willie Wonka candy factory. It'll be ace if we both get to carry for a real pro in the same foursome in front of thousands of people instead of guest hackers or the likes of Toad Fart and Lurch.

Bobby Walton calls Pimples's name for the last loop. "Barton Baumeister, Ocean Links, San Francisco, California." Pimples jumps out of his seat with glee. "Everybody whose name I called come on up. For those who didn't, I'll be posting a list for other assignments at the end of the day."

Owen directs his fury toward me. "I got twice as many loops as you, and you scored a bag in the PGA?" He clenches both fists and grinds his teeth. "You guys from the Hills, always pullin' strings."

I frown and raise my hands in defense. "What are you talking about? I didn't pull *anything*."

He scowls at me like I've stolen his girlfriend and bolts out of the shack. Perhaps I have, thinking of Gigi, but I haven't tugged a single power lever to get this PGA loop. Maybe I impressed the living hell out of Bogart when I caddied for him to earn my honor's badge.

■ ■ ■

At home that night, Virginia has planned a family barbeque on the back patio to celebrate my PGA coup. In his Jack Daniels apron, Pop flips burgers on the gas grill with its fake brown coals and drinks from a can of Stroh's while Mom brings out a pitcher of lemonade. I feel a bit like a rock star, or at least a roadie to a rock star, or in Winston Somerset's case, a roadie to the warm-up act.

"Who's Winston Somerset?" Kate asks as all four of us lounge around the patio, watching Pop fiddle with a spatula. I love when Pop's responsible for dinner because he always serves tasty meals: powdered sugar pancakes and bacon, pigs in a blanket, grilled cheeseburgers, Watergate salad, Little Caesars Pizza.

"He's a superb club pro from New Hampshire." I know squat about Winston.

My sister skips over to an elm stump and waves a croquet mallet. "Come on, let's play."

After leaning mallets on the stump, Kate begins to dot the backyard with wickets. A game of croquet is a Quinn family tradition, like polo is for the Rockefellers. I stride toward Kate, and she hands me a mallet. Billy lounges in a patio chair with his knees slid up to his chin, drinking a Faygo Redpop. Kate looks at my brother. "C'mon, go, Billy. Get off your butt for once."

"Fine, but only if Dweezel Butt over there caddies for me. We'll call it the Quinn Open. And if we win, I'll let you in my room, Fordo."

"I guess you're a pro now," Pop shouts out, placing cheese singles on sizzling burgers.

"Yeah, he's the best slave on the plantation."

Normally I'll say something to shut Billy's trap, but instead I laugh, thwacking the ball toward the first wicket. Kate strikes her ball, and it rolls past mine before settling in the long blades of grass. Billy doesn't move a muscle to play. Kate makes it through the first three wickets while I struggle on number two. You have to be firm with the croquet mallet when striking the ball, but not too firm.

"How'd tennis tryouts go, Kate?" Pop yells across the lawn.

Virginia gives Pop a funny frown to hush him up. Kate was fourth team doubles on last year's freshmen team. She's worked hard this summer to try to make junior varsity singles.

"I'm stuck on doubles, fourth team again. Brenda Richards and me." Kate gives the ball a hard whack, and it careens off the side of the wicket, nestling up against a tree trunk.

"I'll bet your friend Penelope made it. She's a helluva athlete."

"She made varsity." *WHACK!*

"Varsity? As a sophomore? Wow, she's sure something." Pop flips a burger, puts down his spatula, and tugs out an American cheese slice from its pillowcase.

"Why can't you play that well? You practiced every day this summer."

A sharp crack of mallet on ball. "I don't know, *Dad.*"

"Boy, that Penelope. What about Vicky Fontaine?" Pop slides cheeseburgers onto a silver tray.

"She made singles, only junior varsity, though."

A looping swing of the mallet. A sparrow dives and splashes in the bird bath. Chimney lifts her lazy head from a sunny spot in the grass.

"Singles? Wow."

WHOP! Chipmunks scatter in the flower bed.

"That's out of bounds, Kate," I say. "You can have a mulligan, though."

I know *exactly* how Kate feels. Ever since the fourth grade, it's always been Jack Lott did this or Jack Lott did that. Another "helluva athlete." I've never minded too much, though, because I've always admired Jack, and he's humble as all get-out.

Mom brings out a plate with tomato slices, sliced onions, relish, and bottles of mustard and ketchup. "Supper's ready."

I let Kate win the Quinn Open.

■ ■ ■

Bogart snared Gigi a PGA job in a private room inside the clubhouse, serving hors d'oeuvres to VIPs. Although Owen didn't get a bag, Gigi tells me he'll be carrying a scorecard for one of the groups on Friday. That night, I dial Owen's motel room number a zillion times until Jake Rooney finally picks up.

"Think you're the dog's bollocks now? Owen tells me to tell you to go shove a lobster roll up your arse." *Click.*

For a millisecond, I think about handing my PGA loop to Owen. It takes me less time to drop that idea. If my guy raises the Wanamaker Trophy above his sunburned forehead on Sunday afternoon, it'll be a life changer. Hell, my life has already changed, and we haven't even teed off yet.

The day before the first round, Bobby Walton hands us a sheet of paper with all the pin placements on each hole. Golf isn't like bowling. You need to know the precise location of the hole for both the yardage and the slope of the green. (New holes are cut into the greens every day.) You want to be "below" the hole because uphill putts are straightforward and downhill putts are slippery and dangerous, leading to soul-crushing three-putt greens. Nothing ruins a golfer's morale more than three-putting because you're basically just pissing shots away. A caddy has to be spot-on with clubbing his player, or he'll throw you off the course in front of a million people.

All caddies have been issued a paper yardage book. The layout of each hole is drawn out on each page of the little red "Bible," as we caddies call it, with distances from various sprinkler heads to the green. I've spent the evening penciling in the pin positions in my yardage book and noting the levels of the green around the flag stick. ^^^^^^^ means the green slopes down and away from the pin and >>>>>> means uphill and ------- means level surface, aim straight at the pin.

I've been nervous before but nothing like when Pop drove me to the PGA. I have a tight knot in my stomach, and I think my gallbladder might burst. Cars are parked like canned sardines up and down Kensington Road, and spectators are bused in from the Pontiac Silverdome parking lot, twenty minutes away.

When my player approaches me in front of the clubhouse, I can't look him in the eye on account of Winston's wife. Mrs. Somerset reminds me of Phyllis George—only with golden blonde hair and cleavage the size of the Grand Canyon. The pro sees me eyeing his wife and says. "Snap out of it, Fahd."

She makes her way off to the beverage tent, saying, "Good luck, Winnie!" Winston Somerset sizes me up and down while picking food debris out of his teeth with a golf tee. "How young might yah be, son?"

Great start, he thinks I'm ten. "I'll be fifteen in three weeks."

"Ayuh. How well do yah know this coorsh?"

"Very well, sir." I pull my yardage book out of my back pocket. "I have this red book with the yardages to the hole from anywhere on the course."

"No need to call me sir, now. Winston's just fine and dandy with me."

"Yes, sir ... Winston."

"Listen, kehd. I got a wee little problem. I have to whiz all the time." He points at the Bible. "Draw me a picture in that little red book of yours of all of the hoppers ya got on this course. Keyna do that?" I figure a hopper must mean a Porta Potty, so I nod. "Now, let's warm up at the range."

Sir Winston is thirty-seven years old, his career on the downslope, along with his kidneys. This tournament is definitely his last chance for glory. Four buckets of balls wait for Sir Winston at the practice range. He warms up with his 9-iron before pulling a driver from his bag. A few people watch the pros strike balls behind a yellow rope. A player next to Sir Winston finishes up, and a caddy with a huge gray afro and walrus mustache around Rat's age walks up carrying a large bag with a bear's head covering the driver.

Someone behind the ropes yells, "Hey, Angelo!" The caddy celeb saunters over to the rope and signs his autograph. *Maybe I'll give Virginia and Kate my autograph after the tournament.*

Sir Winston turns around. "Da ya know who that iz?"

No clue. "I've seen him somewhere."

"Yawh, like the tube." Sir Winston yanks his driver out of the bag and tosses me the head cover. "He totes for the Golden Bear."

It isn't more than a few seconds later when a bunch of "Hey, Jacks" ripple through the air. A yellow-shirted Jack Nicklaus strides up to his caddy, who holds out a 3-wood for him five yards from where I'm standing. Right then, I'm damn proud of Sir Winston. He barely glances at Jack before resuming his warm-up routine, like he hasn't noticed the greatest player of all time standing right next to him.

■ ■ ■

After the range work, we make our way down Yellow Brick Road and to the first tee. The south course is swarmed with bodies, fans craning their necks over the ropes to get a glimpse of the famous pros: Nicklaus, Palmer, Trevino, Chi-Chi, Johnny Miller, Watson, Fuzzy, Gentle Ben Crenshaw, Raymond Floyd. Golf-hat heads become the rough. Sounds awfully snobbish, but they trample the grass, which royally ticks me off. This isn't the State Fairgrounds down on 8 Mile Road. Most of these people never get a chance to set foot inside the pearly gates of Kensington Hills Country Club unless they work here, like me. I suppose caddies can get snobby and jealous, too.

Don't fook with my golf course.

An announcer is stationed at the first tee. The first player in our group strikes his ball, and a flag rises in the far distance to mark the landing of the ball. If you are caddying for the pros, they don't make you search for your player's ball. Even the caddies get the royal treatment. The announcer steps forward. "Winston Somerset from Nashua, New Hampshire."

Faint claps filter through the air. Sir Winston settles into his golfing saddle and launches a cruise missile straight down the fairway gut. Nerves of Iron Man. For the first time, what I say on the course impacts another person's life. Unlike a typical loop, a five-yard error on my yardage estimate to the hole can be the difference between a birdie or a bogey and a tee time or a plane ride home for Sir Winston on Saturday morning—if a player doesn't score in the top fifty after the first two days, he's cut from the tournament.

There isn't a large gallery following our group, but there are tons of people roaming the course and glancing over at you, so it feels like the whole world is watching you. Pop proudly follows our group, snapping photographs with his Polaroid while Mrs. Somerset trails behind in the rough in a white billowing skirt and sun-visor hat.

The first hole tests my caddy wits. Sir Winston strikes a fine 6-iron seven feet from the cup. He crouches behind his ball on the green, trying to study the slithery sideways putt for a birdie while I lurk behind his right shoulder, sizing up the line.

"Where should I pahk this cah? Looksh left to right."

I shake my head. "Right to left, but don't give up the hole." In caddying lingo, this means don't roll the ball outside of the cup's diameter.

He answers, "Ayuh ... ya betta be right."

If I miss this putt read, my pro career might be over after 444 yards.

Sir Winston strokes his gold Bulls Eye putter blade; the ball curls around the lip, then drops with a rattle into the cup. He raises his hand in triumph. "Wicked pissah!" He slaps me a high five and runs off to the nearest hopper.

If you're a pro, you need to shoot birdies—one below par (a three on a par four gets you a bird, a two an eagle, a one a rare double-bald eagle). An early bird in the round gives a player confidence and faith in his caddy. Sir Winston and I are now a bit like Batman and Robin.

Par, par, par, par…

On the fifth hole, Owen Rooney holds a group's scoreboard. He notices me, and I'm about to raise my hand to wave a proud hello when he flips me the bird, still pissed he didn't get a bag, like it was somehow my fault.

Kiss my PGA-baggy arse, Owen.

Sir Winston Somerset plays out of his freaking N'Hampshah mind, and after nine solid holes of golf, only two shots separate us from the leader. Then downright miracles start happening on the back nine.

"I don't have anythin' to lose naw, do I, Fawd?" This mental state frees up his swing, and he's in the zone. (Golf's all rhythm. Nothing kills a golfer's swing more than tension.) Sir Winston birdies holes 10, 11, and 12.

Good things happen in 3s!

We find ourselves with a one-shot lead. My feet step through country club grass, but my mind orbits the moon. Sir Winston shoots even par the next five holes, and then birdies Number 18 after holing a sand shot, to lead the field by two shots in the clubhouse. Off the green, a reporter from ABC in a brown coat and orange tie shoves a microphone under Sir Winston Somerset's chin, with yours truly standing at his side.

"I had it goin' wicked with those putts fallin' more than soda water down a bubbler," Sir Winston says to America.

That night, the Quinn phone rings off the hook after Max Robinson of ABC News announces Sir Winston is the improbable leader of the PGA. They run a clip of the interview off the eighteenth green, showing me gazing into the camera with the goofiest grin you would never want to see. For twelve hours, I'm semi-famous in Kensington Hills. If this doesn't get Cleo's attention—and even Nick Lund's—then what more can I do to impress them?

Jack Lott and Fat Albert come by my house, listening like mad as I recount every birdie putt Sir Winston holed today. I tell them how I'd been a few feet from the Golden Bear on the range. Fat Albert asks me if I'd scored Nicklaus's autograph.

I tell him, "Geez, that's bogus. It'd be like Muhammad Ali's trainer asking for Frazier's autograph or vice versa."

"Makes sense."

The next morning, the *Detroit News* runs the headline on the sports page: "New Hampshire Club Pro Surges to First Round PGA Lead." If Sir Winston wins, he'll be Rocky in golf spikes, and I'll turn pro and caddy for him in next year's Masters tournament at Augusta. That's a caddy's wet dream. Hell, maybe I'll travel around the golf-globe with him—Europe, Asia Minor, and Australia, where I'll visit Rocket at the Aussie Open.

During Friday's round, pressure starts to tighten Sir Winston's swing, and the previous day's steely nerves turn to jelly. He has trouble finding his putting stroke on the slick greens. Kensington's greens are notorious for being tricky and treacherous. He manages to strike the ball firmly enough from the fairway, but his ball keeps landing in the most unforgiving spots on the green: vicious hollows, sharp slopes, furry fringes.

A golfer can lose a lead quicker than Tang down the throat of a thirsty three-year-old. We climb the five-par twelfth hole tee box six strokes off the lead, still having a puncher's chance to make the cut but little hope of winning the tournament. I'm hoping now just to put $200 in my pocket to buy a new set of MacGregor persimmon woods from the pro shop.

We stand at the thirteenth par-three tee, high above the hog-back green, which sits in the valley below, surrounded by seven Japanese sand trap mines.

"How fah ah we?" By this time in the second round, Sir Winston trusts my judgment. I survey the distant pin, check my Bible—the depth of the green states twenty-five, and I figure it's a tweener—between a 7-iron and an 8-iron.

He steps forward. "Wehhll?"

"Pins down below. Eight-iron, sir. Definitely an eight." The dance floor is two tiered with a high shelf and a low shelf, like you'd see at the edges of continents if you emptied the oceans.

Sir Winston swings his 8-iron silky smooth. A slingshot toward the pin followed by a disappointing groan from crowd surrounding the green. From the tee, we can't see where the ball lands. Sir Winston ducks into a Porta Potty while I head down to the green with my fingers crossed to survey the damage. The ball has flown short of the green, nestled in the lip of a front dinosaur trap. Only half of the ball's shell is visible in the white sand. A fried egg—a golfer's worst nightmare. I've misclubbed him. We should have played a gentle 7-iron rather than the 8. A slight western breeze in our face betrayed us.

Sir Winston Somerset comes bounding out of breath down the cart path toward the green, adjusting his fly. A search for his ball, and he sees me standing next to the trap with a sand wedge dangling from my hand. "That's my baaawwll?"

"Yes, sir."

"Don't 'yes, sir,' me."

"Sorry, sir."

"Sorry, my ass."

Sir Winston's voice booms over the gallery gathered around the fringe. "You gave me the wrong club, did yawh?"

An ABC camera on a platform above my head rotates in slow motion toward me, and necks strain from under white golf hats in the gallery stands built for the special occasion.

"How old awh ya, kehd? Fourteen? This is the biggest tournament in the world, and I'm stuck with a teenager?"

He unleashes a Hercules swing. A sandstorm peppers my jumpsuit. The ball soars satellite high before landing a stunning two feet from the cup. The crowd roars. A high-pitched yell from the gallery. "That's my Winnie!" A gimme putt. An amateur could take a million swings from that nasty lie and still not come that close to the cup.

On the notoriously tough fourteenth hole, the approach shot to the dance floor is tricky as all get-out due to the downward-sloping green. Most players take one less club, which allows the ball to land in front of the green and slowly drain down toward the hole. Any shot that lands on the carpet inevitably rolls off the back.

Still furious I misclubbed him on the previous hole, Sir Winston doesn't bother to ask me for advice on the next shot. He yanks a 5-iron out of the bag. Too much stick, but he doesn't ask me. The hell with him—he can crawl back into his shire to his daddy. He hits the ball, and it flies straight as string toward the pin. Winston beams like he's landed it stiff.

"Han' me mah puttah," he says, but I know he won't be needing that. It's *my coorsh*, after all. The meteor lands a foot past the cup and slides off the carpet into Bogeyville like a kid down a backyard hill on a Wham-O Slip'N Slide.

A girl holds a flag up next to Sir Winston's ball. *Cleo?* I can't talk to her because she's backed away to let Sir Winston pass by. I rest my bag next to the ball, and he pulls out his wedge. He pitches past the hole and misses his putt. I scan for Cleo, but she's disappeared. A different girl holds the flag; perhaps I'd only witnessed a Cleo mirage.

After the bogey on fourteen, the wheels come off Sir Winston's cart. He's caught a bad case of the yips, and it's bogeys all the way home, missing several short putts along the way. He pees after each hole and earns a yellow warning card for slow play. The worse he plays, the more he whizzes.

After missing his par putt on eighteen, he threatens to break his putter in half over his thigh, but at the last second, he shakes his head.

"Here, yawh take it. I don't caah to see that thing again." Sir Winston hands me his golden Bulls Eye putter with its fine black leather grip. "Go home to your mom fah suppah." He slaps me on the back. "Maybe next year."

The club pro from New Hampshire misses the cut by four lousy strokes. In addition to the putter, he pays me $250. That's a fortune for two days' work. I'll be buying that set of MacGregor woods after all. Despite coming unglued from the pressure on the back nine, Winston Somerset's my hero.

On the weekend, I roam the course, following various foursomes. On late Sunday afternoon, Rat's player loses the PGA in a sudden-death playoff. After the tour-

nament ends, I sit, deflated, on the fringe of the eighteenth green, as the crowd melts away, thinking about
what might have been with Sir Winston Somerset. If
he'd won, I'd have been the talk of Kensington Hills.
Darkness settles in, along with the stars and scent of
damp grass. A crow squawks in the woods.

Out of nowhere, a voice says, "Hey, Quinn."

Jason Sanders appears. He notices my PGA-issued
caddy jumpsuit. He sits down next to me. "I saw you on
the national news after the first round."

"My player missed the cut by a few shots." I hurl
a pebble onto the green, and it skids past the hole like
one of Sir Winston's putts. Golf trash wagons with lights
flood the grounds for the post-PGA cleanup.

"Do you know over a million people probably saw
you on TV?"

I shrug. "S'pose so."

"I'd have lost my load."

After I tell Jason about the Bulls Eye putter Sir
Winston gave me, he invites me to play the famed south
course where the PGA has just been held. (Caddies only
get to play the north course, except for the annual member-caddy golf tournament held on the south course.)
He says this without a giving a rat's ass about my caddy
status and former membership in the leprosy colony at

Holy Redeemer. Maybe it'll give me another chance at winning the Lund Gang sweepstakes.

That evening, I phone Owen again, hoping he isn't still sore about my PGA loop. He won't take my phone call—all the more reason to join the Lund Gang. No Rocket. No Owen. But there might be Jason, Jack Lott, and Fat Albert. And I can put up with a bit of ribbing from good old St. Nick as long as I'm part of the Cool Zoo Crew.

I've taped a postcard I got from Rocket on my bedroom wall, showing a koala bear with her cub in a tree, watching a cricket match in a huge stadium. He's scribbled a note on the back: "Ford. Never thought I could get bored, but no one here's as cool as you. No trampolines, but lots of wading pools and howling dingoes. See you on the other side of the world. G'day, mate. Rocket."

22

"I'd give my eyeteeth to play on that course," Pop says, clipping the shrubbery outside our dining room window while I chip a plastic golf ball at an elm tree under menacing clouds. Pop only plays on the two nine-hole public dog tracks in town. He points the clippers at me. "Remember, keep your head down and follow through. And repair your divots."

"I know, Pop, I know." *Don't worry, Dad, I won't embarrass you.*

"By the way," he adds. "Tryouts for the high school golf team are coming up."

"Sounds great, Pop." I hadn't thought about that option. I've been playing and learning a ton about golf this summer. Perhaps that's something I can play in high school instead of getting my brains bashed in by playing football. "You have to carve out your niche in life," Uncle Fred once told me.

A Yamaha motorcycle with chrome fenders screams to a stop next to the large boulder at the edge of our driveway. It's the coolest, far-out thing on two wheels I've ever seen since Nick Lund brought home a stainless steel, gull-winged DeLorean. The driver keeps his helmet on and twists his wrist to rev the idling motor. Kate rushes out the front door past Pop's shears toward the motorcycle. The biker removes his helmet, shakes out his brown hair, and gives Kate a huge smooch.

Really, Kate? Theo? Again? Kate hops on the bike, fastens her hands on his hips, and Theo reverses out of the driveway. She taps his shoulder to stop the bike in the middle of the street.

"Hey, Ford," she yells over the sound of the motor. "Some girl stopped by last night, and she's called you a hundred times." The Yamaha purrs. "Cutesy blonde in a green-mesh shirt ... Fooord's got a girlfriend."

Theo punches the throttle, and the Yamaha's wheels burn rubber down Dot Ave. I've been ignoring Gigi, still holding out hope for a Cleo reunion. Mr. Sanders's white Eldorado drives up, the trunk pops, and I throw my clubs inside, praying for sunshine.

We arrive at the club, and as I carry my bag past the caddy bench and over to the first tee, Count Bogart's voice thunders from inside his vampire hollow. "Where the hell's your caddy uniform, Quinn?"

In a bright, boastful tone, I say, "I happen to be *play-ing* today, Mr. Bogart."

He leans his head out, and venom oozes from his pores. "Think you're hot stuff, huh?"

Why shouldn't I play the south course? I've earned a special member's invitation.

■ ■ ■

My tee shot on Number 1 flares hot down the middle of the fairway. *Take that, Bogart.* A quick glance back toward the clubhouse. The caddy master stares at me with his hands on his hips. Bobby Walton tips his golf visor to me as if saying "Good fer you, Quinn."

Our group doesn't have any caddies, thank God, which would have been strange and uncomfortable. Jason and I carry our own bags, and his hockey-playing dad rides in a cart with a guest, some management type from the Red Wings, and without a cart jockey. My playing's superb on the front nine. Along the way, I give golf-course tips to Mr. Sanders and his guest on what clubs to hit and the best angles to approach the green for any easy two-putt. On Number 9, a nice little draw lands softly onto the back of the pear-shaped green from my shiny new MacGregor 5-wood.

A thunderstorm rumbles in as we descend a big slope on the lengthy 3-par. Rain soon swamps our heads; the wind blows fierce; umbrellas bloom and careen from the hands of their owners. Lightning flashes in the distance and thunder booms—a death knell for golfers. A siren sounds from the clubhouse. *Game over.*

Mr. Sanders says, "Jump aboard, boys." We hop on the back of the cart like it's a trolley car and head for shelter.

A winding staircase leads us to a mahogany-paneled basement. Jason's dad and his friend peel off to the upstairs bar. A painting of a golfer in plaid knickers on a foxhunt hangs from a far wall above a fireplace fit for an ancient warlord. Two kids in Polo shirts play bumper pool. A waitress takes our order—7 Ups and cheeseburgers. Two girls saunter in with wet hair and tennis racquets. It's no fake mirage this time. My heart pumps wildly in my chest.

"Our tournament got rained out," a girl says, sitting down next to Jason.

"This is Pippa and Cleo," Jason says. Pippa wears an all-white tennis outfit with a skirt and an Evonne Goolagong perm.

"I know Cleo." *Doesn't she hate this Pippa bitch?* I barely recognize Cleo from the girl with the Egyptian headband I'd met in the spring. She dons a fake smile, like she's the daughter of one of the Stepford wives. There's something missing in her eyes since I last saw her—wide but lifeless. I figure she really must have undergone electric shock therapy, dulling her senses.

Figures she's hanging out with Pippa Farnsworth now. Kate told me once that Pippa is the most stuck-up person on planet Earth, and her dad owns some colossal salt plant that supplies Mr. Peanut. Maybe Cleo's gained admission into the Pippa Gang or has been sprinkled with Pippa pixie dust. A frightening thought occurs to me. What if Cleo spills the beans that I'm a space nerd named Gifford and keep a telescope in my bedroom? I'll never hear the end of if it from Nick and his gang. Then I thought, *You dimwit. Cleo won't say a thing for fear you'll tell Pippa about her visit to the nuthouse.*

"Jason, are you going to the dance here Saturday night?" Pippa says, pulling her hair back in a ponytail and tying it off with a pink ribbon. "Mother's chair of the social committee and wants a good showing or I'll never hear the end of it."

"Yeah, you're my date." He fingers some peanuts from a bowl. "Did ya forget?"

"What about Cleo here?" Pippa asks.

"Take Ford." Jason pats me on the head like a pet poodle.

Pippa emits a long, drawn-out sigh. "But *he's* not a member."

Cleo comes to the rescue. "Relax, Pippa. He'll be my guest. Besides, who's going to know?" She gives me an approving nod, and I think about our night in the tent. Perhaps she hasn't changed at all.

"Pip, does he look okay to you?" Jason asks.

Cleo serves me up a Pippa-clone smile and answers instead. "Sure does."

After that, I play the greatest song in my head. Bowie's "Hey Man."

Pippa scans my rain-soaked head. "I s'pose ... if we can dry'im off by then."

"Can you manage that, Ford?" Jason asks.

"I think so." *Hell yeah.*

Pippa waves her precious hand, trying to get the attention of the waitress. "The help around here blows." Her eyeballs scrutinize me up and down. "Do you even own a blue blazer ... or khaki pants? The club has a strict dress code for dances, you know."

I swear the sly fox moves in the painting on the wall.

"Stop with the inquisition, Pippa," Cleo says, coming to my defense again. "You sound like my mother."

Pippa returns serve with a sarcastic "Sawr-ee."

"It's settled, then." Jason raises both hands above his head in touchdown style. "We'll have the time of our lives, Ford. Trust me."

Cleo scribbles something on a piece of paper with a miniature golf pencil. She leans over and whispers in my ear. "Here, take this, Giff. You can read it later." She hands me the secret note, which causes goosebumps to ripple and sprout on my skin, and I bet it's her phone number (like I'll ever forget that) or a message to meet her somewhere to have some long overdue alone time together. I shove the note in my pocket, figuring I'll take a fake bathroom break and read it then.

The waitress returns with two virgin strawberry daiquiris for the girls. "Are you Ford Quinn?"

"Who wants to know?" Jason asks the waitress.

"Pimples. He's calling from the bag room."

Can this come at a worse time? I know what Pippa is thinking now—how'd he get in here?

Jason bails me out this time. "Ford's famous for being on national TV."

Pippa raises a cynical chin. "And what might that be for?"

"Caddying in the PGA, Pip," Jason says. "A close-up camera shot off the eighteenth green. His player had the lead after the first round."

"No big deal," I say, thinking I'm cocky as all getout. "Looks like I'm going to have to take this call." I think back to that bus ride with Reagan Paulson and how lucky I was to ask him for career advice. Maybe a member from the country club wants to interview me about my PGA experience. I've heard some of the PGA caddies, like Chip, have been getting calls from the tournament committee to get input on any issues that need improvement because Kensington Hills will be hosting the 1983 U.S. Open. It'll be the summer after my senior year. By that time, I'm sure to get my choice of bags, not just some lame-o club pro like Winston Somerset.

I pick up the wall phone to Pimples's voice. "Bogart wants you ... now."

"Tell Bogart you couldn't find me. I'll owe you one, Pimples." A waiter brushes by me, carrying a tray of champagne flutes for a wedding reception upstairs.

"Not a chance. I ain't takin' any heat for you." A few weeks ago Pimples had been promoted from caddy to the bag room—the most choice job in the club next to Bobby Walton's starter position.

The long phone cord snakes around my neck and tightens its grip. "Why in the hell does he want to see me?"

"I guess you'll find out when you get here."

I slam the phone down. *What right does Bogart have to pluck me from the clubhouse, 'specially when he knows I'm hobnobbing with members?* My cheeseburger hasn't even arrived yet. A member's invitation is supposed to be a get-out-of-jail-free card or an invisibility cloak for caddies. I take a trembling walk back to the table, trying to play it like Cool Hand Luke. "I'll be right back. I need to take care of some business."

"The clock's tickin', Giff," Cleo says in a bouncy tone, smiling brightly. Never seen Cleo this happy go lucky before.

I trudge up the stairs, cross under the veranda, up Yellow Brick Road, and past the practice putting green to the first tee. The hard rain has stalled to a drizzly whimper. Two soggy loppers stand at attention with their bags.

Gigi.

And Rat, two bags in front of him.

A fourth bag lays on the wet sod—Father Steve's.

Bobby Walton stands slack in his rain slicker. "Bogart's inside, wants to see you."

Inside the shack, Bogart leans over his chair and spits chew into an empty red Hills Bros. coffee can. Several spikes are missing from his worn black golf shoes, matching the tooth gaps in his mouth.

"You wanted to see me?" I ask in a get-off-my-ass voice. I fight the urge to tell him: "I'm with a member and that means I'm *above* you on the pecking order till *I* decide to don my green-mesh shirt."

He raises one eyebrow, taking note of my haughty tone. "We run out of caddies." He dips into his Red Man and fills his gums. "Need you on a bag."

At that very moment, I peer through the small window and see a few green shirts loitering on the bridge. No golfers in sight except for the players on the first tee. "You can't make me go out now. I'm a guest of a member." A desperate glance down Yellow Brick Road, hoping I'll see Jason Sanders coming to my rescue. Nothing but bluish-green grass shavings from a predawn trimmed practice putting surface.

Bogart spits more chew in his can, then emits a mockingbird hoot. His fat belly shakes, tobacco juice leaking from his mouth onto his swivel chair. His face turns a shade redder than normal, which I didn't think was possible. Then the words come out of nowhere. "*Who* the hell do you think got you a loop in the PGA, Quinn?"

"What do you mean?" A roulette wheel of names spins in my mind—Bobby Walton, Father Steve … Chip?

"I did. As a favor to you know who. And now you think you can tell me you can't go out on one stinkin' loop?"

"But I earned it." Least that's what I was thinking all along, not having asked for a favor from one single soul.

Bogart scoffs. "The hell you did. There are boys here who have three times the loops you got. You owe me big, Quinn, now get your ass out to the first tee, or you'll never see this club again."

I shake my head and plod sorrowfully out to the first tee, passing two other caddies on the bench. With his ball perched on a tee, Father Steve practices his penguinlike swing.

Gigi serves me a heaping of deviled-egg eyes. "The least you could do is thank me."

Blood leaks from my lower gums after a silent "FOOK OFF, BOGART" escapes under my breath and my upper teeth scrape my lower lip. "You had sumthin' to do with this?"

"I saved you from them." She swipes a trace of blood drool from my lips and wipes it on Mr. Valentine's towel. "After the time we spent together the other day, I figured you'd rather be with *me*."

"Gigi, I'm here as a guest." I nod toward the clubhouse. "They're waiting for me."

She pouts with her pouty lips. "Well, so am I, and you haven't even called me."

I have no excuse. "I've been pretty busy."

"Busy doing what? Who gives a crap, anyway? They're all stuck-up A-holes." She crosses her arms in a fit of anger. "I'd rather kill myself than hang out with the likes of them."

"You don't even know them." This is true. Sure, Nick's a bit of a prick and enjoys the charisma of an undertaker, but Jason and Jack Lott are decent guys. Their parents' membership in a country club doesn't disqualify them as human beings. I've learned that social status doesn't necessarily make the person. If I have to form my own gang, I wouldn't pick the kid based on their parents' income or zip code. My Justice League would include Rocket, Owen, Jason, Jack, Chip, and Pimples. And Fat Albert, too.

Gigi shakes her head. "I don't need to know them. All I know is I have to wipe their parents' balls clean."

"They're not all that bad."

"You think that because you're one of them." She pulls out a club from the bag and shows it to me. "Born with a silver sand wedge in your mouth."

Damn. I have to figure a way out of this with Gigi. I really want Owen back as a friend, figuring he won't resent me forever for getting a PGA loop. Not so for a Gigi loop. "You didn't tell Owen about us, did you?"

The penguin on the first tee waddles and waggles. *CRACK!* A kaleidoscope of Monarch butterflies flutter for cover.

"Don't you worry about Owen." She lifts the strap of the bag onto her bony shoulder. "He's obsessed with his new bass guitar, anyway, not me." So that's the sudden interest in me? Owen's engaged to his Fender bass.

As our group trudges off after their balls, splashing through the swampy grass, I realize I have no way of informing Jason I've been recruited to carry a bag. It's not like we carry walkie-talkies. He's going to wonder why I've disappeared into rain-soaked air. And now Gigi is royally ticked because I don't bother to call her back. I really do like Gigi, but I'm still stuck on Cleo and don't want to betray Owen, but perhaps I already have, and he can't stay sore forever about my PGA loop.

On the fourth fairway, my mind wanders back to what Bogart said about the "favor" he did for me at the PGA Championship. Perhaps Pop lobbied Bobby Walton but didn't want to tell me. But that isn't like Pop; he'd expect credit for something like that. Perhaps Father Steve put in a prayer for me—even Bogart can't refuse a priest; vampires fear the cross. I ask him on the fourth green if he put a good word in for me, but he denies it and says he hates the PGA. I ask him why. Before answering, he jerks his putt past the hole, and it sails toward the perimeter frog hair.

"Grow teeth!" The ball teeters on the edge of a cliff before falling into a deep bunker. "Are you kidding me? Right in the kitty litter." He removes his hat and scratches his head. "What were we talking about, son?"

We exchange sand wedge for putter. "Why you hate that the club hosts golf tournaments."

"Three things I can think of right off the bat. First, the gallery tramples the course. See this rough?" He points the butt end of his wedge toward the ground. "Looks like Hell." He genuflects to the course. "To me, this is a slice of Heaven."

He climbs down into the quicksand and continues to rant.

"I get a low turnout at Mass on Sunday. Plus, I can't play here all week. I need my golf. It's God's way of keeping me humble. You caddies just happen to have the burden of carrying my cross." As he says this, he laughs at his own joke and tops the ball, airmailing it into oblivion. "Why do you ask, son?"

"Nothing."

He reaches his hand up, and I pull him out of the fox hole. "It's something, then. Don't worry, you deserved getting a bag in the PGA, believe me."

At the end of the loop, I lurk around for any sign of Jason. The clubhouse is locked. I check the tennis court, where an employee pushes puddles toward a fence with a broom. No kids in sight. It's then I remember the note Cleo gave me at lunch. She probably wanted to meet me at some secret hiding place along Yellow Brick Road or down at the waterfalls, wondering why I never showed up.

Stupid Bogart! I open the note, expecting an invite to a secret rendezvous and can't believe my bloodshot eyes:

> *Don't rely on other people for your self-esteem. Get inspired*

*and make today your best day
ever! O· P· Peabody·' P·S· I'll
see you at the dance on Saturday
night, Giff· Ü·*

I crumple up the note and throw it off the bridge and under the exhaust systems of Kensington Road traffic. As the cars blur under me, I think of how Gigi has become a super thorn in my ass, and Cleo's become Virginia's little clone. I gaze up to the sky gods. *Why me?*

That night, I interrupt Pop during his evening den time of coffee-mug beer sipping and newspaper reading. "Did you ask Bobby Walton to make sure I got a bag in the PGA as a favor since you know his dad?"

He snaps his newspaper down into his lap. "Are you nuts?"

That's the end of that.

Who gives a damn how I got the PGA loop? I'll take solace in Father Steve's conviction that I deserved it. After all, the PGA loop might be the added bonus on my caddy resume and send me over the top to win the Evans scholarship.

23

I iron my white Izod shirt stone smooth for the dance and pop my collar up and down in front of the bathroom mirror a billion times. Better leave it down. Fads in the Hills change faster than the battleship in *Battlestar Galactica*. I don't need to draw unwanted attention to myself on the biggest night of my life. I steal a pair of Ray-Ban sunglasses from Billy's room and head down the stairs.

Pop spots me from the dining room while eating a heaping of pot roast. "Where do you think you're going tonight, hot shot?"

"He's going to a dance at the country club tonight," Mom says, entering from the kitchen.

"Is this a caddy thing?"

Virginia sets her plate down to eat. "No, he's going with Jason Sanders. His dad's a member."

"You see, Ford," Pop says between mouthfuls. "You hang around the right people, and you can go places. It's all about meeting the right people." He lifts a forkful of pot roast to toast my good fortune. "Good for you."

"Maybe you should go with him, Dad," Billy shouts from the kitchen. I swipe his Ray-Bans off my head and slide them into my pocket.

"Knock it off, Mr. Wiseguy."

Billy has snagged a job uptown at Olga's Kitchen. It's been one whole month, and he hasn't been fired yet, a new record for my brother. Billy can't be working this long at a job unless he's hoarding money for something. He even got his hair cut at earlobe level. *What in the hell is Billy saving money up for?*

Before I leave, I can tell Pop is proud of me. He has that certain twinkle in his eye. *You're on your way up, kid.*

Jason and I ride our bikes to the dance in our sport coats over our Izod shirts. I've outgrown my blue blazer, the sleeves showing my bare wrists. The dance is held down in the basement, where strobe lights hang from the ceiling, and a laser show floods the dance floor. A few couples dance to a syrupy-slow Bee Gees song. A bowl full of punch and pigs in a blanket are in the middle of each table. Pippa and Cleo sit at a table, munching peanuts. An up-tempo song comes on, and we all fly to the dance floor.

We fast dance to "Bloody Well Right," bounce up and down to "My Sharona" (my head nearly pops off), dizzy shake to "Ballroom Blitz," and bump and grind to an extended mix of "I'm Your Boogie Man," "Let's Get Down Tonight," and "(Shake, Shake, Shake) Shake Your Booty." The dance floor swells. Cleo presses up next to me, swinging her hips in time to the pulsating rhythm of the beat. Jason buzz-grins at me as he pulls Pippa's waist close to his KISS belt buckle and his hands Saran Wrap her butt. The speakers thump a new record: "Cool for Cats" by Squeeze. One big wave of bodies sways back and forth before the crowd parts after some spaz starts to break-dance.

The DJ must want to take a piss break because "Heartache Tonight" empties the dance floor.

Polly Ledbetter staggers up to us and slurs, "What're youz loozshers doin' in here … the reel party's ow'side." We boogie up the stairs, push past green and white streamers hanging from the door frame, and fall into the night. A throng of kids surround a guy who is trying to force foamy beer out of a keg on the eighteenth green. Nick Lund and Jack Lott have stretched themselves out in a sand trap on lounge chairs nicked from the pool area. They guzzle beers like they're on spring break in Ft. Lauderdale.

Sanders pours bubbling foam into the hole on the green. "The keg is dead."

"Long live the keg!" says another kid in a nifty light-blue blazer and pressed turquoise Izod (collar popped), who jumps from the edge of the green into the beach party, knocking tipsy Jack Lott off his lounge chair.

Pool water glows aqua-green from underwater lights across the dewy grass. Cleo's face lights up, and she tugs on my lapels. "Let's go swimming in the pool, Giff."

I haven't brought a bathing suit. We'll have to swim in our underwear. *Duh.* I imagine Cleo duck-paddling through the water, her hair floating to the surface.

"Anyone got some beer?" Jason shouts, trying to pump the last beer molecules out of the keg.

Jack and Nick drunk-climb from the beach up to the patio green. "We need a beer medic," Jack Lott says, holding the pin on the green for Lund, who is wearing a red cardigan covering a naked chest. Lund rolls a golf ball with his hand toward the hole. Jack turns and spots me. "Let Ford hold the pin. He's the professional caddy!"

Everyone roars, and I pretend to laugh along, too, although I want to reach escape velocity and exit the country-club atmosphere. There is no way I'll be playing caddy tonight. I hate Jack's guts just then. The last thing I want is the rest of these country-club kids to know I'm a looper.

"I need a beer, too," Pippa pipes in. "Jason, you can *always* get beer."

"What do you want me to do, Pip?" He draws circles in the air with a fake wand. "Presto! Beers appear!"

"Come on, Quinn, show us how to hold this pin." *Shut the hell up, Jack!*

Lund gets into the act, too. "Clean my balls, Boy Wonder."

Nick's quip sends the revelers on the green into hysterical fits of giggles. Lund drops his pants to his ankles, running stumbling circles around me in his boxer shorts before falling back into the beach. The whole crowd starts chanting "clean his balls, clean his balls, clean his balls." The crowd swirls around me, and I want to run from this godforsaken country club full of ass wipes. Perhaps Gigi is right about Hills kids. Of course, I already know that. The crowd turns to a drunken Lund, who rolls around in the sand trap to roars of laughter.

Rocket's beer heist earlier in the summer hatches a daring idea in my brain. *If Rocket can pull it off, how hard can it be?* They'll forget I'm a caddy if I score some booze. Hell, maybe this will be the clincher to get me into the Lund Gang. Nick Lund throws a rake toward my feet, spraying sand on my worn penny loafers. "Rake my assprints in this trap, Quinn," Lund says.

"I'm getting some beer for everybody," I announce to deflect my looper status.

The throng goes orchestra-crowd silent. Nosy crickets chirp and snicker off the green.

Lund peeks over the lip of the trap. "Quinn's getting us beer? Go, Quinn, go."

The chorus starts up again. "Go, Quinn, go. Go, Quinn, go. Go, Quinn, go."

Nighttime sprinklers detonate and quench parched fairway turf.

"What are you waiting for?" Pippa says in her most bitchy tone. "We don't have all night, ya know."

I can't welch on my promise and betray the faces on the green: Jack, Jason, Nick, Pippa. "Jason, you have to come with me," I insist. Cleo starts down a paved path toward the pool, turns, waves me along, and mouths the word *c'mon*. I drift toward Cleo, but Jason grabs my arm.

"Let's go. These thirsty wenches are close to revolting."

Pippa slaps Jason on his chest with the back of her hand. "Nice, Shakespeare."

Cleo stops between the pool and the green, tapping her foot. "I'll be waiting, Giff."

"*Go get the booze, Ford,*" says the Great Gazoo perched on my shoulder. "*Don't blow the chance of a lifetime—in with the country-club kids and dream-dating Cleo.*" I flick the green alien off my shoulder. My confidence soars as we fly down the road on our bikes, shouting the lyrics to the Stones' song "You Can't Always Get What You Want."

"Where are we going, Quinn?" Jason asks, trying to keep pace with me.

"Just follow me, Sanders," I say with cocky confidence. Jason follows me as we coast into the Farmer Jack's parking lot. We ditch our bikes and hide behind a blue van. I stake out the grocery store, watching for any employees or bag boys lingering near the entrance. Enough people roam the store to keep everyone distracted, which opens the door for what I am about to do.

"What the hell are you up to, Quinn?"

A kid strains to push a train of carts toward the entrance.

"Gettin' us some beer."

"You gonna pay some guy to buy beer?" That's the time-tested method, but I don't have a dime on me.

"Do you have any money?" I ask Jason, thinking that's the safest route to take and losing my nerve a bit.

He digs his hands into his pockets. "Not a nickel."

"Okay. Just wait here until I come back." I kneel behind the bumper of the van with stickers that read "SCREW Iran" and "Ellen Ripley for President," wondering if I should risk pilfering some beer just to get in good with the country-club kids. I wish I had an ounce of Rocket's guts. If I return to the party without any beer, I'll get no mercy from Nick the Prick Lund and be the butt of some Pippa joke.

"C'mon, Quinn," Sanders says. "What are ya putzin' around for?"

Now or never. "You'll see."

I grip a lonely grocery cart in a parking space next to the van and saunter scared into the store. The lights shine bright. Three long laps up and down the aisles. A bottle of Mr. Clean—to give me strength—goes in first, followed by Cap'n Crunch from the shelf in the breakfast aisle. A slow lap past a woman headed in the other direction with a toddler fidgeting in the front basket and on past the freezer department toward the beer. Since no one seems to pay attention to me, I load a case of Stroh's and bury it in the bottom of the cart next to a skeptical Mr. Clean. I dash to the next aisle and fill the cart with bags of potato chips, pretzels, peanuts, and then, in a slight panic, cross to another aisle in front of the fruit section, grabbing a head of lettuce and broccoli. A mountain of food blankets the beer.

The cashiers are busy ringing people up, and I don't worry about the baggers—they're teenagers who probably lift beer and cigs every night of the week. After one more scared-to-God-freaked-out spin up and down the grocery aisles, the cart clatters straight out the front door, pulled by some uncontrollable invisible force. The doors automatically open, and tension leaks from my body because I'm in the clear as I search for my getaway man in the dark parking lot, but Sanders is nowhere in sight. I look left, then right. I haven't thought the caper past this point in time. Straight ahead it is, and back behind that van, but I don't see it.

A deep voice shakes me to my core. "STOP!" Another man comes up behind me, wearing a butcher's apron and a nametag that reads "Bob."

I try to think of an excuse. "I'm looking for my mom."

"Right, kid, and I'm Zeus," Bob says.

"Get back inside," the other man orders. He's wearing a short-sleeve button-down shirt with a tie and a nametag that reads "Peter Barger, Fresh Foods Manager." The broccoli stop has done me in. They parade me back through the bright lights of the store, and after a quick glimpse behind me to locate Jason, I pray he'll see I've been busted and call his famous dad from the phone booth in the corner of the lot to save my sorry ass.

They escort me past the frozen-food section and to the back of the store to Mr. Barger's cramped office. A red plastic electric chair for my execution. Mr. Barger squats behind his desk, and Bob from the meat department stands guard behind him. Before they can interrogate me, I start bawling on the spot, thinking my world has frozen in hell.

"Please don't tell my dad," I plead. "He'll kill me."

The meat guy comes to my defense. "He's just a little-shit kid, Pete. Maybe we should just let 'im go."

"No goddamn way, Bob. Punks like him need to be taught a lesson." He rolls up his sleeves and takes out a notepad. "Now what's your name?"

"Quinn, Ford Quinn."

"You got any ID, Quinn?"

I fish out my Kensington Hills municipal pass for the public pool and golf courses and hand it over to Mr. Barger. He scans it and stalks out of the room, leaving me with the meat cutter.

"Pretty dumb stunt you pulled tonight," he says. "If you was my kid, you'd be dead meat."

I eye his apron splattered with cow blood and believe him. My crying slows to a drip, the fear subsiding briefly before I'm overcome with the Regrets. For me, there's no cure. I blame Rocket for showing me the beer stunt, like it's somehow his fault. There's no way in hell he'd ever have been caught, and right now he'd be guzzling a beer in the shallow end of the country club pool with Cleopatra.

Five minutes later, Mr. Barger returns with a policeman in full uniform and a gold badge on his chest engraved with the letters "KHPD." He rests his hand on the brown handle of the gun protruding from his hip holster. The officer must consider me dangerous, or at least desperate enough to try something. If I make a run for it now, I'll be shot dead, which sounds like my best option at this point. I'm half hoping I'll spend the night in jail, not afraid of the cops as much as I'm deathly afraid of facing Pop.

The officer directs me through the store and past the cooler section. I eye the missing space in the row of Stroh's cases, where I'd lifted the beer. People stop their carts to turn around and gawk at the perp walk. I stare straight at the back of the policeman's black hat, praying no one I know saw me. They shove me into the back of a police cruiser, and I see Pop's red Impala drive up. The Regrets turn into the Sweats. Jason Sanders weaves his bike in front of the police cruiser, peering into the windshield, and then peddles through the squad car's light beams, out of sight. My fear shifts from Pop to the country club party. Jason is headed to blab about what I've done, for sure. I'll be the laughingstock of the junior country club set. It occurs to me that Cleo and the chance at that life has just slipped through my sticky fingers.

They release me into Pop's custody, who doesn't utter one single flipping syllable, probably saving up his words for the most world-ending epic tongue-lashing in the history of teen-rearing. The Impala pulls into the garage, knocks over a garbage can, and rear ends the lawnmower. I pull on the inside door handle of the car.

"Don't you move a muscle, buster."

Nothing but deadly silence for an eternity. Through the windshield and the garage window, I see a porch light go on at the Carters and a shadowy silhouette on the porch. *Laney?*

Pop sits staring into the darkness as if figuring out what to say before uttering in his most somber there's-been-a-death-in-the-family tone, "You've let the family down, son. You're grounded until I say so." There's no trace of anger in his voice, just pathetic, sad disappointment. The tone of his voice is the biggest blow I've taken tonight. Not the what-ifs with Cleo and Jason and the boys. But how I've let down Pop.

So much for Golden Boy.

As I traipse through the mudroom, stumbling over unsold Mix-Fare product and Rainbow vacuum accessories, Mom stews at the breakfast table, sucking on a cigarette. She starts blowing rings with her smoke. When I was a little kid, during her peak years of smoking three packs a day, she used to entertain us by blowing rings toward the ceiling, and I'd jump up and try to catch them. I'm pretty sure that's how I'd learned how to count.

"Why did you do that, Ford?" Virginia says with a biting, bitter tone.

"I don't know." A hundred wavy lines next to the wall entering the kitchen from the mudroom get my attention. Faded memories of Pop with his No. 2 pencil in his hand, slashing across our heads to show our growth. Billy's the tallest, Kate the smallest. I'm the middle child, but I'm the only one left still growing. I've been taken down a notch or two tonight.

"Who put you up to it?"

The Great Gazoo. She can't imagine her own son being a thief. It must have been some other kid who'd lured me to sin. That'd be Rocket, Virginia. *G'day, mate,* I can hear him say. *G'damn, Rocket.*

"No one."

Her lips are pursed together before opening to the greatest insult of all. "I'd expect this from Billy but not from you."

"Sorry, Mom." Water splashes from my cheeks and onto the kitchen table, extinguishing a glowing ember in Virginia's ashtray.

"Get up to bed. Your father and I need to talk."

■ ■ ■

I crawl under the covers that night, hoping to wake up on the moon. I conjure up a crazy idea in my head to take a Greyhound bus to Cocoa Beach, where my cousin Mitty lives. I'll pick up some records by the Ventures or some other surf band at Sam's Jams on the way down south. There has to be lots of ex-cons in Florida; I can blend right in on the beach.

Summer might as well have ended tonight.

24

After the failed beer heist, Pop threatens to send me to the public high school, where Billy attended after he flunked out of Catholic High his freshman year. What my parents don't know is it sounds more like a gift to me. No one at the public school would know about my crime, or probably care. Plus, in public school they have live girls in the classroom, unlike Catholic High, where the girls go to a school next door.

With light-years of time on my hands, I make myself a mixtape with a bunch of songs that seem to fit my mood. "The Sound of Silence," "Lost in the Supermarket," "Space Cowboy," "Hey Hey, My My," "Call Me," "Refugee," "London Calling," "Detroit Rock City," "God Only Knows," "Once in a Lifetime," "Moonage Daydream," "Wish You Were Here." After listening to my tape, I lose my mind and mail it to Cleo with one line:

Enjoy!! Ford. P.S. Wish you were here.

One night during my purgatory, Billy knocks on my door. He tells me to follow him into his room. He's never done *that* before. We climb out his window and onto the roof of the garage. Billy pulls out a pack of Kools and shakes out two cigarettes. He gives me one and tells me to light it. I ignite the tip and inhale like there's no tomorrow.

"Hey, you're a natural."

I don't tell him I've done a little smoking this summer. We sit there in silence for a few minutes, smoking and staring up at the stars. "You really surprised me, little bro."

"I guess I surprised a lot of people."

"Dude, it takes some guts to do what you did." Billy breathes in the stars and a Kool cig without a care in the world. "You definitely took the heat off me."

I think of the cash he's been saving up from his Olga's job and think I might not be the only criminal in the house. What's he done this time? "What do you mean?"

He scratches his head and looks over at me. "Mom didn't tell you?"

"Tell me what?"

He takes a long drag on his cigarette. "I might be leavin' the den soon."

"For college?"

"Yeah, with Jenny."

I search the Rolodex in my head and can't find any girl by that name in Billy's life. "Jenny who?"

"Name one Jenny you know."

A cat shrieks next door. Then it dawns on me. "Jenny from next door? Jenny *Clark*?"

Billy exhales a laugh along with a trail of smoke. "Pop doesn't know I'm going to marry Jenny. I've saved up a little dough from work."

"Jesus, Billy. You're barely nineteen."

"Right, but Jenny is totally cool. She's going to study anthropology."

Sounds about right; she's already been studying a primate. Still, Billy's become my hero. "You're going to live together?"

He punches me lightly on the shoulder. "Yeah, you idiot, that's what you do when you get married."

"So you're going to college?"

"Kind of. I'm going to the Ford Motor Institute. Uncle Mitt went to bat for me and got me in. Ford Motor likes to keep it in the family. Grandpa Quinn still pulls weight with them, even though he's been retired for decades. Anyway, they teach you how to sell cars so some day you can run a car dealership. How cool is that?"

Billy flashes a wide grin, and I imagine him with a slew of brand-new Mustangs at his disposal. I haven't seen him this happy in forever. Even Billy has his life figured out overnight, while I'm stuck in neutral. Billy does nothing and gets a potentially great gig. Go figure.

"When Uncle Mitt retires," Billy continues, "he said Mitty and I can take over his dealership in Cocoa Beach."

Surfing *and* driving convertibles up and down the Space Coast? Billy really is a genuine genius.

Pop's going to blow a fuse when he finds out Billy's marrying a Clark, but the Ford Motor Institute will soften the blow. "Have you told Pop?"

"He's thrilled about me enrolling in the Ford Motor Institute." Billy flicks ash at the Milky Way. "But he's not going to find out about Jenny."

"Ever?"

Billy arches his chin at the sky, mulling it over. "I guess he'll have to at some point, but I'll worry about it when the time comes."

Maybe Kate will marry Pauley. Pop would dig his own grave first.

We recline under the stars for a long time, our elbows perched on the shingles and our ankles crossed. I admire Billy for doing his own thing. He lives with total freedom and doesn't give a hoot about what anyone thinks. Why can't I be like that?

I ask him if I can have his record collection before we head back inside. He looks me over. "Why not?"

. . .

A few days after Billy's revelation, Pop hauls me down to the police station on Telegraph Road. The radio blares the song "The Year of the Cat" with its sad horns coming in and out. I think if my parents sang this song about me, they'd change the title to "The Year of the Ass."

A detective leads us into a small room and shuts the door. He flips through the paperwork on me with a puzzled face. I expect him to do the usual Kojack routine: mug shot, fingerprints, black-striped jumpsuit. Detective Reynolds carries a manila folder with "Quinn, Ford, Case No. 80-897812-CV" typed on the side. It seems strange they have a detective on the case when I've been caught red-handed and confessed.

"You've got a clean record with no history of trouble, Ford," the cop says. "And straight As. The grocery store is going to drop the charges, and this won't be on your permanent record when you apply for a job or college as long as you stay out of trouble. You got that?"

"That's it?" I'm off the hook. My heart rate returns to normal.

"No. You need to go through counseling. It's mandatory, even for first-time offenders. We don't want potential mass murderers running loose in the Hills." The detective chuckles to himself. I don't understand what's so goddamn funny.

Pop leans in over the desk. "A shrink?"

In the parking lot, Pop opens his door and says, "Are you still friends with that kid from the country club?"

I shake my head. I haven't heard a peep from Jason Sanders, and I can't blame him one little bit. Nor have I heard anything from Cleo since I sent her my new mixtape. I called her house a few times and hung up because her mom kept answering the phone. One time a familiar male voice I couldn't place answered and said, "No, Cleo's out, but I'll tell her you called, Ford." Click. I'm still waiting for the call back.

Then I think of Gigi. I haven't called her back, either.

25

"Don't relive your past lives. Think anew." (Peabody, *Mensa-Netics*, Volume Three, p. 314) Virginia quotes this bit of philosophy to me before I leave for my therapy session with Dr. Clark to satisfy my criminal counseling sentence.

Pauley greets me at the door and leads me up their creaky stairs to Dr. Clark's office. I notice Virginia's fingerprint—a Rainbow vacuum cleaner behind the door. The room smells of red licorice. Two cats roam the floor.

Dr. Clark waves me in. "Have a seat, Ford."

I stretch my legs onto a red chaise longue. Dr. Clark sits down across from me, and Fluffy's sister jumps in her lap. She strokes the cat's chin. A candle burns on a table with one of its legs carved into the image of an American Indian chief next to that month's *Journal of*

Abnormal Psychology. I wonder: *Does the doctor know the tale about Billy Quinn and Jenny Clark?*

Dr. Clark turns to the door. "You may leave now, Pauley." The door closes, but he leaves a cranny opening. "PAULEY!"

BAM!

I'm careful to speak real soft, fearing Pauley's tape recorder will pick up our conversation. Bracing for an interrogation into my most private, innermost criminal thoughts, I fidget like a pig caught in a volcanic mudslide. The doctor crosses her legs and chews on a red licorice stick. She asks me about my aspirations and what I am *really* passionate about.

We end up talking and laughing all afternoon. Somehow she gets me to tell her I read poetry and have written a few verses of my own, and how it got started in English class after Mr. Garoppolo had us analyze the lyrics of old sixties songs from *The Moody Blues, Dylan, The Byrds*, et cetera. I've never told a soul about that before. I won't tell you everything we talked about, but somehow she made me feel better.

A typical shrink would have probably tried to psychoanalyze why I'd stolen the beer or how I feel about my mom and dad. Or blah, blah, blah. *The Bob Newhart Show* stuff without the corny laugh track. Dr. Clark doesn't even mention the beer heist. All she says is "kids do stupid things;

that's why we call them kids." We talk a bit about Cleo. How I'd helped her, and how I think Cleo doesn't give a rat's butt if I'm alive or dead. She also doesn't give me any of the "plenty of fish in the sea" BS. She simply says, "Cleo's not the same person anymore, Ford. You need to come to terms with that and move on." So what she's really telling me is Cleo moved on *without me*, so get over it.

"I thought she was different, that's all."

"All I can say is she doesn't want to be different anymore." Dr. Clark clasps her hands and leans forward in her chair. "She wants to fit in. Can you understand that?"

"I guess so." Maybe I know that better than anyone.

"Before you go, I want to give you a present." With a bright smile, she hands me a brown paper lunch bag. The paper bag drops from my hands, and out slides *That Was Then, This Is Now* onto the floor. I pick it up and calculate the chances of both of us buying the sequel to *The Outsiders*. Same as me solving Rubik's Cube after a zillion turns—ZERO. Cleo probably gave it back to Dr. Clark without reading a word of it and is on her fiftieth Jackie Collins romance novel.

She tells me I can come back, but I know I won't see her again in therapy. There's nothing else to discuss. I hug Dr. Clark, grab a licorice stick from a jar on the table, and head out the door. There is one thing I don't confide in to Dr. Clark.

Like hell I'm giving up on Cleo.

■ ■ ■

During my purgatory, Virginia and Kate clean the house like mad, right down to using Mix-Fare Super-V cleanser on toothbrushes between the cracks in the blue-tiled bathroom for Pop's prospective house buyers while I coach from the sidelines. A guy in a cheap three-piece suit came by several times in the evening. Pop hoped the man might make an offer. The blowhard went on and on about how his wife would love to live on Dot Ave because it's close to uptown and the schools once they start a family. I figure if Sir Winston had won the PGA, my winning share could have paid off the real estate taxes and given the house a reprieve from its death sentence.

I don't return to caddying right away, too embarrassed to show my face in public. Instead, I hang out at the waterfall with Chimney, lounge around town, and eat baklavas and three-cheese sandwiches at Olga's Kitchen served up by Billy.

One foggy, soupy day, I bump into Fat Albert at Hamburger Heaven, who's shoveling a cheeseburger into his mouth at the lunch counter. One down, three to go. Even though he's already living up to his name, it seems like he's gained a Volvo in weight since he shoved me into the country club swimming pool.

"There's an empty seat. Sit down," Fat Albert says. I figure there's nothing he can do to me in public. Plus, we're headed for high school and will be driving real cars soon, not just bumper cars at Boblo Island. Kids mature as they got older, don't they? So I sit on a stool next to him and order two cheese sliders smothered in grilled onions and ketchup. "Sorry about shovin' you in the pool. Lund just makes you do crazy shit."

"Where is Nick the Prick today?"

"I don't give a rat's ass." Another plate of steaming sliders slides under his chin. "He booted me out of the gang."

I notice his bottom lip quiver and ask him why Lund kicked him out of the Fantastic Four.

"Wendall Lober has somethin' called Home Box Office. It's got ten times the number of channels as ON-TV." He stacks two burgers together and pours ketchup on the top layer. "I became pretty worthless to them. Wendall's in. I'm out."

"Sorry."

"It's okay. Nick's a dick. Plus, we're about to start high school, and he's still reading comic books in his stupid tree fort like he's still in the sixth grade." It occurs to me I haven't read a comic book in ages. "I could pound him if I wanted to." Fat Albert swallows a double-onion cheeseburger whole.

"No doubt about that, Gene."

"Geez, nobody's called me Gene since the first grade. It's always Fat Albert. Hey, you want to come over some time and watch a movie with me? *Mad Max* is showing on ON." A fried onion dangles from his mouth.

"That'd be great." He holds out his oniony paw. I shake it and think *we* don't need Nick.

No doubt we aren't cool, but we're real. I'm not changing for anyone. Why waste my time trying to impress the likes of Lund? I'll take Gene Duncan, thank you very much.

■ ■ ■

Mom starts nagging me to start caddying again. I don't want to go back and face Father Steve. Instead, I ride off in my caddy shirt and towel every day to go to the movies or the arcade. I've now seen *Airplane!, The Blues Brothers, Friday the 13th*, and *The Shining.*

On a beautiful Friday afternoon, as the sky glistens with a fresh coat of light-blue paint, I exit the back door of the movie theater that leads to a field, and beyond that, Freddy's Go-Cart, Slippery Slide and Golf Range. The go-carts and water slide are so fun that kids hardly use the range. After watching a middle-aged man in a dress shirt and loose tie hit worm burners, I realize I miss playing golf every Monday with Owen and Pimples. For five bucks, kids can hit balls all day long at the range. I wander over to Freddy's and borrow a 5-iron. Kids fly around the go-cart track with their hair pressed back while I bash ball after ball off green AstroTurf.

I return to the range early the next day with my own clubs. Mr. Valentine had explained to me once how to play different shots: a fade—open your stance, a hook—close your stance and rotate your grip counter-clockwise, a Texas wedge—use a putter instead of wedge to run the ball up to the green. A great golf shot mirrors the sensation of a slingshot. The ball launches off the clubface if properly struck, along with a small divot. If you hit it sweet, the divot is like the solid rocket boosters falling off the Saturn V at takeoff.

From that day on, I keep my hours at the golf range the same as my caddying hours. That way, Pop and Mom won't suspect I'm not looping. I want a college scholarship, but I figure there might be a better way.

The following week, Pop talks me into trying out for the junior varsity golf team for the upcoming high school year.

"Gee," I lie, "been so busy caddying again, I haven't thought about playing golf much." At this point, I got nothing to lose by trying out for the team.

Tryouts are held at a golf range, where the coach watches us hit balls. At my turn, I hit the ball straight as an arrow ten times in a row. As a freshman, it's hard to make the JV squad because only seven guys are selected. The tryout lasts a total of ten minutes. After watching me for a while, he comes up to me and says, "Kid, you have a real nice swing. Show up next week for the Kensington City Golf Tournament. It's the second leg of the tryout."

I trudge over to Pop's car. "How'd it go?" he asks.

"I made the first cut. I have to play in the city golf tournament for the next round of cuts." A smile emerges from my lips for the first time in ages. I've finally something to look forward to.

"You had the smoothest swing out there." He rolls the window all the way down. "If you don't make the team, that coach doesn't know his head from his ass."

I back away from the car. *Don't worry, Pop. I'll make it.* If I make the team, it'll salvage my summer and give me a head start in high school. If there's one thing I've learned, it's that you have to distinguish yourself in life. Or was it stand out in life? It's Grandpa Quinn's expression, and I know stealing beer isn't what he meant. Making the golf team might make Pop forget about the Farmer Jack's debacle.

26

The following Monday, I show up at the city golf tournament. Nine holes will be played on the first day at Logan Springs, and nine holes the next day at the other public goat track called Willow Hills. Golf has become a serious passion now. A Quinn has to be good at something. I tee off that morning with three other boys while Pop lurks in the shadows of a two-headed maple tree. Three miserable putts and a double bogey on the first hole. A depressing slog to the second tee. I'm hoping Pop has left, but it's too far for me to see him.

Things turn around for me as I manage a tricky up and down for par on Number 2, which settles my frayed nerves. I barely miss a putt the entire day with Sir Winston's Bulls Eye putter. *In the zone!* I fire a personal best of thirty-six, several shots in front of the field. Afterward, I eat a baloney sandwich and bake on a picnic bench as other players trickle in with their scores. A tournament "official" writes the scores on a large board in black magic marker.

Some mom waiting for her son shouts out, "Who's Ford Quinn?" I proudly raise my hand as the owner of the score. "What a wonderful score," she gushes.

The golf coach from Catholic High approaches me and says, "That's quite an impressive score for an incoming freshman. Another round like that and you could even make varsity." After I thank the coach, he adds, "What country club do ya play at?"

Monday's North Kensington Country Club—by special invite only. "I don't belong to any country club."

Playing a varsity sport as a freshman would launch me from the bottom rung of the social ladder to orbiting Jupiter. I'll be heading to parties with seniors, making out with cheerleaders, signing autographs for third graders. Not even football players make varsity as a freshman unless their last name is Lott. Freshman letter winners get to go to the homecoming dance, and I'll have my pick of dates for sure, but I'll take Cleo. *Duh!* I'll be the famous freshman Tiger and maybe even get elected class president. (Plus, players who win the tournament get their photos taken for the local paper, and maybe then Cleo will take notice—and we can double date with Jason and Pip.)

Because it's Monday, I decide to sneak on the north course with Pimples in the afternoon (if you don't caddy over the weekend, you're forbidden to play). I continue to play my A-game that day until my thirty-seventh hole of the day. My tee shot flies straight, and I drag my suddenly tired limbs toward my ball, imagining myself wearing a Tiger's varsity letter jacket. Pop'll be on cloud nine if I make varsity. I waggle in front of the ball and swing my 3-iron from the fairway. The ball flies quail right.

"Nice shank." Pimples knows better. It's taboo to utter *that* word on a golf course. Shanks are balls that barely get off the ground, like a firework dud, skidding dead right. Golf's version of a mosquito bite: The more you scratch the bite, the worse it itches. I shank my way all the way down the rough on Number 10 ... *shank, shank, shank* ... until God dims the lights.

The next morning, Dial-A-Ride picks me up along with my bike and drives me to Willow Hills to play the last nine holes of the tournament. The scoreboard is set up on an easel in front of the tiny clubhouse, which sits on a hill overlooking the course. My name is first on the board for my age group: **Ford Quinn 36**. My nearest competitor lags eight shots behind. With only nine holes left to play, the tournament is all but over, and I'll be hoisting the championship trophy (now sitting on the scorer's table) above my head in two hours' time. Sir Winston Somerset'd be proud as pee.

The first hole at Willow Hills is a par four with a watery grave you have to clear with your tee shot. A small gallery has formed to watch the leaders tee off. I'm last to hit because I had the top score the day before. I overhear someone in the crowd say, "That young kid shot one over par yesterday, can you believe that?"

I wallop my tee shot over the pond and out of sight toward the distant fairway. *Perfecto*. With my first-tee jitters behind me, I strut down the steep hill in cocky Arnie Palmer-style while applause from the gallery fades behind me.

My second shot flies straight as an arrow, landing softly on the middle of the dance floor. After a poor lag putt, I roll in a gnarly ten-foot tester for par, then slip my putter into a fake holster, draw it out, aim, and fire at an imaginary villain à la Chi-Chi Rodriguez. *Eight simple holes to a fresh start in life.* I'll take high school by storm. How silly was I giving two hoots about getting into the stupid Lund Gang?

I have *my game* now. I have *my life*.

The second hole is a short par-three, which can be easily reached with an 8-iron. I swing the club, figuring for a nice draw on the ball because the pin's on the left side of the carpet. The ball skids right instead, rattling through a few tree limbs before dropping straight down.

A shank.

I receive odd looks from my fellow players, but I shake it off. It's only one lousy shot, and besides, I have an enormous lead. I still have a chance to get up and down for par if I cozy my next shot close to the pin. The next shot shanks, too. I skull the following shot onto the dance floor after it rolls through a lipless trap. Two putts for a double bogey.

The shanks continue to plague me on the next hole.

Shank, shank, shank.

I can't shake the shanks. Three holes later, I've lost the lead. It's now a matter of survival. My legs go limp; my nerves turn to jelly. I choke down on the club, aim way left of the target. Nothing works. I should just quit and never look back. I wonder how I've gotten myself into this mess and why I had to shoot the round of my life the day before. If my score had been in the middle of the pack, no one would have noticed or cared about this dreadful round except Pop. I deduce the shanks are from muscle fatigue, due to having played a thousand holes the day before at the country club. Pimples always has to play till dark so he can bring out his stupid puke-green glow-in-the-dark golf balls he'd won at the member-caddy tournament raffle this summer. I've been bitten by a shank-bite, and there is no anti-venom in the pockets of my miserable golf bag.

The end of my misery is in sight—Number 9—a par-three straight uphill toward the clubhouse. I round the pond I triumphantly strode past two hours earlier on the first hole and see that a large throng has populated the back of the green to presumably see me win the tournament by a wide margin. In the crowd, I notice Pop wearing sunglasses and a straw hat, proudly watching me. There's no escape route at this point unless I jump into the pond and swim underwater to the other side, which is tempting.

I place my ball on a peg, aim at the flag on top of the hill, and swing wildly at the ball. Predictably, it skids right, splashing down into the pond. I fish another ball out of my bag, reload, sending the ball into the sea cemetery again. My next shot flutters harmlessly straight and low, about halfway up the hill. I nurse the ball onto the green using a Texas wedge. Three putts later, the sad torture ends. As I creep toward the scorer's table, someone snickers in the crowd.

A boy in my foursome tallies up my nine-hole score and announces, "Sixty-three, Quinn."

Why couldn't he keep his mouth shut? A mixture of murmurs and laughter follow me as I head toward my bike just as the official starts to write my score on the large board. I'll be lucky to make the girls' freshman team with that score.

Pop's vanished. *Thank God.*

I ride my bike out of the parking lot and down a long and winding road toward Dot Ave. The bag makes me tilt to the right, just like my golf shots that day, so I have to jerk my handlebars to the left every few yards. A car breathes down my back tire. It's him. Pop rolls the window down. I sprint away as fast as I can, but he keeps pace. I know what's coming.

"What the hell happened to you out there today, mister?" The car pulls even with my handlebars. "A sixty something? You can forget making the golf team."

"Go to hell," I say, fighting back tears.

"Why didn't you just quit after a couple of holes and tell them your hand hurt or something?"

"What?" I heard him.

"Forget it." He roars off in his old Impala. I throw my clubs on the ground and ride off to the waterfall at Stoner's Lake to drown my sorry sorrows.

The sound of rushing water sooths my anger and keeps me company. Maybe I'll show Pop and not return home, ever. I get now how Cleo felt the night she ran away from home because of the spat with her mom, and

I wish Rocket was still home so we could camp out in his tent together. Yeah, I like to play golf for fun into the twilight hour when the blades of grass turn purple-black and the curtain rises for the cricket choir. But it's Pop's dream that I play on the high school golf team or become the next Winston Somerset, not mine. I'd sooner read a Steven King novel or write poetry or listen to music or skateboard or play video games or gaze at the night sky or Cleo's navel. At least, that's what I'm trying to convince myself.

I once watched a black-and-white documentary about Robert Frost in Mr. Garoppolo's English class. Mr. Frost grew up in the city but loved spending time with nature because it propelled his poetry writing. I know how Mr. Frost must have felt, and I'm missing the country club course. There's something peaceful about just walking around a beautiful golf course like Kensington Hills. Closest man-made thing to Heaven. You soak up the sights and sounds (if you don't count golfers cursing), and poetic lines just spontaneously erupt in your head. (I sometimes jot them down in my caddy yardage book with my miniature golf pencil.)

On the other hand, playing golf is a whole different feeling. If you attack the golf course by playing risky shots over water or sand traps, you're just fighting an uphill battle, and a nice walk soon becomes a battlefield full of mines. A lovely oak or bubbling creek turns into a hazard rather than God's creation. But still, there's nothing like draining a lengthy birdie putt from across the green to send a shot of adrenaline through your veins.

■ ■ ■

Besides failing to make the cut, my second-biggest disappointment from bombing at the tournament comes two days later from the *Kensington Hills Observer*. The front page of the sports section has an article about the tournament, listing the winners and showing a photograph of a smiling Dennis "Freaky" Fredrickson, standing with my trophy in his hands. The article states "Fredrickson was twelve shots down at the start of the day before rallying for victory."

Rally, my ass. How about a total collapse on my part?

I mope around the next few days, repeating in my head why I had to play all those holes at the country club that day. What really bugs me is knowing that Cleo should have seen *me* holding that trophy in the newspaper, not Freaky Fredrickson.

On Friday, Gene and I bump into Gigi and Owen inside the arcade at the Thunder Bowl. Owen has just finished a record-breaking game of *Asteroids*. He's an ace video player on account of the endless free games he gets at the Palms Motel.

"Quinn, heard ya scored the first Harvey Wallbanger in Michigan golf tourn'ment history." He's wearing an old leather mod jacket with the collar turned up. A Harvey Wallbanger—or Flaming Dr. Pepper or Irish Car Bomb—is not only a cocktail but caddy slang for when scores on the front and back nine are reversed. 36 and 63. 35 and 53. 37 and 73.

Gigi doesn't give a whit about my golf score, but she laughs right along with Owen, too. I've had it with Owen and Gigi. From the concessions, I turn my head toward my old friends, who are at the exit, their arms locked around each other's waists and each hand in each other's back pocket. A quick glance outside the storefront window, and I see them zoom off on Owen's new Vespa scooter—and out of my life.

At home, I find a lumpy, sealed letter on my bed and notice the handwriting on the envelope. I feel a small, hard rectangular object in the envelope, hoping the chemical-potion songs I've sent to Cleo worked a spell on her. Of course, those songs were made for my ears only.

Kate pops her head into my bedroom. "Who's the looovve letter from, Ford?"

I frantically check to see if the seal has been broken by my nosy sister and can tell it's been tampered with. *Jesus, Kate, ever heard of a little privacy?* She probably read my poetry verses, too. "How's Theo?" My best counterattack to shut her mouth up.

"None of your business!" My door bangs shut.

I pull out the letter along with the cassette tape.

Dear Giff: Thank you for another mixtape. Most of those songs are pretty dark and out there. ☹ Pink Floyd? Even Pippa agrees. But I guess you would know that bx you made it. Duh! Anyway, we made a new tape for you with some more uplifting songs. ☺ Pippa picked most of these. Cleo P.S. We just taped over your songs & figured you wouldn't mind. Sorry!

What the hell did she mean "we"? I thought the mixtape thing is an "our" thing, not a "we" thing. I figure Pippa Farnsworth is still into the Carpenters or Barry Manilow or Seals & Croft. I stick the tape into my Sony Walkman, slide on Billy's Technics linear drive headphones, rest my head on my pillow, and press play. "Misunderstanding" begins. "Miss You" would have been perfect from her right about here, but what comes

next is "All Out of Love." Then "I Can't Tell You Why"
... "Hurt So Bad" ... "Slip Slidin' Away" ...

▪ ▪ ▪

The man in the three-piece suit puts an offer in on our
house. Pop accepts on the spot. Two days later, he tells
the guy he'll renege on the deal unless he pays a couple
of grand more. That is just like Pop, and my last glim-
mer of hope that my childhood home will be saved. The
man not only agrees but throws in an extra thousand
dollars to cover our moving expenses.

Our new home will be a red-brick apartment building close to uptown. There will only be the four of us,
plus Chimney and Fluffy, because Billy is relocating to
K-Zoo with Jenny Clark.

27

In the morning before Virginia starts her first day at her new job in Detroit, she can tell I'm down in the dumps, so she gives me a self-help lesson from her Mensa-Netics brainwashing manual. She tells me to stand in front of the mirror and imagine myself standing in the Evans scholarship house on the University of Michigan campus, about to head out the door to an astrophysics class. Oddly, Mom's self-image drivel casts a positive spell on me like it did for Cleo.

"It's time for you to join the living, Ford." She grabs my cheek and stretches it across the room. "You're still so cute."

"Stop it, Virginia."

With my inflated self-image, I muster up some Quinn courage and ride my bike to the country club, determined more than ever now to get the Evans scholarship. I can go from the Regrets to Redemption—a true Holy Redeemer. Chip shouldered 306 loops last year. Next year, I'll shoot for some new Guinness Book of World Records for loops—140 golf days times 2.5 loops = 350. Maybe Mom can quit working, start a fresh business scheme with Pop, and not worry so much anymore.

I pump my pedals faster and faster, past the beautiful rows of colonials, and forget how the Quinns have been a bunch of fakes living in a neighborhood we can barely afford. Maybe I should turn back and cut all ties with the country club. But I'm a Quinn, and there's no quit in Quinn men. I refuse to give up on life just because I got busted for stealing some beer. I pedal on toward the club.

At the foot of the bridge, I eye the turf, turned black-green by the shade from the clubhouse. The beauty of the golf course hits me: the sloping lush fairways, the finely cut blades of dew-soaked grass sticking to my high-tops, the morning fog huddling in the hollow bunkers. Now I understand how the Apollo 8 astronauts felt when they orbited the moon for the first time, transfixed by the bright, luminous sphere rising above the moon. They could almost touch the lunar craters, but what really struck them was the beautiful blue living Earth, rising above the gray, dull surface of the moon. Earthrise. The Earth was alive and breathing above the desolate shores of dry lake craters. The Kensington Hills course is alive and breathing for me, too.

My own green Sea of Tranquility.

That afternoon, I cross the bridge to the caddy shack and feel at home amid the pinball noise, the snapping croc towels, and the monument of King's big blond head behind the counter. At that moment I know I've found my true calling in life. While Father Steve has found it in grace and salvation, I've found it in straight tee shots and eagle putts. Perhaps caddying at Kensington Hills will become a permanent occupation for me like it is for Rat and the priesthood is for Father Steve. I picture future loopers lounging around the caddy shack, waiting for a call across the bridge from an 85-year-old Bogart, saying, "That's Quinn. He's a lifer." With my confidence restored, I'm ready to caddy again. My resurrection is here.

The ink's barely dry on the caddy list when Commandant King tells me Bogart wants to see me. I grab my towel and run across the bridge ready to do the work of the golfing gods. I'll see some fine golf, stop after the front nine to receive communion from Myrtle (chocolate milk and fried dog), and then finish my first round by 3:30. Then I'll be glad to start my service again.

Before I even see him, I hear Bogart bark my name from his office. I enter his palace, and he sits as usual on his swivel-chair throne with his feet up on the counter, chewing his soggy cigar. "Quinn, I ain't got good news for you." I figure he's sticking it to me for being out for so long, a well-deserved punishment I'll take in stride to reclaim my caddy pride. "You won't be loopin' anytime soon."

No problem. "I can wait for a loop." A picture on the wall shows golf legend Ben Hogan smiling with his U.S. Open trophy in hand next to what looks like a young Bogart.

Did Bogart caddy for Hogan in a major? That'd make 'im a looper legend.

"You'll be waiting a long time, 'cause you're relieved of your duties at the club."

My heart plummets thirty thousand leagues under the Sea of Tranquility. "I don't quite catch your drift."

He removes his soggy cigar from his mouth and leans forward, elbows resting on his desk. He smells of smoked Vick's Vapor Rub and day-old whiskey. "Catch this. You are FIRED. Canned. Finished."

"I'm fired?" I shake my head. "Nooo."

"The country club's got a code-of-conduct policy that applies to employees." He raises two fat fingers in the air. "And you broke two of 'em. No employees can drink booze on club property, and no employee can have a criminal record."

"But Farmer Jack's dropped the charges. You can't do this." I stumble backward against the wall.

"Did ya forget I'm the caddy master?" he snarls. "I can do what the hell I please, and what I want is never to see your butt here again."

"You don't understand … I have to caddy."

Fruit flies disguised as caddies stick to the window.

"Then go caddy somewhere else, or wash dishes down at the Fox and Hounds, where all you fancy folks hang out."

"Fancy?" *You don't know me from Farmer Jack, Bogart.* "I need this job to get the Evans scholarship."

"What world are you living in, Quinn?" Bogart snaps. "A kid from the Hills thinks he's earnin' a caddy scholarship? That's for poor kids who can't afford to go to college."

"But you don't understand—"

"I understand plenty. You think with the size of that house you live in you're going to be an Evans scholar? I'd sooner be the King of England." How's Bogart know the size of my house? Then I say it to myself for the first time: My *old* house. "You can't even be nominated for an

Evans scholarship unless I give the okay, and right now you're finished. I don't want to see your sad ass anywhere near this club." Bogart rises. "Now beat it, kid."

"Who told you about my house? About the beer?"

A moment of silence.

"Tweety Bird."

I scramble out of his hut, rip off my badge, stuff it into a trash can, and make my last trip across the bridge. *Who ratted me out? Pippa Farnsworth? Gigi?* I don't think she gives two hoots about me and just wanted to crash at my Hills pad or make Owen jealous. *Did you ever call her back, Casanova?*

It doesn't matter now. How can I go back to Virginia and tell her the caddy scholarship is lost? Pop will think I'm a fired loser, just like Billy. I steal a golf cart and drive back across the bridge, motoring through the parking lot to avoid the first tee.

The happy sounds of country-club life echo around my ears: splashing swimmers, giddy golfers, boozy members on the patio. I drive past the pool of lost opportunity. How things could be different now if I hadn't ridden off to steal that beer. I picture me and Cleo reunited in the pool that night and then making mixtapes together for the rest of our lives.

I pull up next to the golf range and notice a girl hitting booming, dead-straight tee shots. Cleo. *Where'd she learn how to swing a golf club like that?* Wow! I didn't even know she played golf. She wears red-and-black checkered Capri pants she probably borrowed from her reclaimed best friend, Pippa, and socks with little cotton balls on the heel above her golf shoes. She swings again. *Thwack.* Her ponytail shakes cutely. The ball sails out of sight.

I abandon the cart and sneak along a fence that separates the tennis courts from the golf range. A crowd of boys wearing red Bjorn Borg headbands files out of the clubhouse in their white tennis shorts and Tretorn shoes. Cleo finishes her practice swings and skips happily past the fence. I duck down below some manicured box shrubs and think of what I should say to her. Some lame explanation as to why I didn't come back to the country club party, like I fell into quicksand. She strolls right past me and up Yellow Brick Road. The mood ring she took from me at the falls early this summer glows deep blue on her ring finger. I'm about to shout her name when a boy approaches her. She hugs him and gives him a peck on the lips. The boy places his arm around her shoulder. My eyeballs bulge; my stomach turns.

Jack Lott.

The Human Torch.

I've been burned.

Cleo transforms into the Invisible Girl to me as they disappear down Yellow Brick Road toward the land of Ozzie and Harriet. I jump back into the golf cart before they can see me, thinking Doctor Doom-revenge thoughts. Pushing hard on the pedal, I Starsky & Hutch down Yellow Brick Road, drive past Bogart's hovel, past Pimples's pimply head hanging out of the bag room, past a row of stunned caddies on the green bench, and past Bobby Walton at his starter's lectern.

Cleo and Jack are nowhere in sight. They must have ducked into the pro shop to buy new gear or gone into the club for a romantic lunch. I hear the rumble of a cart driven by Bobby Walton, and I suddenly realize he's chasing me. I take a U-turn and roar past the tee box on eleven and down the long slope that leads to the twelfth fairway before cutting over to the fifteenth rough and toward sixteen.

Bobby's gaining on me. "Quinn. What do you think you're doing?"

A pair of yellow polyester pants appears five feet in front of me. I turn the wheel hard to the left; the golfer nosedives out of the way, and the pond on Number 16 opens up wide in front of me. A sharp turn of the wheel.

"Shhhiiit!" *CRASH!* The cart remains on dry land, but I'm thrown helter-skelter out of the cab into the deep, wet abyss. I sink to the bottom. Lonely white golf balls dot the bottomlands, the drowned remains of failed shots at the sixteenth green.

Two large hands pull me by my armpits, up out of the water, and sends me crash-landing to the ground. I struggle to rise. A hand presses me to the sod and says, "Stay down and relax."

I knock his hand aside and rise to my feet, but he holds me down. The hands finally release their grip. Rat, again. "Quinn, you're going to get canned for this." *Too late for that, Rat.*

As I sit on the ground, I see Mr. Valentine approaching from the tee toward his second shot on sixteen. One hundred seventy-five yards to the green. All carry. A firm 4-iron would do. *You are better off long and sandy than short and wet.* Chip lumbers up with Mr. Valentine's bag; Jake Rooney shoulders Father Steve's. The priest gets to me first because he sliced his drive. I fear Father Steve will give me my last rites—well deserved if he does. Mr. Valentine follows with a 5-iron in hand. Chip must have told him to go for the left front of the green and not the pin—a safer shot with less water hazard to carry.

Mr. Valentine eyes me like a bad lie in the rough. "Are you okay, son?"

I'm scared to raise my sorry, soaked head, so I stand up. "Yes, sir."

Father Steve turns and whispers in Jake's ear. Jake jumps in the cart and drives toward the clubhouse. Mr. Valentine and Chip walk off toward the shady, undulating green. Father Steve waves the other players along to go ahead of us. Mr. Valentine fades around the bend of the artificial lake toward the green.

Bobby Walton rides up in his cart, steps out, removes his hat, and rubs his curly hair. He radios someone at the first tee, but I can't make out the words. "Come with me, Ford."

Father Steve comes to my rescue. "I'll take him from here, Bobby." Bobby drives off in his cart back toward the first tee. "You can carry my bag, Ford." I pick up his bag from the ground and expect a sermon. "Who do you think got you that round in the PGA?" Father asks.

Not certain why he's asking me that now. "I'm not sure."

"Mr. Valentine." It doesn't register in my mind why he'd do that. I reply with a blank stare. "Swear to God." A warm smile appears on Father's sunburned lips. "He owed you one, Ford."

As far as I know, he's paid me in full for every round I've carried for him, plus a healthy tip to boot. "How so, Father?"

"You helped his daughter."

Thor summons a lightning bolt to strike me on my head. Cleo's *his stepdaughter*. I never made the connection because they don't share the same last name, but then I recall the pharaoh-shaped name tag and King Tut towel hanging from his bag. *No bigger clues than that, Sherlock.* No wonder Cleo knows how to hit a golf ball. "I guess I messed up."

He tosses me a towel to dry my hair. "How about carrying two more holes for an old priest?"

"If you say so, Father, but it'll be my last."

"Why is that, son?"

I pause and sigh deep. "Bogart fired me for some reason." *Yeah. Gigi, I'm guessing, but who knows or cares now?*

"Why might that be?" He wants details, and I figure I owe him as much for being mighty kind to me this summer. "I'd normally only hear a confessional in church, but I consider this God's sacred pasture."

I confess to stealing the beer, blowing off Gigi, and losing the Evans scholarship.

Father performs the sign of the cross. "Three Hail Marys and two Our Fathers. That's your penance, son."

"Yes, Father." I lower my chin to my chest, start murmuring my amends while we make our way over to the Number 17 tee box, a long uphill par-three. He gives me time to finish. I perform the sign of the cross and hand him his 3-wood. Father Steve places his ball on a tee and swings. The ball sails over the front bunkers and disappears onto the distant green. We trudge up the hill.

A shadow grows over our feet on the green, and the pin bends horizontally from a sudden northern gust. Father Steve braces himself against the wind by digging his spikes into the turf, holds his hand over his golf hat before taking it off and pressing it between his knees.

"You're free from the bag now, Ford." He lags his putt short of the hole for a gimme, returns his hat to his head, and hands me his putter.

"But, Father—"

"You can put down that cross you've been carrying."

"But—"

"It's not your burden. Let caddying go." I follow him down a slope toward the last hole. "Just *be* a kid. You have four years before you grow up and go to college. Enjoy yourself. I did."

"You did?" Of course he did. Priests don't grow from the womb.

"I didn't go from altar boy to priest." He rests the shaft of the club under the crook of his elbow and fixes his eyes on some distant memory. "I was young once, too."

. . .

A few days later, I fill my backpack with things I need for my trip: bathing suit, Neil Armstrong biography, *That Was Then, This Is Now*, a family photo of all five of us at Niagara Falls, my new mixtape, Cleo's mixtape, and my expandable telescope. The timing for getting the hell out of Dodge is actually good, because this weekend the movers are coming to the house. Most of our stuff can't fit in the new apartment, so it's either been sold or put into storage, like my late grandmother's claw-foot antique dining room table that would have taken up most of the living room in our new apartment.

I clean out my closet and throw out all the dopey stuff I've collected over the years—my model airplanes, walkie-talkie (what good is it now that Rocket's Down Under?), jackpot bank, comic books (I'll be bringing my baseball card collection, though—never let those go), metal race cars, skin-diver calendar watch, and toy soldiers. In the back of my mind, I don't think my folks are ever going to buy a new house again. For a split second, I think about going next door to talk to Dr. Clark for life advice, but I nix that idea. You have to learn to do things on your own, just like Uncle Fred once told me.

I want a new start in life—a place to start over where no one knows me from Adam West.

A lady at the Greyhound Bus counter hands me a one-way ticket to Cocoa Beach to see my cousin Mitty and Cape Canaveral again. She tells me I have to transfer to a different bus in Atlanta, Georgia. My parents can wait until I get to Florida to find out I've been fired. I leave a note that I'll be sleeping over with Owen at the Palms Motel for a few days. They don't know he hates my guts.

I fall asleep before jolting awake from a nightmare just past the Kentucky border. I dreamt I was at a funeral. I sat down in a pew. Bogart and Commandant King were there, along with Gigi and Gigi's mom, who I've never even met, but somehow I knew it was her. Fellow green shirts showed up, including Rat, Chip, Owen, and Pimples. Rocket sat next to me in the pew in his Australian school uniform: shorts and long gray socks pulled up to his freckled knees. Father Steve stood at the altar ready to give the sermon, dressed in golf knickers and spikes. He had a ball on a tee for some reason, and it kept falling off, and he'd put it back on, and it would fall off again, and he'd put it back on. This kept going and going until I woke up.

The next day, I arrive in Georgia to the blinding noon sun. A kid with a red balloon steps off the bus with his mother in front of me and into the waiting arms of a wrinkled old man.

"Grampy," the boy says as he jumps into his grandfather's arms.

I stand frozen on the last step of the bus from the street. The bus driver says, "Kid, this is the last stop. Get off the bus, okay?"

After pacing back and forth for an hour in downtown Atlanta, I lose my nerve and miss the transfer bus to Cocoa Beach. In the late afternoon, a park bench gives me refuge from the unrelenting sun as I watch pigeons circling a statute of a woman being lifted from a fire by a large-winged bird. A plaque reads: "Phoenix Rising from the Ashes." I've never been this far from home alone. Everywhere I turn I witness families meandering about the streets hand in hand together, and I think of Virginia and Pop and even Billy and Kate.

But it's Chimney that I miss most of all. I've left my dog behind. *Dog's worst friend.* She always waits for me at the bottom of the stairs till I get home at night, and then we go up together to sleep in my room after a quick peek at the night sky. I picture a lonesome, sitting Chimney at the foot of the stairs, forever waiting with her tongue hanging out for me to return home.

After wandering the streets of Atlanta, I'm dead tired and rest on a bench across from a post office. Sweat pours down my face. I recall Virginia harping from time to time about confronting your troubles, not running away. Perhaps she's right for once. Early in the evening, I buy a slice of pizza and a Coke, lie down on a park bench, and start reading *That Was Then, This Is Now* before falling asleep.

The next morning, I wake to pecking pigeons, sleepwalk to the train station, and hop on a bus headed for home, mostly because I miss Chimney. Two cramped legs later, I crack open a window and slip Cleo's farewell mixtape onto the I-75 highway, imagining it crushed by rubber wheels into a million tiny bits.

At some point during this bus trip, I realize I don't want the new Cleo; she's not the one I fell in love with in my bedroom playing Nerf, in Rocket's tent listening to Pillow Talk, in the hospital psycho ward inventing souls. She's just like the rest of the Hills girls now. Gigi's the one I'm missing all of a sudden, but her punk, bad-ass spirit matches Owen's to a tee. I put in a new mixtape I'd made just before I left, kickstarted with old-school Bruce—"Growin' Up"—and tell myself high school will be a new start at life in the fall. New friends, no history.

28

The new apartment isn't too bad, although I can't find a single kid my age in the building. There's a middle-aged couple on the first floor with no kids and a pet ferret. A young divorcée lives above us and blares Gordon Lightfoot and Chicago all day long. Kate reunites with her long-lost pal from the second grade, Candy Montgomery, who lives on the third floor with her mom and stepdad. (Kate could meet old friends in Siberia.) Because our apartment has only two bedrooms, I let my sister have the extra one, because teenage girls need their privacy. I sleep on the old TV-room couch in the new "living room." Chimney pants on the floor at my feet on a worn green shag carpet that Virginia vows to replace.

Both Kate and I get regular jobs at Olga's Kitchen carving a spigot of lamb-beef and making pita sandwiches and Greek salads for the Hills people. Olga herself shows me how to carve the meat into papery-thin slivers. With Billy having worked there, Olga's becomes a Quinn family tradition.

One Saturday morning, I'm dribbling a basketball between cars in the parking lot when I hear Virginia scream. I sprint up the steps into the apartment after she's just hung up the phone and see her sobbing. My first thought is a dead relative. "That was Mrs. Olivehammer."

My jaw drops to Earth's inner core. "Don't tell me something's happened to Rocket?"

She holds her head in her hands, then comes up for oxygen. "No. Those bastards are bulldozing our house."

It turns out the man who bought our house had no intention of living on our street after all; he works for a real estate development company. His wife never dipped one toe into Dot Ave water, let alone set two eyes on the house. And for good reason. They are destroying my childhood house so they can make way for two brand-new houses, narrow enough to fit within the zoning footprint of the two lots. Pop's been bitten once again by a Kensington real estate shark.

I try to renew Virginia's spirit with some Osmond P. Peabody slogans, but all she says is "I loved that house … I loved that house … I loved that house."

The more I consider the demolition of our house, the more I know it's absolutely the right thing to happen. No one else should be living in the Quinn house, sleeping in my room, playing in my basement, eating prime rib in our dining room, watching "rain" in my TV room, reading newspapers in Pop's den, smoking cigarettes in Virginia's kitchen, or sitting on top of our garage roof with *my* view of the sky and the stars and the moon and the sun. It's better this way, I tell Virginia. It isn't right for any *outsiders* to create new memories in Quinn-space, so be damned with 'em all, as Uncle Fred was fond of saying.

■ ■ ■

A week later, I come home after bumming around uptown, and Virginia tells me Chimney hasn't been seen all day, which isn't like my dog. I holler at Kate for letting her wander outside all alone in a strange new place. Losing Chimney would be like losing my left testicle. Normally, Virginia's high-pitched wolf whistle will cajole my dog home, but it only attracts complaints from our new neighbors. It's weird living with strangers under the same roof, but there's walls and ceilings, and I suppose I'll get used to it.

Three days drag by, and we all hunt for Chimney, shouting her name around town. They say the chances of a dog coming home diminish by ten percent each day they're gone. We're now at thirty percent. Kate and I put up posters all over town with Chimney's picture from the *People* magazine shoot, along with a reward of thirty dollars, the last of my caddy earnings. I cry myself to sleep for three days straight.

After work on day four, I'm wandering lonely around town, nailing up more lost-dog posters for Chimney, when the cancer-dog trainer walks out of Peabody's with a mustard stain on his shirt. He reads the poster I've just tacked up on a telephone pole and frowns at me.

"Dogs are really smart, and they eventually find their way home," he says. "I knew a dog once who got lost on vacation and then somehow turned up at home two months later. He'd traveled over two hundred miles."

I shake my head in despair. "Chimney's been gone for almost a week now."

"Don't worry; she'll come home."

The cancer-dog trainer's last word hit home to me— literally. *Home.* The apartment isn't home to Chimney; our old house is home to her. I drop my armful of posters and sprint as fast I can toward Dot Ave.

"Hey," he yells after me. "You forgot your posters!"

A thousand exhausting breaths later, I reach the rubble of my old house and wade through the debris. A man in an orange hard hat leans against a dump truck, eating a baloney-and-cheese sandwich. There's nothing but the first-floor flooring left, and wood has been piled up where the garage once stood. I step onto the linoleum kitchen floor and can see scuff marks from the years of Quinn wear and tear. A remorseful jolt hits me in the chest, but I shrug it off. I have to find my dog.

The hard-hat man storms up to me. "Hey kid, this is a construction site. Beat it."

"No, it's not. It's the house I grew up in!" I stand on old brand-new-looking linoleum floor in the footprint of our old stove. Fallen noodles crunch under my feet.

The worker takes pity on me. "Sorry, kid. That's a tough one."

I whip my head around, scanning for dog fur. "Have you seen a dog around here?"

"Nope."

The unthinkable suddenly dawns on me. We had a dog chute in the mudroom. That way Chimney could come and go as she pleased. The old mudroom has been demolished, and the floor is covered with wood. My arms flail. Wood boards fly from the pile. The man churns his feet through the wreckage. "Be careful. There's nails in there."

"Shut up," I cry.

"Okay, okay. Let me help you, then."

For the next two hours, we excavate the mudroom site. I find Chimney's dog tag before realizing it's an old one from when she was a puppy. I put the metal tag in my pocket. I'm exhausted from moving the wood pile and wander into the backyard, leaning up against our wood fence. The six-foot solid board fence is the only thing that still exists from the Quinn era, unless you count the patio bricks and dirt. I remember Pop built that fence when I was about ten after a fight with some new neighbors that had moved in and replaced the Weber family.

It hasn't occurred to me until I look up from the fence that the bloody, greedy bastards have already cut down most of the beautiful elm trees in our backyard to make way for the two new houses. Kate will be crushed if she ever comes back to review the remains of her childhood home. I sit down on one of the freshly cut stumps. On the bottom of the stump, I see a carving in the wood: K ♡ T.

I try to stop myself from thinking about Chimney to avoid crying, so I pinch myself hard on the fat part of my calf. I've spent half of my life chasing Chimney around the backyard. Now she's gone and disappeared, along with everything and everyone good in my life. Rocket. My house. My dog. My country-club golf course. Owen. Cleo. I retrieve the dog tag from my pocket and rub the dirt off of it with my thumbnail. It reads "I'm Chimney Quinn, 678 Dorchester. If you find me, please return me to my family."

I fight off some tears, and I'm about to leave when I hear some muttering from the driveway next door at the Clarks'. *Pauley?* I'm in no mood for him whatsoever. The muttering ceases. I glance over and can see him pulling back some branches, peering through the shrubs. He sees that I've spotted him and cuts through the hedge toward me.

Before I can move, Pauley appears in front of me but doesn't say a thing. His head swivels back and forth from me and my destroyed house, like he's just noticed it's been nuked by a Soviet warhead.

"Whatta bummer," he says.

The sun's in my face, and I have to squint to look at him. His hair has grown past his shoulders. He wears a pair of cut-off jeans and no shirt, his hands greasy from working on one of the Clarks' motorcycles. He wears a perplexed face, like he is trying to solve a riddle in his head. "Where do you live now?"

Should I give Pauley my new address? At least he doesn't give two rips where I live or what kind of house I live in. "A building uptown called Paradise Garden Apartments."

"Sounds nice."

"Splendid." I notice a deflated football by the fence line. Rocket and I used to play catch in the backyard for hours on end.

"Too bad they don't allow dogs."

The word "dog" gets my attention, but the word "they" doesn't register with me at first. "What do you mean *they*, Pauley?"

"Your dog doesn't live with you. They must not allow pets."

I leap off the stump and stand eye to eye with him. "What do you mean? Have you seen Chimney?" My nose practically presses up against his. Maybe Pauley killed my dog.

"Yeah, I've seen her."

I put my hands on my head in despair. "Jesus, Pauley!" Maybe I'll kill *him*. "Where the hell is my dog?"

"In my room, sleeping." He scratches the back of his neck. "She looked lonely and hungry. My mom's been out of town, and I didn't have your new phone number to tell you. I was beginning to wonder if I should just keep her. She's pretty nice."

A million tons lift from my shoulders, and I give Pauley Clark a huge Bigfoot hug. After taking one long, last look at the remains of my childhood home, I hurry next door to get my dog, tears of relief washing down my face.

29

On Labor Day weekend I hear from Kate, who heard from Vicky Fontaine, that there's a party going down at the park, and there might be a fight between the private and public schoolers. Gene comes by the apartment, and we head off together to watch the spectacle and attend the last summer party before high school kicks off.

Tonight it's muggy cool. Swirls of tumbleweed gusts blow in from nowhere. Energy fills my bones as we step into the park, and it seems just about every kid knows this is the last summer gig before the adults run or ruin our lives again. A moth flaps its wings at me and flutters off.

I ponder where the rumble will start or if it's just tough talk. Catholic High vs. Kensington High. There's a big rivalry between the two schools. Usually fights end on the football field, or you hear about an occasional brawl somewhere. We stumble upon a keg of beer. I grab a foamy cup and roam the park with Gene.

Is that Cleo nuzzled up to Jack Lott against a Corvette convertible? She's left a deep wound in my heart that hasn't healed yet, and I wonder if it ever will. A boy with shaggy brown hair turns around and grins. It isn't Jack and Cleo, just another mirage in the social desert.

Droning mosquito kamikazes blitz and feed on my sweaty neck. I bump shoulders with a guy and spill his beer. "What the hell, dickhead?"

"Sorry."

We move on up a hill and hear yelling coming from over a distant ridge, and I wonder if the rumble has already started and what side I'll be on if I ever muster the courage to join the fray. *Maybe I should go to unschooling school with Pauley.*

In this section of the park, I notice a few public schoolers I'd played baseball with a few years ago, and we exchange hellos. A girl appears from the crowd in a pink sweater; tight, flared Jordache jeans; and pearl earrings. Her face doesn't register with me because I haven't seen her outside the boundaries of Dot Ave. She stumbles up to me, and her beer breath almost knocks me over.

"I know *you!*" A wasted smile spreads across her lips, and she spills her drink on my shoes. "They knocked your entire house down and," she slurs, "I watched the whole thing from my front yard."

I'm trying to get away from that old life, but she keeps going. "And ya know what? I wrote a poem about it. *The Fall of the House of Quinn.* I write poetry, too."

Too? It finally dawns on me that she's Laney Carter from across the street, and I remember that according to Ralph Lord, she writes poetry. How the hell does she know about my poetry writing? The only two suspects are Pauley and Kate, unless Laney combed through the wreckage of my house and unearthed stuff from the rubble.

I recall Virginia saying during the frantic move before I left for Atlanta, "You can't take all your books to the apartment ... it's too small. You could fill a library with all these books." Maybe Laney bought my poetry book at Mom's last garage sale on Dot Ave from the ten-cent bin. Then I trash that idea. Perhaps Cleo stole my notebook, and it made the rounds of the Hills girls in-crowd before winding up in the hands of Laney. Who the fook knows?

"Turn around, will ya?" She presses a piece of paper against my back and chisels numbers across my spine. She spins me around and shoves a piece of paper in my front pocket. "You hear about the showdown?" A piss-drunk kid stumbles into her backward, suffers a laughing fit, then rolls into the night. "Some bullshit dare Nick Lund made. Just like him."

I wonder how she knows Lund, and a faint memory of Pop ranting about Mr. Carter belonging to the Hunt Club kicks in. The Lunds are members there, too. It's just like adults to have some pretend club name from England, like they actually hunt foxes in Kensington Hills. Who do they think they are? Nobles, earls, lords, kings, and queens? I think of our apartment building and the serfs we've become. Grandpa Quinn's probably twisting in his grave. Not sure what Uncle Fred would think. For once, I feel bad for dear old Pop and decide maybe I should become a lawyer and fight for the little guy against the likes of Mr. Carter, Mr. Fitz, and all the other fox hunters.

Nah. I love space too much to piss away my life just to get revenge for Pop's lot-scheme debacle. Plus, Laney Carter's pink sweater is lingering in my mind like the funny-smelling smoke wafting through the park air.

She stumbles off into the night. Maybe some kids like her care more about what you *do* than where you live. Farther into the park, a circle of kids surrounds two dark figures squaring off with each other. I squeeze into the circle to get a better view and see Gorilla flexing his muscles inside the circle—the same guy who'd beaten Rocket's face to a fine pulp.

My anger rises. I throw the cup I've been holding on to the ground and squeeze my way to the front of the throng. Gorilla throws a punch, and the kid he hits doubles over and twists around so I'm face-to-face with his next victim. A frightened, helpless Nick Lund stares into my eyes.

"Help me," he says. "Fantastic—"

Gorilla turns him around and punches him in the windpipe. Lund stumbles, regains his footing, and throws a pathetic jab that the bully blocks. I don't see any Holy Redeemer in sight, let alone a member of the Fantastic Four. The only guy I know who could take on the Gorilla is Jack Lott, and he's probably snuggling with Cleo on the suede beanbag in his basement. I'm the only one who can help hapless Nick.

For me, this has nothing to do with private schoolers versus public schoolers. Nothing to do with Hills kids versus any other kids. This is about avenging Rocket. He's never let me down—ever. Lund deserves to get his ass whipped for once in his privileged life. But what I'm about to do has nothing to do with Lund or his silly middle-school gang. I'll avenge my friend.

The public schoolers egg their man on, and Gorilla throws a punch. Lund ducks, and Gorilla's fist grazes off his temple. I have to make a move, or he'll kill Lund. Gorilla holds up his hand and clenches his fist for all to see. Lund straightens, turns up his chin, and raises his left arm in self-defense. He takes two wobbly steps backward before the crowd pushes him forward like ropes in a boxing ring. I close my eyes and sprint toward Gorilla and tackle him in the knees like I'd done to King. But there's no Rat to save me. I'm on top of him now. He throws me onto the ground like a rag doll.

Gorilla rises.

I know I'm burnt toast. He coils his arm and makes a fist to turn my face into a tossed salad. His gold ring glints on his right knuckle. An epic, primal scream silences the crowd. Gorilla's eyes grow wide. He puts down his arm and rotates his head. I lift my chin off the ground and see Gene's giant fist hurtling through the night air.

Gorilla ducks and avoids the punch. He does an Andre the Giant move on Gene, picking him up by the waist and body slamming him on the ground. Gorilla backs up against the human ropes and runs toward Gene, flying off the ground and landing on his fat stomach. Gene screams and throws him off. Gorilla aims a roundhouse to finish my buddy off.

I crawl forward on my knees and divert Gorilla's attention toward me. "Hey, asshole!" I'm fast enough to run away if I want to, but Gene'll never make it out of the ring alive.

Gorilla's eyes drill on mine, and I'm dead scared he's going to kill me. He rubs his hands together, clenches his fist in and out, and I quickly get to my feet, thinking the best shot I have to stay alive is by doing some Muhammad Ali rope-a-dope. As I back away in one frantic, spastic motion to get some distance between us, he raises his knuckly fist. Courage drains from my arteries and leaks from my shoelace holes into a muddy puddle on the ground. I close my eyes to meet certain death.

I open my eyes and wonder why I'm still breathing. Silver flashes in front of my petrified face. Owen Rooney's wearing his knee-long army parka and is in a low fighting stance, waving his Swiss Army knife under Gorilla's chin. He slashes at Gorilla's knee, and blood spurts out, suspended in midair before dropping liquid on Gorilla's shoes.

Gorilla cries in agony and swings an off-center punch at Owen, missing his head, but he clips his hand, and the knife goes flying. Owen clocks Gorilla straight in the nose. His knees buckle, and Owen lands another under his chin. Gorilla goes down as the crowd falls silent. The Red Sea of kids parts, and we scramble past the stunned crowd. Police sirens blare in the hills. We make a run for it, but I look back, and no one dares to follow.

On the narrow exit path in the park, Owen and I trek stride for stride, and Gigi comes up from behind.

She nudges in between us and places an arm around each of us while Gene trails us. None of us need to say a thing. And we don't. Sometimes kids can show what they're feeling through telepathy or just a small gesture like the slight grin Owen gives me as we exit the park. I know he's saying in his head, "Us mod loopers need to stick together."

A warm electric glow spreads through my body, and a comet trails through the black sky, reminding me of Rocket. He'll be back next year, I just know it. "Jake scored tix to The Who. You wanna go with us?" When two kids get in a fight together, it forms some kind of a blood bond I can't explain.

"Bloody hell yes."

Owen and Gigi raise their fists in the air and do an epic rebel yell. "Yaah." They peel off from us, holding hands, into the blissful night air.

Under a lamppost, I feel a tap on my shoulder, followed by his voice. I turn and see Nick Lund with a small shiner under his eye. He looks different, small and weak. I wonder why I've been in awe of him all of these years and know now if I'd confronted him at some point in grade school, he'd have never bothered me again. On the other hand, maybe I would have been just like him or been part of his lousy gang and turned up my nose at guys like Rocket and Gene. But I doubt it.

"You guys saved my life. You want into the gang?" He grins stupidly. "We'll call it the Justice League."

"No thanks," I say. "I'll stick with Marvel comics."

Gene and I let out hyena laughs. "Gene," I say, "take care of good old Nick for me, will ya?"

Gene raises both of his gigantic fists high in the air in Lund's direction. Nick backpedals and falls on his stuck-up ass. He scrambles to his feet and runs off into the distance.

A long wade through the woods leads us down a dirt trail before we empty into a paved alley uptown and head toward my new home at the Paradise Garden Apartments. Somehow I know that everything will be all right this coming school year at Kensington High with Owen, Gigi, Pimples, and eventually Rocket. I'll follow Billy's path to public school no matter what Mom and Pop say.

Pop may hate her dad's guts, but all I can think about when I get home is Laney Carter, so I write a poem in my head about holding hands with her in some land far from the Hills, perhaps Iceland or Scotland. I'll send Aunt Shirley hundreds of postcards with verses of a poem the length of *Beowulf* about the summer of '80 that she can piece together and translate into her adopted Scots language and mail back to me. I'll place the epic poem in the time capsule NASA intends to send into space for future Martians to translate and get someone at *People* to do another story.

An Earthling Sends a Poem to Mars.

ACKNOWLEDGMENTS

I would like to thank the following people for their generous support and invaluable assistance in writing this novel during its various stages. My lovely wife, Marcia (who was the first to see potential in this book), Sharon Umbaugh (editor extraordinaire), Fiona Tobin (and her mum who coined the term 'Mocker'), Natalie Wright, Ranee Stemann, Dana MacLean, K.A. Tutin, Diane Yamashiro, Janie Rose, Bob Rose, and the wonderful copy editors at Pikko's House: Crystal Watanabe and Cheryl Lowrance.

Cover design by Renée Barratt at The Cover Counts. Thank you Renee. Amazing work.

Permissions granted: David Wallechinsky for *The Book of Lists*. Thank you.

ichael Conlon is a graduate of the University of Michigan and Wayne State Law School. In a former life, he caddied in the PGA Championship and U.S. Senior Open. This is his debut novel. His forthcoming novel *The Monks' Cross* will be published in 2019. He resides in Traverse City, Michigan with his wife, three children, and dog, Sumo.

Mr. Conlon can be reached at michaelconlonbooks.com and Facebook.